Tyler thought of the s... even the coed prosti... thought of the old bastard Anderson McClintock, who had run the city like a feudal overlord. He thought of his brothers, Kieran and Bryce, whom Tyler had seen occasionally on the streets or in the stores, but had otherwise avoided.

Now that he'd committed to writing this book, he was going to have to return to Heyday sooner or later. He was a good reporter, and he wouldn't leave all those stones unturned.

But he remembered the Heyday residents who hated his guts. He particularly remembered Mallory Rackham, who had run the Ringmaster Café, where the Heyday Eight had gathered to make their dates and count their profits.

Mallory, who had let Tyler spend so many hours there, chatting her up and complimenting her coffee, never guessing that he was gathering notes for his exposé.

Mallory, beautiful and ridiculously naive, whose husband had been one of the Heyday Eight's best customers. Mallory, who had tossed a plate of French fries, complete with ketchup, into Tyler's face when she found out who he really was.

Mallory, who for some strange reason was the only person in ten years to put Tyler's disciplined objectivity and emotional distance in jeopardy.

"All right," he said, ignoring the wriggle of doubt. "I'll come back to Heyday."

Dear Reader,

It's not easy being the older sister. I should know—I've got one, and I've spent most of my life driving her crazy!

My sister is only two years older than I am, but in our family she's called the "mother pretend." At five, I was afraid to go upstairs alone, so she trotted up into the darkness at my side. At ten, I broke the priceless Oriental vase, but she told our parents she did it. Later she pierced my ears, cut my hair and taught me that sometimes less is more, especially in bad boys and blue eye shadow. She played ambassador ("Let her go, he's a nice guy"), counselor ("let him go, he's a jerk") and cheerleader ("look at her go, isn't she super?"). I didn't ask her to do these things. I didn't have to.

So when I had to write the story of Mallory Rackham, who suddenly finds that protecting her troubled younger sister will be both frightening and expensive, I knew where to go for inspiration. All I had to ask myself was—what would my sister do to save me? The answer was simple. Anything.

A woman like that deserves a special man, someone who understands all about love and loyalty. But sexy Tyler Balfour hardly fits that description. The third brother in the complicated McClintock clan, Tyler is a confirmed outsider. He has no interest in getting involved.

Then he meets Mallory.

I hope you enjoy their story. And if you have older sisters or brothers like mine, give them a hug today. They've undoubtedly earned it!

Warmly,

Kathleen O'Brien

P.S. I love to hear from readers! Please write me at P.O. Box 947633 or stop by my Web site, KathleenOBrien.net.

The Stranger
Kathleen O'Brien

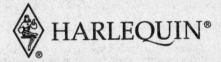

HARLEQUIN®

TORONTO • NEW YORK • LONDON
AMSTERDAM • PARIS • SYDNEY • HAMBURG
STOCKHOLM • ATHENS • TOKYO • MILAN • MADRID
PRAGUE • WARSAW • BUDAPEST • AUCKLAND

ISBN 0-373-71266-9

THE STRANGER

ABOUT THE AUTHOR

Three-time finalist for the Romance Writers of America's RITA® Award, Kathleen is the author of more than twenty novels for Harlequin Books. After a short career as a television critic and feature writer, Kathleen traded in journalism for fiction—and the chance to be a stay-at-home mother. A native Floridian, she and her husband live just outside Orlando, only a few miles from their grown children.

Books by Kathleen O'Brien

HARLEQUIN SUPERROMANCE

HARLEQUIN SINGLE TITLE

SIGNATURE SELECT SPOTLIGHT

*Four Seasons in Firefly Glen
†The Heroes of Heyday

Don't miss any of our special offers. Write to us at the following address for information on our newest releases.

Harlequin Reader Service
U.S.: 3010 Walden Ave., P.O. Box 1325, Buffalo, NY 14269
Canadian: P.O. Box 609, Fort Erie, Ont. L2A 5X3

CHAPTER ONE

MALLORY RACKHAM LOVED many things about owning a bookstore in Heyday, Virginia, but balancing the bank accounts wasn't one of them.

Balance? What a joke! Watching the numbers on her computer screen cling to the "plus" column was as nerve-racking as watching an acrobat bicycle across the high wire without a net.

And she hadn't even entered this month's sales-tax payment. She typed a few keys, and, sure enough, the dollar total tumbled off the tightrope and somersaulted straight into the red.

She put her head in her hands and groaned. Apparently living your whole life in Heyday did things to your mind. Heyday had been built around a circus legend, and from the Big Top Diner to the Ringmaster Parade it was a one-theme town. And now she was even going bankrupt in circus metaphors.

"Mallory?" Wally Pierson, the teenager she'd hired to work the cash register in the afternoons, stuck his head through her office door. "The guy from the place is here. He wants to know if you need some more thingies."

She looked at Wally, wondering when teenagers had stopped using nouns. She was only twenty-eight, but Wally always made her feel old, with his tattoo and his piercings and his multicolored hair.

"You mean the sales rep? About the bookmarks?"

"Yeah." Wally clicked his tongue stud against his teeth. "So you want some?"

She stared at the computer screen. She wanted some, all right. They sold well, and the markup was extremely advantageous, much better than some of the books. But how was she going to pay for them?

"Yes. But tell him just to replace what's sold. Nothing new until next month."

Wally nodded and disappeared, leaving her alone with the computer screen, which was still blinking bright red.

She was going to have to borrow money from her personal account again this month. She began typing. Goodbye to the haircut, even though she'd put it off three months now and her "breezy, low-maintenance" cut stood up in spikes that made her look slightly electrified. Goodbye to the steak dinner she'd been going to cook for Roddy Friday night—he'd have to settle for pasta, though if ever a man was a born carnivore, it was Roddy Hartland.

Goodbye, goodbye, goodbye. When she saw the final number in the home account, she grimaced. Not even enough for pasta. She felt herself sliding toward self-pity, so she closed her folder of bills briskly and wiggled her fingers to shake it off. Roddy was a millionaire. She'd make him take her out to dinner.

"Mallory?" Wally's head was in the door again, so she arranged her face in a calm smile. He knew she was doing the books, and of course he knew business had been off lately. Wally's weekly paycheck wasn't huge, but it was important to him. No need to make the kid wonder where his next Whopper was coming from.

"Phone's for you. Some rude guy, won't give his name. Just said to tell you it's about your sister's wedding."

Mindy's wedding. Oh, hell. Mallory had completely forgotten that the first check was due to the country club at the end of the month, to reserve the room. Her eyes instinctively darted back to the computer screen. If she typed that entry in right now, the whole thing would probably explode in a storm of flying red numbers.

"Another salesman, do you think?" The minute Mindy's engagement had hit the papers, the phone had started ringing. Apparently people assumed that when you married a state senator's son, you had a fortune to spend on satin and lace and geegaws. They seemed to forget that the bride's family paid for the wedding.

"Doesn't sound like a salesman," Wally said, toying with the silver ring in his eyebrow. "Sounds like a weirdo, actually. Voice like Darth Vader."

Great. Just what she needed. Darth Vader peddling pink votives and silver-tasseled chair shawls.

"Thanks, Wally," she said. "I'll handle it."

He ducked out, clearly relieved that she hadn't asked him to get rid of the caller.

"Good morning," Mallory chirped as she pulled the phone toward her. *You've reached the offices of Maxed Out and Dead Broke.* But when she picked up the receiver, sanity reasserted itself, and she merely said, "Rackham Books. This is Mallory Rackham."

"Good morning, Miss Rackham," a strange, electronic voice said slowly.

Mallory's hand tightened around the telephone. How bizarre. The voice didn't even sound quite human, and yet it managed to convey all kinds of unpleasant things with those four simple words. Everything from an unwanted familiarity to a subtle threat.

That was ridiculous, of course. A threat of what? She was a small-town bookstore owner, not James Bond. And yet this voice was mechanically altered. Why would anyone do that?

"Who is this?"

"I want you to listen to me carefully. I have some instructions for you."

"Instructions for *me?* Who *is* this?"

He ignored her question again. "I want you to go to the bank this afternoon. I want you to get fifty twenty-dollar bills and wrap them in a plastic baggie."

Oh, good grief. This was ridiculous, like something out of a gangster movie. Did she recognize anything about this voice? Could it be a joke? Roddy loved jokes.

But the hard kernel of anxiety in the pit of her

stomach said no. She didn't begin to understand what was going on here, but she somehow knew it was no joke.

"Look, I don't know what you're talking about, but I don't like your tone. I'm going to hang—"

"I'm only going to say this once, Mallory, so you'd better listen." The metallic voice had an implacable sound, a cruel sound. She felt her spine tingle and go soft. She leaned back against her chair and tried to think clearly. Who would dare take this tone with her?

"Put the baggie in a small brown lunch bag and close it with packing tape. Then take the bag to the Fell's Point Ferry tomorrow morning."

In spite of her confusion, in spite of her outrage that anyone would talk to her this way, she instinctively reached for a pencil and began to make notes.

"Buy a ticket for the 11:00 a.m. trip," he continued. "The Green Diamond Ferry. When you get on, go immediately to the front. Put the bag under the first seat on the left, the one closest to the bow. And then get off the boat and go home."

She scribbled, her mind racing. Not because she had any intention of taking orders from an anonymous blackmailer, but because, at the very least, she should have some concrete record to show the police.

"Did you get that, Mallory? Do you know what you're supposed to do?"

"Yes," she said. She put down her pencil. "What I don't know is why you think I would agree to do it."

He chuckled. It was a terrible sound, full of unnatural metallic reverberations, like laughter emanating from a steel casket.

"You'll do it because you're a good sister. You'll do it because you love that spoiled brat Mindy, and you wouldn't want to see anything happen to that classy wedding of hers."

Mallory scalp tingled. "Her wedding?"

"Yes. You wouldn't want me to ruin her wedding, would you? Senator Earnshaw's son…Frederick, isn't it? He's such a good catch. So handsome, so—"

"How could you do that?" She reached out blindly and clicked off the computer screen, her body on auto-pilot while her mind struggled to figure out what was going on. What was he getting at? What exactly was he threatening to do? "How could you possibly ruin my sister's wedding?"

He laughed again. "Easy," he said. "I'd just tell the senator and his son about Mindy's nasty little secret."

For a second Mallory couldn't answer. She was suddenly aware that her heart was thumping, hard and erratic, like a fish struggling on a wooden dock.

This wasn't possible. This couldn't be happening. No one knew about…*that*. Not even Tyler Balfour, big-time, muckraking, investigative journalist, had discovered Mindy's part in the whole—

"Are you there, Mallory?" The voice slowed, no doubt savoring her shock. "Are you thinking about it? About the scandal? Mindy's always been a little weak, hasn't she? Not too stable. God only knows what she'd do if her fancy wedding fell apart."

Mallory opened her mouth, but in place of her normal voice she heard only a strange, thin sound, so she shut it again.

The electronic voice hardened. "Be on that ferry, Mallory. Or I'll have to tell poor Freddy Earnshaw that his lovely bride is nothing but a two-bit prostitute."

FOR AS LONG AS she could remember, when things got a little bumpy, Mallory had turned to her smart, sensible mother for advice and comfort.

Elizabeth Rackham had a straightforward approach to life. She called it "Eliminate Step B." Life was as simple as ABC, she said. Everyone faced problems—that was Step A. Most people dithered and worried and agonized, which she called Step B. Then they reacted, which was Step C. Elizabeth's theory was that, if you could just discipline yourself to eliminate Step B, you'd make much better decisions about Step C. And save yourself a lot of grief in the process.

So naturally, as soon as Mallory closed down the bookstore that night, with the ugly echoes of the metallic voice still ringing in her ears, she headed straight for a visit with her mother.

The Heyday Chronic Care Center was brightly lit and welcoming, though it was late by the time Mallory arrived. The nurse at the front desk smiled and waved her back to the private rooms. No one bothered to make Mallory sign in anymore. They all knew her too well. She'd been coming through those double glass doors almost every night for two years now.

Her mother's room was dim, and the satellite television was set to a classical music station. Small white letters inched their way up the black screen. *Verdi,* the letters said. *Rigoletto.*

In spite of everything, now that she was here, Mallory felt herself begin to relax. Her mother always had that effect on her. Even now.

Dropping her heavy purse on the floor, she plopped down onto the bedside chair, kicked off her sandals and took her mother's hand in a warm hello squeeze.

"I'm sorry I'm late, Mom," she said. She leaned her head back against the soft headrest and shut her eyes. Verdi washed over her like a bath, cleaning away the dirty feeling that had clung to her ever since she'd spent five minutes on the telephone with a blackmailer. "It was a crazy day."

But where should she begin? Ordinarily, on these visits, she kept the conversation light and upbeat. She didn't burden her mother with the petty problems of everyday life. She didn't mention the overdue bills or the crummy book sales. She didn't mention that Dan, her bum ex-husband, who had never forked over the last installment of the divorce settlement, was now dating a teenager and said it was "serious." Not that Mallory cared, except that apparently this teenager was expensive, which meant that Dan was even less likely to get around to paying up.

And, of course, she never, ever mentioned what she had discovered about Mindy. How could she? They'd all been so horrified when Tyler Balfour had uncovered a prostitution ring at Moresville College. And when they had learned that the Rackhams' own little café had been the headquarters, the rendezvous point for the girls and their customers, her mother had been furious and mortified.

Then, about three months later, one of the betrayed wives whose husband had been "outed" in Balfour's story had thrown a gasoline can through the front window of the café and followed it with a lighted match. Heyday firefighters had done their best, but the place, which Elizabeth Rackham had built from scratch after her own divorce twelve years ago, had burned to the ground.

"I've got a big problem, Mom." Mallory didn't open her eyes. She just held on to her mother's soft, graceful hand. Elizabeth Rackham was fifty-five, but she didn't look a day over forty. Everyone said she was the most beautiful woman they had ever met.

"It's about Mindy. She's fine right now—the wedding is only eight weeks away. Frederick is crazy about her, it's really sweet to see them together. But there's someone—someone who would like to spoil things. I think I can stop this guy, but I'm not sure it's the right thing to do."

She felt hot moisture pushing at her eyelids, so she squeezed her eyes even more tightly. She would not cry. Crying over a problem fell into Step B, and strong women never indulged in Step B.

"What should I do, Mom? Should I protect Mindy, no matter what it takes? I just don't know what she'd do if she lost Frederick now. She's better, really she is. It's not like before, when she…when she didn't even want to go on living."

Her throat closed painfully as she remembered that horrible time. The blood all over the bathroom, spilling over Mindy's pale wrists like red lace cuffs.

Finally she opened her eyes, letting the tears fall silently down her cheeks. She looked at her mother. If only she would answer her. If only she would give her some advice, tell her what to do.

But she wouldn't, not ever again. Elizabeth Rackham looked as if she were peacefully sleeping, but it was nothing as natural as that. She'd had a stroke two years ago, and the doctors told Mallory that, according to all the tests, her mother wasn't aware that her daughter was in the room.

The next morning, Mallory got in the car, a brown paper package on the seat beside her, and drove carefully through the silver spring rain. She passed the police station. She passed Roddy's house. She passed the Heyday Chronic Care Center. She found the sign that said "Maryland—Fell's Point Harbor" and she hit the gas. She'd have to hurry if she was going to be on that ferry before eleven.

CHAPTER TWO

TYLER BALFOUR WAS running late, and he didn't like that. He refused to spend all day playing catch-up, so he pulled out his cell phone, called his assistant and, after about two seconds' hesitation, told her to cancel his lunch with Sally.

The two seconds were because Sally, a beautiful blonde with the temper of a blazing redhead, had warned him that the next time he canceled a date she would assume he was canceling the whole relationship.

She didn't mean it, of course. It probably wouldn't take him more than another two seconds to sweet-talk her out of her snit. But he realized suddenly that he probably wouldn't bother. Sally was gorgeous, but the thrill was gone. She was too high-maintenance anyhow. Two seconds here, two seconds there…it added up.

On the spur of the moment, he also told his assistant to ditch his three-o'clock interview. That interview was worthless. The guy might be a U.S. Senator, but he wouldn't ever talk on the record, and Tyler hated anonymous sources.

Besides, he needed to free up some serious time. The man he was on his way to meet right now might be a lot less exalted, but he was a whole hell of a lot more interesting.

Dilday Merle was the chair of academic affairs at tiny Moresville College in Heyday, Virginia, which meant that, in the grand scheme of things, he was pretty much nobody.

But when Professor Merle had called Tyler yesterday and asked for an hour to talk about the Heyday Eight, Tyler hadn't even hesitated. Hell, yes, he had time. He'd *make* time. The Heyday Eight had won Tyler a Pulitzer when he broke the story a few years ago, and they were expected to make him a couple of million dollars next year, when he published his detailed hardback version of the scandal.

He'd taken his time finding the right publisher, though several houses had been interested. He wanted to find someone who would let him tell the story straight, not just as pure exploitation. And, of course, he'd wanted a lot of money.

It was ironic, really. Eight ditzy blond college girls who spanked grown men with toy whips, then bedded them for fun and profit, had done what a decade of serious investigative reporting couldn't do. They had set Tyler free from the underpaid grind of life at a daily newspaper.

No clock-punching for Tyler anymore. Mostly he worked on the upcoming book, which the publisher wanted to call *Shenandoah Sex Circus,* though Tyler was fighting to keep it simple. *The Heyday Eight* was good enough.

If he wrote anything else these days, he did it for magazines. In-depth and on his own schedule. In fact, his *New Yorker* piece should have hit the stands today. He had arranged to meet Dilday Merle in front of Bennie's News Stand on M Street. If he hurried, he might get there early enough to grab a copy before the professor showed up.

Bennie had been selling Tyler newspapers and magazines for more than ten years, ever since Tyler was a senior at Georgetown and working on the school paper. Back then, Tyler had bought the *Washington Post* the way some men might buy a lottery ticket, just holding it reverently and praying that maybe, someday, it would be *his* byline on the front page.

"Hey, there, big shot! Who's the *man?*" Bennie hailed Tyler with enthusiasm from the shadows of his crowded counter. Though it was a muggy spring day in D.C., Bennie wore his usual uniform, a pair of black sweatpants and a black sweatshirt with a hood pulled up over his balding head. He held up a copy of the *New Yorker.* "Who's famous today?"

Tyler pulled out a couple of bills and traded them for the magazine. "I believe that would be me," he said with a smile. He leafed through the pages to his story, scanned it to make sure they hadn't cut him too much or spelled his name wrong. Good—they'd given him great play. Six pages, with full color.

Snapping it shut, he looked back at Bennie. "Did you read it?"

No one ever actually ever saw Bennie reading the merchandise, but he was the best-informed man in Washington, so Tyler assumed he must be doing it on the sly.

"Yeah," Bennie said. "You're slick, man. Real slick. You did a tap dance on that oil boy. You fishing for another Pulitzer?"

Tyler rolled up the magazine and stuffed it in his pocket. "It's the Ellies when it's magazines. But no, I'm not fishing for anything. I just tell the truth. I just tell it like it is."

Bennie stuffed a sweet-smelling slab of gum into his mouth and eyed Tyler speculatively. "So you say. But is it really as easy as that? You gonna sleep okay when oil boy's busting rocks in the slammer?"

Tyler thought of oil boy and his bankrupt company, his laid-off employees, his creditors who were basically screwed, and his investors who were suddenly destitute. One of them, an eighty-year-old man, had already shot himself to death rather than end up a burden to his children.

"You bet I will," Tyler said. "Like a baby."

Bennie looked as if he might enjoy a good debate, but Tyler, who had, as always, been subtly scanning the other customers—just in case the vice president's wife had chosen this spot to rendezvous with her boyfriend, or the local minister was shoplifting a copy of *Penthouse*—realized that one of the old guys reading in the back of the store looked vaguely familiar.

He narrowed his eyes. Who was it? Thin, stooped,

with shaggy white hair. Even from the back, the man was obviously not a local. His clothes were too ill fitting and tweedy for D.C.

Finally, the light went on. It had been almost three years since Tyler had seen him, but this had to be Dilday Merle.

He cleared his throat. "Good afternoon, Professor."

Bennie's store was small enough that Tyler didn't even have to raise his voice. Which meant, of course, that Merle must have been able to hear every word Tyler had said since he walked into the newsstand. Tyler wondered why the old man had kept silent so long. The last time they'd met, when Merle had been trying to talk Tyler out of printing his story on the Heyday Eight, he hadn't exactly been shy.

Merle turned around with a smile, and Tyler saw that the professor was holding the current copy of the *New Yorker.*

"Hello, Tyler. I've just been reading your latest article." Merle glanced down. "Still chasing the bad guys, I see. Your style hasn't changed much."

A small chuckle came from Bennie's side of the counter. "Perhaps not," Tyler said neutrally, watching as Merle walked toward him. "But then, the bad guys don't change much, either."

Merle gazed at him through his thick glasses, which made his eyes seem large and owlish, as if they didn't miss much. "And you're still not losing sleep over it," he said. He glanced at Bennie. "Or so I hear."

Bennie laughed outright at that. "If you're looking

for a bleeding heart, man, you better look somewhere else. Mr. Tyler here, he traded his heart in ten years ago. Got himself a bigger brain instead."

Tyler shot Bennie a hard look. Surely he knew better than to bring up that ancient history. What happened ten years ago was none of Dilday Merle's business. It wasn't any of Bennie's business, either, but unfortunately Tyler had been young at the time, and emotional. He'd talked too much.

But Merle obviously wasn't interested in Tyler's past. He stopped, set down the magazine and held out his hand. "I'm glad to hear that," he said. "Because I don't need a heart this time. I need a brain."

"Oh, yeah?" Tyler shook Merle's hand, noting with surprise how firm the grip was. "Why is that?"

Merle looked at Bennie, and seemed relieved that the vendor was fully absorbed with another customer.

"Because I'm being blackmailed. And I want you to catch the bastard who's doing it."

Twenty minutes later, when they were settled at Tyler's favorite café, and the waiter had taken their order and departed, Tyler knocked back some scalding black coffee and turned to the man beside him.

"Okay," he said. "Let's start over. Slowly. From the beginning. Because I'm having a little trouble believing I heard you right."

"You did." Dilday Merle had ordered bottled water, and he was carefully decanting it into the empty glass the waiter had provided. "I'm being blackmailed."

This time, Tyler was better able to control his shock.

But still…it was insane. Seventy-something-year-old Dilday Merle, with his old-fashioned etiquette and his bow ties, and his owl eyes?

This stuffy, ivory-tower academic was being black-mailed?

Though it was the lunch hour, and dozens of people thronged the quaint little café, the anonymity of the crowd provided its own privacy.

"What the hell could anyone blackmail you about?"

"Hell is the perfect word for it." Merle's voice carried some heat. He might be close to eighty, but there wasn't anything frail about him. "Some bastard has been calling me up, ordering me to pay him a thousand dollars every two weeks or else he'll tell the board of regents that I was mixed up with the Heyday Eight."

Tyler, who had just lifted his coffee cup, froze in place. He felt the steam moisten his lips, but he was too distracted to drink.

Dilday Merle and the Heyday Eight?

He didn't want to fall into stale clichés about old people, but *come on*. His mind tried to picture Greta Swinburne or Pammy Russe straddling this elegant, elderly man, snapping their little black whips across his bony backside.

No way.

"For God's sake, son, get that look off your face." Merle tightened his mouth. His high forehead wrinkled in an intense scowl. "It isn't *true*."

As if the projector of his life had started rolling

again, Tyler blinked back to reality. He sipped at his coffee, trying to look unfazed.

"Of course it's not true," he said. "Greta gave me the complete list of their customers when I broke the story. You definitely weren't on that list. I would have noticed."

"And plastered my name all over your story, no doubt."

Tyler shrugged. He was used to this attitude. He hadn't made those stupid college girls buy rhinestone-studded sex-whips, and he hadn't made those pathetic men buy their services. He'd just let the world—including the girls' parents, the men's wives, and the local police—know what was going on.

You'd think they might even be grateful that he'd brought an end to something so fundamentally unhealthy for all concerned. But about ninety percent of the people in Heyday had automatically hated Tyler Balfour's guts.

Oh, well, it was an occupational hazard for journalists. Everyone liked to shoot the messenger.

Still, he wondered what the huffy Heydayers had thought when they'd learned who journalist Tyler Balfour *really* was. When they learned that he was a McClintock by birth and had inherited a third of their precious little town.

But that was another story.

Merle was still frowning. "Wouldn't you?"

"What? Publish your name?" Tyler returned Merle's gaze without flinching. "You are a high-profile community leader. You worked with those girls at the college, in a position of trust. At least part of your salary comes from public funds. So yeah, I probably would have put your name front and center."

Merle snorted softly. He managed to make even that sound elegant. "Fair enough. Well, anyhow, this accusation is a bunch of baloney. But the blackmailer obviously knows that, in my position, I can't afford to have charges like that leveled at me. The school can't afford it, not after the scandals it's already been through."

Tyler nodded. "The guy sounds pretty clever. He's made the payment just small enough that it'll hurt less to pay it than to fight it. That's what usually trips black-mailers up. They get greedy and they ask for too much. Their victim is left with no choice but to call in the po-lice."

Merle offered him a one-sided smile. "Two thou-sand dollars a month hurts plenty," he said. "Not all of us just inherited a small town, you know. In fact, I have to tell you it still seems positively feudal that anyone *can* inherit a town."

Tyler chuckled, then leaned back as the waiter ar-rived with their meals. It did sound ridiculous, which was why he didn't intend to touch this inheritance with a ten-foot pole. He had left a standing order to sell everything, as soon as there was a legitimate buyer. So far he hadn't been able to unload any of it. Property in Heyday, Virginia, wasn't exactly in high demand.

Neither of them spoke until the waiter had gone through the requisite frills and flourishes, asking them three times if they needed anything further.

Finally they were alone. Merle looked at his dark green and yellow salad as if he'd never seen anything like it before. Then he put his fork down and gave Tyler another of those appraising stares. Tyler had to smile. He could just imagine how effective that glare had been in the classroom.

"I've always wanted to ask you something," Merle said. "When you came to Heyday and uncovered the prostitution ring, no one had any idea you had a connection to the town."

While Tyler waited for Merle to continue, he chewed a mouthful of sprouts and spinach. Georgetown college students were way too health-conscious. Even the dressing was clear and artery-friendly. The damn thing tasted like wet grass.

Merle was still staring at him. "No one knew you were related to the McClintock family."

"Right." Tyler washed his grass down with coffee. "But you said you wanted to ask me something. I haven't heard a question yet."

"I'm asking if it was just coincidence. Because I don't buy it. I don't buy that you just happened to be passing through the very town where your natural father lived. I don't believe that, out of all the insignificant little burgs on the map, you stumbled by accident onto Heyday."

"Of course I didn't. I went there to check out

McClintock. I had just found out about him. My father—"

Tyler paused. It had been several years now since he'd learned the truth, but it still caught him by surprise to think that Jim Balfour was merely his adopted father. It still disappointed him, too. Jim Balfour was a great man, quiet and introverted, but more decent and loyal than anyone Tyler had ever met. Anderson McClintock, on the other hand, had been something completely different. Fiery, self-indulgent, opinionated, arrogant. The classic rich SOB.

He started over. "The man I considered my father, Jim Balfour, decided that I ought to know. My mother had just died. She was the one who had been determined to keep it all a secret. I think she was ashamed. She and Anderson hadn't ever married." He forked another clump of grass. "Although, when I did my research, I discovered that she was probably the only woman in Virginia he *didn't* marry."

Merle smiled. "That's overstating it, but not by much."

"Whatever. So I went to Heyday to get a look at the guy. I didn't announce myself, obviously. I wanted anonymity, in case I—"

"Hated him?"

Tyler chuckled softly. "Now *that's* an overstatement. You can't hate a total stranger. And frankly I don't waste energy hating anybody. I like to keep things simple, that's all. The whole thing—second father, second family, second set of entanglements—

sounded far too complicated. I thought it quite likely I wouldn't want to get involved."

Merle had an infuriatingly unconvinced expression on his face, as if he didn't believe a word Tyler was saying. Well, too bad. Ten years ago Tyler had learned to keep a safe distance from messy emotional situations, and once he learned a lesson, he never forgot it.

"Must have come as a shock, then," Merle observed dryly, "when Anderson put you in his will. Inheriting almost a full third of Heyday, just like his other sons. Your brothers, who were, of course, just as shocked as you were, I'm sure. Kind of hard to keep your distance from that."

Tyler put his napkin on the table and gave up all pretence of eating. "Look, Merle, I don't mean to be rude, but maybe we should get to the point. You didn't come here to talk about the complexities of life as Anderson McClintock's secret baby."

Merle tilted his head. "No. You're right. I didn't."

"So let me tell you what I think this is all about. You obviously heard I'm writing a book on the Heyday Eight. You knew I'd be interested—more than interested—to learn there are new developments in that situation. A blackmailer operating nearly three years after the girls were put out of business is definitely great copy."

Merle smiled wryly. "I hadn't thought of it quite like that, but—" He nodded. "Yes. I was hoping your curiosity would be piqued. I'm checkmated here, Tyler. If I don't pay him, he'll smear me, I'll be ruined, and the police won't ever expose him. They won't even have enough incentive to try very hard. But you might. Naming the blackmailer. Having an arrest. That would make even better *copy,* right?"

"Right."

Merle sighed heavily, as if a weight had been lifted from his shoulders. "Then you'll find out who this guy is? You'll come back to Heyday?"

Come back to Heyday.

Tyler thought of the silly little city, where everything, even the co-ed prostitutes, had a circus theme. He thought of the old bastard Anderson McClintock, now dead, who had run the city like a feudal overlord. He thought of his brothers, Kieran and Bryce, whom Tyler had met, but had deliberately avoided getting close to.

Obviously, now that he'd committed to writing this book, he was going to have to return to Heyday sooner or later. He was a good reporter, and he wouldn't leave all those stones unturned.

But he remembered the Heyday residents, who hated his guts. He particularly remembered Mallory Rackham Platt, the sexy young woman who had run the Ringmaster Café, where the girls had concocted the Heyday Eight and had gathered to make their dates and count their profits.

Mallory, who had let Tyler spend so many hours there, chatting her up and complimenting her coffee, never guessing that he was gathering notes for his exposé.

Mallory, beautiful and ridiculously naive, unaware of what was going on under her nose. Mallory, whose husband had been one of the Heyday Eight's best customers. Mallory, who had tossed a plate of French fries, complete with ketchup, into Tyler's face when she found out who he really was.

Mallory, who for some strange reason was the only person in ten years to put Tyler's disciplined objectivity and emotional distance in jeopardy.

"All right," he said, ignoring the wriggle of doubt. "I'll come back to Heyday."

CHAPTER THREE

MINDY RACKHAM'S turquoise bikini was the most fantastic article of clothing she had ever owned. She had maxed out her MasterCard to buy it. She had almost been able to hear Mallory's shocked disapproval as she signed the charge slip.

But the minute she saw Freddy's face, she knew it had all been worth it.

"Wow," he said as he wrapped his arms around her. "You're absolute dynamite today, lady. You've just guaranteed Dad the vote of every male under ninety."

She nuzzled into his shoulder happily. He was wearing his own swim trunks, and his strong, bronze, beautifully shaped torso was pretty marvelous, too. He might have been a statue of a god, except that his skin was velvety warm from the sun.

His curly blond hair was wet, dangling adorably into his forehead, and he smelled of suntan oil and cocktails. Of course, he'd already been at this party for hours. She'd had to work half a day, so she'd had to arrive alone.

That was one of the main reasons she'd indulged in this designer swimsuit and cover-up. She knew she was probably the only nine-to-five working gal here. Every other female was either the wife of a rich man, or the daughter of one—or a self-made woman who wouldn't stoop to punching clocks or filing papers.

If the women here had jobs, they were high-powered positions with glassy offices, six-figure salaries and secretaries of their own. They were public-relations specialists and college professors and museum curators. They were speechwriters, magazine editors, airline pilots and congresswomen.

Mindy Rackham, low-level secretary at the corporate offices of a snack-cracker company, already felt inferior enough without having to arrive at this elite affair looking shabby and off-the-rack.

Freddy kissed the top of her head, and a honeyed calm slid down, from the contact point of his lips all the way to her pink-painted toes. *Much better.* With Frederick Earnshaw's arms around her, how could any woman feel insecure? She could already feel the jealous eyes of the other women boring a hole into her bare back.

Everyone knew Freddy was the hunkiest guy in Richmond. And the sweetest. And the richest.

He could have had any girl he wanted. So why on earth, they whispered to each other, had he chosen little Mindy Rackham, a nobody from nowhere? From Heyday, which was actually even worse. When Freddy introduced her to people, they always seemed surprised that she could speak in complete sentences and didn't have hayseeds falling from her hair.

The truth was, she didn't understand it herself. Which was why she dreamed every night that Freddy took back his ring, and every morning awakened, heart pounding, with tears in her eyes, thanking God that it had only been a nightmare.

"Come on, honey, let's get you a Coke, and there's somebody I want you to meet."

Freddy put his warm hand against the small of her back and guided her toward the others. The Olympic-size pool was as turquoise as her bikini, and shimmered under the beautiful afternoon sun. The people who stood around it were tall and elegant, murmuring to one another in low, laughing tones, making a collective sound that Mindy had come to associate with money.

White-coated waiters braided through them with trays of cocktails, and constantly refilled the beautiful tables piled high with pyramids of fruit and clear crystal vases of orchids.

For a minute, Mindy was afraid her feet wouldn't move, but somehow she forced herself to be steered into the crowd. She couldn't ever admit to Freddy that she was afraid. A politician's wife had to be good with people. Outgoing, glib and graceful.

He had told her that when he asked her to marry him. He loved her, he'd said, but he couldn't ask her to share his life without being completely honest about the responsibilities that came with the job.

Completely honest...

Her face had burned as if someone had lit a fire

under her skin when he'd said that. She'd almost told him the truth right then. But of course she had chickened out, as always.

How could she take the piece of heaven he'd just handed her, and give it back? How could she resist the joyous security of being the cherished fiancée of Mr. Frederick Earnshaw—and go back to being poor little screwed-up Mindy, who had no future and way too much past?

"Jill, I'd like you to meet Mindy. Mindy, this is Jill Sheridan-Riley. *Judge* Sheridan-Riley," he added with a teasing smile at the other woman.

Mindy smiled, too, without the teasing, and held out her hand, trying to remember, among all the things she needed to remember, that she had to shake firmly enough to look confident, but not so tightly as to seem absurd.

How could Freddy feel comfortable calling such an imposing woman "Jill"? She must be almost six feet tall, six feet of elegant, dramatic bones—collarbones, jawbones, wrist bones, cheekbones—every inch of her was jutting and determined. Dark hair and dark, intelligent eyes. Not yet forty. Still beautiful, but an uncompromising, unconventional beauty.

Judge Sheridan-Riley was one of those women who always made Mindy feel ridiculous, as if being short and blond was a character flaw. As if wearing lip gloss was a sign of weakness. Jill Sheridan-Riley hadn't spent two hours getting ready this morning. She hadn't needed to. She'd been born ready.

"Hi, Mindy," Jill said. Her voice was dark, too, thick and elegant, but it held a surprising warmth. "I've been telling Freddy that if he didn't introduce you soon I'd hold him in contempt." She laughed and patted Freddy's arm. "I've been dying for a chance to say that."

She turned back to Mindy with twinkling eyes. "I've only been a judge about a week."

Her laughter was infectious, and as Mindy chuckled she felt the knot in her stomach relax a millimeter. Maybe she could do this after all.

But just then, in the depths of the clever turquoise macramé drawstring purse Mindy had purchased to match her bikini, her cell phone began to ring.

Freddy shot a quick glance at her, and, her cheeks heating up, she shrugged helplessly. *Dumb, dumb.* She should have put it on mute.

She squeezed her hand over the purse, hoping to muffle the sound, but Freddy shook his head. "Go ahead, answer it," he said in an understanding voice. "It might be Mallory. It might be about your mother."

She nodded gratefully. He was such a special guy. He always seemed concerned about her mother's health. He didn't even seem to mind that his new fiancée came with so much baggage.

She excused herself from the other two as she dug out the small, silver phone. The caller ID showed that he'd been right. It was Mallory.

Mindy found a quiet corner, between an untended

bar and a trash can, the least picturesque square foot of the entire party. She clicked the green answer button.

"Hi, Mallory," she said. "Is everything all right?"

"Mom's fine," Mallory said. That was the first sentence of every conversation they had. "I just wanted to talk to you for a minute."

Mal sounded a little edgy, Mindy thought. Her own guilty conscience pictured the overpriced bikini. But there was no way Mallory could know about that. Mindy had bought it with her own credit card, and she'd pay for it with her own paycheck. Somehow.

"Okay. What's up?"

"I just—" Mallory stopped. She sounded uncertain, which was unlike her. She was the big sister. Now that their mother was…sick…Mallory was the boss, and the job suited her. Just like Mom, Mallory had always been completely sure of herself and her decisions. Of all the Rackham women, only Mindy was tormented with self-doubt.

"I just wondered," Mallory said slowly, "if you've thought any more about when you're going to tell Freddy."

God, that again? At a time like this? They'd just had this conversation three days ago, and Mindy had promised to think about it, to look for the perfect moment. They both knew she was going to have to tell him. Even in Mindy's most selfish dreams, she didn't imagine that she had the right to marry him without telling him the truth. It was just a matter of when.

"Mal, it's a little awkward to discuss this right now. I'm at a party. With Freddy. It's a political thing."

"Oh. Oh…well."

"What's wrong?" Mindy could tell that Mallory was upset. "Can't we talk about this later?" She lowered her voice to a near-whisper. "You know this kind of thing intimidates me, Mal. But I'm doing pretty well, I think. I just can't let myself get upset now."

"Yes, of course, later is fine." Mallory's voice resumed its normal, brisk, cheerful tones. "I'm sorry. I didn't remember that the party was today. Good for you, honey. I'm really proud of you for deciding to go after all."

Mindy remembered sheepishly that she'd told Mallory she might plead a headache, or the flu, and skip the party. She was so afraid of letting Freddy down. She was so afraid that someday, at one of these functions, the mist would fall from his eyes and he'd see her as she really was.

Too young, too gauche, too shy. Pretty enough to be a trophy wife, but not worthy in any other way.

In the end, a liability.

"Thanks," she said self-consciously. "Well, I guess I'd better go see what Freddy's up to."

"Of course." Mallory was back in cheerleader mode. "I'll bet you look like a million bucks, kiddo. Now you go out there and just be yourself. Show them how sweet and smart you are. Before this party is over, they'll all love you just as much as Freddy does."

As Mindy put her phone away, she watched Freddy and his friend the judge, who had been joined by three other suave people with drinks in their hands and clever laughter on their lips. She tried to convince herself that Mallory was right. They would love her, too…love her just as much as Freddy did.

But that was the question, really, wasn't it? How much did Freddy love her? When the time came, would it be enough?

FORGET FRIDAY THE THIRTEENTH, Mallory thought as she opened the last of the day's mail. Thursday the twenty-second was every bit as evil.

So far her day had consisted of two obnoxious publisher's reps, one carton of damaged books, three hefty returns, one irate mother who apparently didn't know that a CD called *All Night Long* might contain sexual content, and a call from Valley Pride Property Management Inc., notifying her that they planned to raise her rent.

But she could handle all that. She'd been a bookseller for almost two years now, and she could count on one hand the days that hadn't included similar frustrations.

In fact, ever since last week's call from the blackmailer, she'd decided that, as long as she didn't hear from *him,* every day was a good day.

But the piece of mail she held in her hand clearly

hadn't come from any blackmailer. This new insult was even more personal. It shouldn't really upset her at all—she'd been half expecting it for weeks. And yet, strangely, it did, if only because it reminded her what a fool she'd once been.

She slid her forefinger under the flap of the big, showy, pink-flowered envelope, already sure what it was. It was a supertacky wedding invitation—the kind Mallory would never encourage Mindy to select—and it was addressed in an almost illegible curlicue calligraphy.

Which meant that her ex-husband Dan and his pretty fiancée, Jeannie, who was nineteen but clearly had the taste of a middle-schooler, were actually getting married.

And they wanted Mallory to show up and watch.

The arrogant bastard. Mallory tossed the invitation, which was embossed with silver wedding bells that looked like scratch-off squares on lottery tickets, onto the counter. She'd show up, all right. She'd sit in the front, and when they asked if anyone knew any reason why these two should not be joined together, she'd stand up and say, *I* do! Dan Platt is a hard-core sleazeball, she'd say, and even this ditzy little airhead deserves better.

Out of nowhere, a new suspicion skittered across her mind. Her blackmailer with the metallic voice couldn't have been Dan, could it? When they'd been married, Dan had never had enough money. And he had always resented the way her family spoiled Mindy. He'd called her "the little princess."

And, since he was one of the Heyday Eight's customers, he might have known about Mindy's involvement.

But this was ridiculous. Dan was definitely a jerk, but he wasn't a blackmailer. She was just getting paranoid. She'd noticed it the very first day. Every male customer—or female customer, for that matter, if she had a deep voice—made her nervous. Everyone from the postman to the sales reps, from the mayor to the cop who patrolled Hippodrome Circle looked suspicious.

Was it you, she'd ask mentally? *Or you? Or you?*

"Mallory, stop daydreaming and get me a copy of *The Great Gatsby.*" Aurora York was suddenly standing in front of the counter, the blue feather on her pillbox hat trembling, which always meant Aurora was in a temper. "I need to show that fool Verna Myers something."

Mallory smiled at her favorite customer, glad to have something fun to take her mind off the annoyances of the day. And any meeting of Aurora's book club, Bookish Old Broads Incorporated, or Bobbies, as they called themselves, was bound to be fun.

The group met here every Thursday at six, for cookies and coffee and spirited debate. Last Thursday, Verna Myers, who worshipped at F. Scott Fitzgerald's literary feet, had been so enraged when Aurora criticized *Tender is the Night* that she had stood up, sputtering indignantly, and yanked the feather right out of Aurora's hat.

A hush had fallen over the entire bookstore. No one, but no one, touched Aurora's feathers. Wally said later that he'd been expecting a catfight. But Aurora was a lady. Instead of scratching Verna's eyes out, she had merely taken her copy of *Tender is the Night*, torn out a page from the middle, and used it to wipe the cookie crumbs from her mouth.

Frankly, Mallory had been surprised to see Verna show up again this week. But Verna probably enjoyed the rows as much as Aurora did. And, since the wealthy old ladies always paid for anything they ruined, it was lucrative for Mallory, so everybody came out a winner.

"*Gatsby?* I'll go look," Mallory said obediently. No one who knew Aurora really minded her bossy tone. Underneath the haughty Queen Victoria exterior beat one of the kindest hearts in Heyday.

But wouldn't you know it? She was completely out of *Gatsby*. The high-school seniors were writing research papers on Fitzgerald this year, and they'd all come rushing in at the last minute and picked her shelves clean.

She had her own copy upstairs. Rather than disappoint Aurora, Mallory decided to go get it.

"Wally, will you watch the register for a minute?"

Wally, who was shelving CDs, his favorite task, frowned. He was an artist—a budding film director, at least in his own mind—and he thought handling money was crass. But he was deeply in hock to the photography store down the street, so he didn't dare annoy the one employer in town who would put up with his attitudes, not to mention his multicolored hair.

"Sure," he mumbled, and began to shuffle in her direction.

Mallory's shop was actually two storefronts combined into one large bookstore on the bottom. On the upper floor, though, the building was divided into two snug but charming apartments with porches overlooking the tree-lined, curving Hippodrome Circle. Mallory lived in one. The other had been empty ever since Christmas, when her neighbor, a local chef, had taken a job at a fancy restaurant in Richmond. She still missed the great aromas that had always seeped from his apartment to hers.

Both apartments were accessed by the same outside staircase, so Mallory exited the bookstore, drank in a little of the sparkling Virginia spring air, and then climbed up to see if she could hunt down *Gatsby* in the jungle of books in her living room.

She kept admirable order downstairs—customers had to be able to find books before they could buy them. But up here, where she stored everything that wouldn't fit in the shop, as well as her own ever-growing collection of books, the situation was a mess.

Gatsby…Gatsby… When had she last read *Gatsby?* Probably around the holidays…which meant it would be beneath the "summer reading list" books that had just been delivered, but not so far down as the "back to school" books from last fall.

It took forever, so she wasn't surprised when she

heard footsteps on the outside staircase. Wally, undoubtedly panicked by being stranded with the Bobbies, must have left the register untended—the ultimate no-no—and come up here to drag her back downstairs.

She grabbed *Gatsby,* knocking over three Pilchers and a du Maurier in the process, and hurried to the door. "Darn it, Wally, I'm coming," she called. "Now get back down there before someone robs us blind."

But it wasn't Wally.

The lovely spring sunlight, so bright in her many-windowed living room, didn't quite penetrate this narrow hallway that ran behind both apartments. She blinked as her pupils tried to adjust, but she couldn't make out the person's face.

His back was to the open stairway door, and the sun haloed around him, leaving just a black silhouette, like a moving shadow. Still, she saw that he was tall, much taller than Wally. More substantial. Wally had a boy's shoulders. This squared-off breadth belonged to a man.

With no warning, fear tingled across her scalp, and she instinctively took a step backward, toward the shelter of her own doorway. This was Heyday, where dim corridors rarely posed a threat to anyone, and she was no coward, but ever since that call…

Things had changed.

Once again she asked herself…could this be the man, the faceless blackmailer with a distorted metallic voice?

But then the man spoke and the fear disappeared, replaced by a sudden, flaring fury.

He said just one word. Just her name.

"Mallory." The word was uttered softly, almost apologetically, as if he knew how she would hate seeing him and wished he could spare her the pain.

"Mallory," he said again.

No, this wasn't the blackmailer—it was someone she despised even more.

At least the blackmailer was ashamed enough to hide his true identity. This was someone who made money by exploiting other people's misery, but did it right out in the open, as if it were something to be proud of. The blackmailer at least announced right up front that he was just trying to weasel something out of you. This man masqueraded as a friend, drank your coffee and pretended to care about your problems.

And then, like a kick to the gut, he betrayed you.

This was Tyler Balfour.

CHAPTER FOUR

WOW. TYLER PAUSED in the half-open doorway. Three years hadn't softened Mallory Rackham's heart much, had they?

The hall in front of him was dim, but the afternoon light behind him streamed in over his shoulders in two bright bands, one of which caught Mallory's face and illuminated it. The venom with which she eyed him now was just as potent and undiluted as it had been the day she read his first story about the Heyday Eight and saw her husband's name.

At least she wasn't holding a plate of greasy French fries this time. He glanced at the book in her hand. A small paperback. Good. He probably wouldn't even bruise if she decided to chuck it at him.

He guessed he had at least a few seconds before that happened. For the moment she seemed paralyzed with shock and the slow awakening of long-buried anger. So he slung his suit bag over his shoulder and moved carefully toward the apartment that would be his temporary lodgings, all the while fingering his keys, trying to locate the right one.

When he reached the door, which was only about four feet from her own, she finally spoke. "What the *hell* are you doing here, Tyler?"

Okay, that was a start. She had used profanity, which he knew she rarely did, and her voice was pointed and frosty, like a dagger of ice, but at least she hadn't tossed the book. And she'd used his first name.

About a six, he figured, on the hostility scale. Nothing he couldn't handle. He'd once investigated a senator who'd been taking bribes, and though that guy had been hostile enough to consult a hit man, Tyler had still managed to get the story.

He'd get this one, too, including her part of it. He couldn't leave her out, even if he wanted to. She'd owned the café. She'd been married to one of the johns. Her little sister had gone to school with the Eight. He needed her in the book, and he'd get her.

At first, Tyler had wondered if moving into the apartment next to her was the best plan. He'd been afraid she might feel crowded. But now he saw that his instincts had been right. He was going to need the proximity, the frequent meetings, to break down long-entrenched barriers like these.

"Well?" She was gripping her book so tightly the pages curled into a circle. "Tell me. Why are you back?"

"I'm going to be staying here for a while." He held up his key. "I inherited the building, as I'm sure you've heard."

"Yes." She still clenched her jaw, which distorted

her normally musical voice. "But I also heard you were trying to sell it."

He smiled. "Did you want to make me an offer?"

"Don't be ridiculous. I just want to know why you're back in Heyday. *God.* Haven't you done enough damage already?"

"Damage?" He looked her straight in the eye. "Are you sure you don't have me confused with someone else?"

The light in the hallway wasn't great, but he could tell she flushed. Deep inside, she must know he was right. She must know that Tyler hadn't caused her husband's infidelity. He'd just exposed it.

But clearly she wasn't planning to admit it.

"Don't pull that crusading white knight routine with me," she said, her voice a shade too loud in the empty hall. "You didn't write your series to rescue the sad little girls of the Heyday Eight. You wrote it to make yourself famous. And you have absolutely no idea what kind of wreckage you left behind. You were too busy scurrying out of town to collect your Pulitzer."

Man, she really was furious. Tension crackled off her like electricity. He wondered what fed it, kept it throbbing and vital all these years. Surely she wasn't still breaking her heart over that no-good bastard ex-husband of hers.

The guy hadn't ever deserved her, but Tyler was well aware that love was illogical and unpredictable.

Which was why he always steered his own life a hundred miles in the other direction.

"I know you got divorced," he said. "And I know that, however embarrassing it must have been to discover he'd cheated on you, you're smart enough to realize you're better off without that scum bucket."

She didn't respond at first, though her flush deepened. Maybe the word had been too harsh. But Dan Platt *was* a scum bucket. What kind of sleazy moron paid for kinky thrills with a silly teenage hooker while a woman like Mallory waited for him at home?

Mallory was one of the few natural beauties Tyler had ever known. Even better, she was—or had been—lighthearted and full of life. She had smiled a lot, and laughed a lot, and let her short blond hair tumble all over itself in a way that was somehow ten times sexier than anything he'd seen at a White House ball or a Kennedy Center gala.

Some of that vibrant energy had been dampened, he saw now. It wasn't that she looked older, for the three years had hardly touched her in that way. The difference was more subtle. She looked subdued, as if her colors had faded. This face was still lovely, but it had new shadows.

He felt an odd prick of guilt, knowing that his series had helped to put some of those shadows there.

Finally she found her voice. "I am not going to discuss Dan with you. But if you think my divorce was the worst thing that happened around here in the wake of the great Tyler Balfour, you're very wrong."

He gave her a half smile. "You underestimate me, Mallory," he said. "I'm a journalist. I know all about

the developments of the past few years. I know that
eighty students pulled out, and the college almost
closed. I know there were six divorces, including
yours, one suicide attempt, one illegitimate baby and
two county commissioners ousted in the next election."

He paused, in case she wanted to break in, but she
didn't speak. She just looked at him, as if she were
hypnotized by his litany of misery.

"I know that Sander Jacobson's loony wife set fire
to the Ringmaster Café, illogically blaming your family for her husband's sins. And I know that, after the
fire, your mother had a stroke. A stroke from which
she hasn't yet recovered."

Again he paused.

Mallory's eyes were bright, but her chin was high.
"Is that all?"

He thought about Dilday Merle and the mysterious
blackmailer. But he wasn't free to talk about that.
"Seems like enough, doesn't it?"

Was it his imagination, or did she seem relieved?
She certainly took a deep breath, and when she spoke,
her voice was steadier.

"Impressive," she said. "I knew you spied on us
when you were in Heyday. I had no idea you had continued to do so from Washington, D.C."

"I just followed the story. I follow all my stories.
And this one is particularly important to me."

She laughed harshly. "Why? I hope you aren't
going to say it's because of me, because we were

'friends.' I quit believing in that fairy tale three years ago. Although I have to admit you had me fooled pretty thoroughly for a while there."

Again that slight sting of conscience. Had he gone too far back then, while he was digging for the story he suspected was buried in her innocent little café? Had he played the role of friend and confidant so convincingly that he had actually hurt her?

He hadn't meant to. Ordinarily he knew just where the ethical lines were drawn. Sometimes, though, he had forgotten it was a role. Sometimes, while he sat at the counter late at night and ate her amazing blueberry pie, he had forgotten that he was a reporter. Sometimes, when she had hinted at how unhappy her home life was, he had been forced to fight the urge to take her hand across the counter.

Sometimes he had almost forgotten to take notes.

Almost.

But he'd done plenty of soul-searching back when it happened. And he'd decided that, though he might have touched the line with his toe once or twice, he hadn't ever actually crossed it.

He wasn't going to cross it now, either. Even if it made the reporting more difficult, he was going to play it straight with her this time.

"No, it's not because of you," he said. "It's because I'm writing a book about the Heyday Eight. For that, I'm going to need all the information I can get."

"You're writing a—" She swallowed, and, as if her fingers had gone limp, the book dropped to the wooden floor. She didn't seem aware that she no longer held it. "A book? About those poor girls? *Why?*"

He retrieved the mangled paperback, which he saw was a copy of *The Great Gatsby.* "It's what I do, Mallory," he said quietly. "I'm a writer."

She looked at him. She opened her mouth, as if she were about to say something. And then, without another word, without even taking her book from his hand, she moved past him and went out the side door. He heard her footsteps disappearing fast along the stairs.

Well, hell. What exactly was that all about?

He'd known that seeing her again would be awkward. He'd expected her to be angry that he was going to tear up her town again when the book came out.

And she had been angry, damn angry, at first. But then, after he mentioned the book...

He stared at the empty rectangle of light for a long moment, trying to sort through the signals his instincts were sending him. He had talked to a lot of people about a lot of difficult things, and he had learned to read them pretty well.

Unless he had completely lost his touch, Mallory Rackham wasn't merely angry anymore.

She was flat-out scared.

A WEEK LATER, Mallory was on her way to the Windjammer Golf and Country Club. She was going too fast, and her thoughts were so agitated she almost drove her Volkswagen into the faux-marble haunches of one of the zebra statues that stood guard over the winding, green-bordered entry.

A caddy working the seventh hole glared at her, shocked that anyone would disrupt the pastoral harmony of this elite club.

But Mallory didn't care. She almost wished she *had* hit them. Those zebra statues were stupid.

Not as stupid, however, as *she* was.

Yessir, Mallory Rackham took the blue ribbon in Abject Stupidity.

She shook her head, muttering to herself as she guided the car more carefully up toward the clubhouse. What fantasy world had she been living in? Had she really believed the blackmailer would just send her a nice thank-you note for the thousand-dollar payment and then scratch her off his list? Hadn't she ever read a detective novel, or watched a crime show on TV? Heck, a five-year-old could probably tell you that, once you paid a blackmailer, he'd just keep coming back for more.

But not Mallory. Idiot that she was, she'd actually been stunned to hear the man's electronic voice on her telephone again this afternoon.

He'd told her he wanted another thousand dollars. Only two weeks after the first payment.

When she'd asked him where he thought a small-town, small-business owner was going to get that kind of money, he had laughed—that horrible, tinny laugh she remembered so well.

Maybe, he'd said, she should consider taking up

where Mindy had left off. Mallory might not be a teenager anymore, but she was still a good-looking woman. Did she know how to handle a whip?

Without thinking, Mallory had slammed down the phone, too furious to calculate the wisdom of such a move. But almost instantly she regretted it. During the long two or three minutes she'd waited to see if he'd call back, she was racked with fear that he might not, that the next call he made might be to Freddy Earnshaw.

Or what if he'd heard that Tyler Balfour was writing a book? How much, she wondered, would Tyler pay for juicy information like this?

Finally, the phone had run again. She picked it up, her fingers trembling. The metallic voice was colder and harder than ever. That little insult had cost her, he'd said slowly. Double the pain. This time he wanted *two* thousand dollars. Tomorrow.

But she didn't have two thousand dollars. And, because she was a shortsighted fool, she hadn't made any provisions for getting it. She could have taken another loan on the business, maybe, if she could persuade Doug Metzler at the bank to stretch the income/debt ratios a little. Or she could have accepted one of the offers for credit cards that clogged her mailbox daily. She could have sold some of her own collection of antique books—well, *all* her collection, probably.

But the point was, if she hadn't been such an idiot, she could have done *something*.

Instead, she was going to have to get desperate.

She was going to have to borrow the money from Roddy.

Not that Roddy cared. Roddy had been born middle-class, with a curious mind that got him into a ton of trouble as a child but had made him several million dollars as an adult. Roddy was always inventing things—things that weren't necessarily sensible enough to make it to the market, but which were just interesting enough to bring in huge option purchases from big businesses.

His latest idea had been a "flip-flop clip," which kept the cuff of your slacks from tucking under when you wore sandals. Even his best friend, Kieran McClintock, had laughed at that one, but when a major beachwear company had paid him a hundred thousand dollars for it, Roddy had thrown a bikini-beach party at the country club and invited the entire town of Heyday.

So, after running around mentally like a rat in a maze for a couple of hours, she'd finally called Roddy on his cell, taken a deep breath, and asked if she could borrow two thousand dollars. Today.

"Okay," he said in his typical laid-back style. He was the only man she'd ever known who wouldn't ask why. "Want to come get it now? I'd come there, but I can't leave for another hour or two."

She knew where he was, of course. He was always at the country club's bar, the Gilly Wagon, after four o'clock, when he finished his last hole of golf for the day. He played poker, flirted with the married women, watched CNN and drank ginger ale for at least three hours every Tuesday, Wednesday and Thursday. Friday and Saturdays he switched to beer and single women.

And no one could tell him to leave. He'd single-handedly built the Gilly Wagon with the proceeds from his crazy idea for fake fingernails made of candy.

"You've got that much money *on* you?"

He chuckled. "Well, you know. In case I have to flee the country unexpectedly, that kind of thing. Come on over."

"I guess I could," she'd said. Wally could close up. "But, are you alone?"

"No. But I am amazingly discreet. Never fear, Mallory dear. The hand is quicker than the eye."

And so here she was, parking the car at the country club and heading into the Gilly Wagon, which at this hour would, she hoped, be mostly empty.

It was. Other than a foursome in the corner arguing about how many strokes it had taken one of them at the ninth hole, Roddy and Kieran were the only ones there.

She said hi to the bartender, who doubled as the waiter and was hurrying over to seat her. She waved him off, pointing toward Roddy. The man nodded gratefully and went back behind the bar to finish washing the glasses for the coming rush.

"Hi, guys," she said as she approached the table. Kieran, that handsome, golden-haired sweetie, half rose immediately and gave her a kiss.

She hugged him briefly. "Where's Claire?"

Kieran chuckled. "She said she'd rather stick bamboo shoots under her fingernails than be a part of this little adventure of Roddy's. But I assume she's not actually doing that. She's probably rolling Stephanie around the park, trying to get her to go to sleep."

"Roddy's little adventure?" Mallory turned to Roddy with a smile, noticing that he hadn't bothered to rise, leaving the graceful manners to Kieran.

Roddy Hartland was nowhere nearly as classically handsome as the McClintocks, with his freckles and his unruly brown curls, but he was pretty darn sexy, once you saw the intelligent laughter in his eyes and the easy tolerance in his smile. And he had a wonderful, strong body.

Mallory and Roddy dated each other more often than either of them dated anyone else, but they both understood it would never come to anything. Though no words had ever been spoken on the subject, she knew that he'd always been half in love with Mindy. Sadly, the ten-year age difference had proved fatal. Roddy wasn't willing to declare himself and risk rejection. Mindy, young and self-absorbed, had never even guessed.

"What trouble are you trying to stir up today?"

Roddy blinked innocently. "Trouble? Gosh, you say that like I do it all the time."

"That's because you do," Kieran put in, his mouth full of ice. He held out his empty drink. The bartender nodded and turned to retrieve the bottle of imported single malt Scotch whiskey they kept on hand solely for the McClintocks, who might not be the only ones in Heyday who could appreciate it, but were just about the only ones who could afford it.

· Kieran turned his gorgeous blue eyes toward Mallory. "Don't tell Claire I was drinking. But this is one stunt I just can't pull sober."

"You're not pulling it, you coward." Roddy shook his head. "I am."

Mallory growled. "Will someone please tell me what's going on?"

Kieran waved the question to Roddy, who grinned happily and sucked down some ginger ale, clearly just to prolong the suspense.

"Roddy Hartland…"

"Okay, okay. So you know Doug Metzler, right?"

Mallory frowned. "Yeah. Of course."

"And you know he's an unmitigated stuffed shirt, right?"

Mallory smiled. "Um…he holds three loans of mine, Roddy, so I'm not sure I want to call him that out loud."

"I do. He's a pompous zebra's ass, and I've decided to give him the apoplectic fit he so richly deserves."

Kieran began to chuckle. "He *will* have a fit." He drank some of his new Scotch. "Really. When he sees you, he'll have a fit and turn purple."

Mallory still didn't understand a thing. She glowered at Roddy, who was trying so hard to hold back his laughter that he was getting a little color in his own cheeks.

"Okay, look. Here's the deal. Metzler is the current president of the country club. And frankly, the man's got a stick up his—" Roddy wrinkled his nose guiltily. "I mean, he's so uptight nobody can stand him. Yesterday he had the nerve to issue a *dress code* for the club. No sandals. No T-shirts. According to Doug-God-complex-Metzler's official memo, you won't be served if you aren't wearing closed shoes and a shirt with a collar. "

Mallory shrugged: "Well, you *are* wearing a shirt with a collar."

Kieran, who had just swallowed, choked on his expensive liquor. "Yeah, but that's not all he's wearing."

"What?" Mallory narrowed her eyes. Roddy leaned back, looking insufferably smug, delighted with his own ingenuity.

And then she finally caught on. What else was he wearing? Scooting her chair back, she ducked her head under the tablecloth and took a peek.

Oh, my God.

A skirt.

An honest-to-God, bonafide skirt, the kind the Heyday cheerleaders wore. The navy-blue pleats folded gracefully around Roddy's tanned, athletic thighs. His muscular calves were bare and a little hairy above his sneakers.

She started to laugh as she lifted her head, and in her helpless mirth she banged it noisily on the underside of the table. Still, she had to thank him. He had not only agreed to loan her a fortune, he had made her laugh on a day when she hadn't thought that was possible.

"Oh, Roddy," she said. "You goof."

Roddy was back to looking innocent. "What? I read the official memo word for word. It didn't say anything about skirts." He reached out and gave her hand a tap. "But actually, sweetie, you might want to scram before Doug gets here. Things are likely to get ugly."

"Hell, yeah, they will," Kieran said to Mallory earnestly. "I've seen him standing up in that skirt. The man's so bowlegged it's tragic."

Still smiling, Mallory gave Roddy a hesitant glance. "But—" She tried to think of a subtle way to remind him why she was here.

"Go," he said firmly, and squeezed her hand. "I'm sure you have at least *two thousand* more important things to do than messing with Doug Metzler's mind."

The grip was unusually firm. He was trying to tell her something. She glanced down at her purse, which, she saw, now had a bright white envelope sticking out of it.

The money was already there. How had he done that? When had he done it? Perhaps when she and Kieran had been kissing each other hello? Roddy really was a magician. And she could use a magician right about now. If he could make a treasure appear out of nothing, maybe he could make Mindy's past *disappear...*

She smiled at him, hoping he could see her heart in her eyes. She wished she could tell him this was for

Mindy. But he had no idea that Mindy had been involved in the Heyday Eight, and she'd never disillusion him about the girl he silently adored.

"All right," she said. "If you dorks really are going to start a brawl in here, I guess I *would* rather be someplace else."

She reached over and gave him a kiss. Usually they pecked on the cheek, but this seemed to call for something more heartfelt. She pressed her lips to his, and as she straightened up she whispered, "Thanks."

He winked and grinned. "No problem, sweetie. But look. Here comes our resident stranger. I hear he's your new landlord."

She turned quickly. It was true. Tyler Balfour had entered the Wagon. She hadn't expected him, and, unprepared, she caught her breath, struck anew with his good looks. How had she not realized he was a McClintock the last time he was in town? Only the McClintock genes produced men this dangerously virile.

"Oh, yeah." Kieran was nodding, motioning Tyler over. "He's here to see me. We've got business to do."

Maybe that was true, but as Tyler approached his gaze seemed locked on Mallory. He was probably a great poker player, she thought. His handsome face was as blank as a mannequin's. Clearly he had been trained to observe, and not to care.

Well, fine, she didn't care, either. She had been humiliatingly gullible the last time he was in Heyday. Emotionally tangled in a failing marriage, she'd been so grateful for the calm sympathy he had projected. Over the weeks, she'd even begun to dream about him, about his comfort turning to something warmer…

He'd kissed her once. Only once. She was still married, on paper anyhow. And the next day his story had come out.

As he drew nearer, she gave him a deliberately fake smile. He must know she wasn't pleased to see him. She'd managed to avoid him for a full week now, even though sometimes she was piercingly aware that they were just inches away from each other, with only a piece of drywall between them.

Sometimes at night she could hear him on the phone in his apartment, though she could never quite make out the words. She filed that information away, though. If she could hear him, he could hear her.

"Hi, Tyler," Kieran said, smiling and rising. "Thanks for coming over. I'll be ready to leave soon, but I promised Roddy I'd wait a few more minutes. He's going to put on a fireworks show for us."

Kieran seemed to remember suddenly that Tyler was a relative stranger to Heyday. "Oh, sorry. Have you had the chance to meet Roddy Hartland?"

"I don't think so." Tyler held out his hand. "Our paths didn't cross when I was here before."

Which was a polite, secret-code way of saying Roddy hadn't been listed as a client of the Heyday Eight. Mallory felt a flush of indignation. As if Roddy, with his muscles and his millions, would ever need to buy sex from anyone! She put her hand on his arm, instinctively protective, though he obviously had no need of protection from Tyler or any man.

Tyler saw the touch. She felt the flick of his eyes like the tip-touch of a whip. Yes, she told him with her own gaze. *I was lonely back then, and you played me for a fool. Yes, I wanted to trust you. I even wanted to kiss you. But he's the one I'm kissing now.*

Roddy must have felt the currents of tension, but with his usual composure he took her hand and, holding it, he rose and held out his other hand to Tyler.

"No, we never met," he said, grinning. "You were in Heyday looking for secrets, and frankly I haven't got any. With me, what you see is what you get."

Tyler's focus fell slowly to Roddy's ridiculous skirt. It barely skimmed his knees.

"So it would seem," Tyler said. "If only that were true of everyone, my job would be a whole lot easier."

He smiled when he spoke the words, but Mallory couldn't help thinking the comment had been directed at her. She hugged her purse to her side and smiled right back.

She wasn't afraid of him. She had the money she needed. She would buy the blackmailer's silence for another couple of weeks.

And during that time, somehow she'd find a way to keep her little sister's name out of this son of a bitch's sleazy book.

CHAPTER FIVE

Two hours spent in the company of Kieran and Bryce McClintock only confirmed what Tyler had suspected about his "family."

They were nuts.

First, Kieran had been sitting at the country club bar with a guy wearing a miniskirt, which apparently they had arranged for the express—and somewhat juvenile—purpose of annoying a balding guy who came in later wearing neon-green pants. If you asked Tyler, it was a toss-up who looked stupider, the guy in drag or Mr. Greenpants, who began sputtering convulsively the minute he caught a glimpse of the skirt.

Now, though the three of them had arrived at the Valley Pride real estate offices and were trying to review an offer Kieran wanted to make on one of Tyler's properties, they kept getting interrupted. Apparently every single tenant insisted on seeing the McClintock brothers personally, about everything from busted sewer pipes to leaky window caulking.

If Tyler had run this ship, he would have fired Elton Fletcher, the prissy pencil pusher at the front desk, who clearly didn't want to get his hair mussed by tangling with the clients. None of these lunatics should ever have made it past the first pair of double doors.

Especially not this new one, a fifty-something, wild-eyed tenant named Mrs. Milligan, who had entered ranting five minutes ago, and, as far as Tyler could tell, hadn't drawn a breath yet.

She seemed to focus her wrath on Bryce, and was leaning over him, wagging her finger in his face.

"And if you think you can scare me just because you have a reputation for shooting anyone who crosses you, you're quite mistaken, my boy. I've got a Doberman who's been waiting a long time for a nice dish of McClintock stew. He'd have you by the throat before you could get your finger on the trigger."

Bryce looked over at Kieran with a tilted smile. "Is that really my new reputation? Gunslinger? What happened to the trashy man-slut thing? I think I liked that one better."

Kieran shrugged. "Now you've got both. Congratulations."

Bryce sighed and returned his gaze to the wild woman standing over him. "I don't shoot women, Mrs. Milligan. Not unless they're coming right for me. It's just that you've had two and a half years of living rent-free—"

She drew herself erect, in clear offence. "There were extenuating circumstances."

"Yeah. I know. Your sister was kidnapped, and you had to pay the ransom. Your dog needed extensive psychiatric help." Bryce shot a quick look at Kieran, but somehow both of them managed to keep straight faces. "So what is it this month?"

"It's…it's *classified*." She pursed her lips and lifted her chin haughtily. "If I told you, good men would die."

Kieran made a strange sound, but he quickly buried his head in a file and wouldn't look at anyone. Bryce sighed again, shut his eyes and put his hand up to massage his forehead.

While both of them were distracted, Mrs. Milligan turned abruptly to Tyler and gave him an unmistakable wink, a theatrical expression so broad it screwed up one entire half of her face.

The old scamp! This was just a game to her. Tyler wondered if the McClintock brothers knew that, or whether they really thought she was insane.

Without thinking, Tyler winked back. And then Bryce opened his eyes. Smiling, Mrs. Milligan returned to staring him down.

"Well?"

"Well," Bryce said slowly. "I wouldn't want anyone to actually die."

"That's what I thought." She picked up her purse. "You have enough blood on your hands already, don't you?"

Bryce held his palms up, obviously outmatched. "Yes," he said. "I mean, no. I mean…forget about the rent, Mrs. Milligan. If the time ever comes that you're in a position to pay, you know where to send the check."

"Of course I do." She turned from the doorway. "But don't hold your breath."

When she was gone, both brothers leaned back in their chairs, shaking their heads and chuckling.

Kieran turned to Tyler. "Sorry about that. I didn't realize she'd be here today. Wouldn't you just know it? After we waited all this time for you to get here, I had hoped—" He dropped the file on the desk. "We certainly can't be making a very good impression on you, can we?"

"This is how it is," Bryce said dryly. "This is life in Heyday. Tyler might as well know that from the get-go. That way, if he decides to run for his life, he can at least get a head start."

"Run?" Kieran's face sobered. "Surely you're not leaving right away, are you? We've got a lot to catch up on."

Tyler took a moment to frame his answer. He was eager to liquidate his inheritance and get out of here. He'd spent the past week visiting his new holdings, working with Elton Fletcher, the front-desk neatnik, and a real estate agent he'd brought in from Richmond.

Things didn't look promising. Though months ago he'd left instructions to sell anything at almost any price, so far he'd been able to dispose of only two properties. Some guy named Slip-something who owned a bar just outside the city limits had wanted to expand, so he'd bought the Black and White Lounge. And now Kieran wanted one of Tyler's empty lots by the river.

At this rate Tyler would be free in about, oh, ten years.

Too bad he didn't have more empty lots. They'd be a lot easier to unload. This town, with its circus fetish, was just too kitschy for words, and the architecture was a nightmare. He had one lovely plot at the edge of town, but the house on it had been designated a historical building. He wasn't allowed to pull down the ridiculous ringmaster statue by the front gate or replace the hideous stained-glass windows depicting leaping zebras.

"Maybe you could give it a little time," Kieran said. "Believe it or not, Heyday kind of…grows on you."

God forbid. Tyler shifted his feet, as if he could already feel weeds and vines trying to wrap themselves around him, rooting him to this eccentric little backwater.

Still, Bryce and Kieran seemed to love the place, and there was no need to be callous. They weren't such bad guys, actually. They clearly wanted to reach out to him, which was a little awkward. He'd dodged their phone calls and dinner invitations for a full week, determined to make it clear he wasn't interested in being drawn into the bosom of the family, hailed as the beloved long-lost brother.

But inevitably they'd met in town from time to time. He'd pegged their types right away, a knack he'd developed over the course of about a thousand interviews. Kieran was the solid one, the brother who couldn't bear the thought of hurting anybody, the one who would be a bad liar and would do the right thing if it killed him. He was probably buying this lot just to be nice.

Bryce was only about half as cynical as he pretended to be, but that was plenty. He prided himself on being a dark, sardonic devil with attitude to spare.

So yeah, Tyler understood them. He even liked them. It wasn't their fault he felt no real sense of connection, no call of blood to blood. How could he? He wasn't a McClintock, whatever the DNA might say. He was a Balfour. And he had no interest in being anything else.

Bryce, who clearly wasn't the patient type, cut through the stretching silence. "So what's the answer, Tyler? Do you intend to cut and run?"

"Not *run,* exactly," Tyler said with one his most neutral smiles. "I told you about the Heyday Eight book. I've got a lot of interviews to do before I can leave. But I don't have any plans to stay longterm, if that's what you're asking."

Kieran looked somber, almost disappointed, but Bryce just laughed. He had been casually tossing a small football-shaped paperweight from one hand to the other. Suddenly, without warning, he lobbed it over to Kieran, who caught it as easily as if the whole thing had been scripted.

"No one ever *plans* to stay in Heyday, my friend." Bryce stood and, loosening his tie, moved toward the door. He paused by Tyler's chair long enough to give him a brotherly pat on the shoulder.

"But somehow, in the end, you just *do.*"

WHEN MALLORY APPROACHED the ferry at Fell's Point Harbor that stormy Friday morning, dressed in dark jeans, black T-shirt and hooded gray raincoat, she felt strangely excited. Almost happy, in spite of the fact that it was a dreary day, and she'd hadn't slept all night.

She looked at the choppy water, which was the unappealing color of tarnished silver. Little frothy whitecaps promised the ferry customers a bumpy ride.

But yes, in spite of all that, she felt *happy*.

Because the blackmailer didn't know it, but the rules of this game were about to change.

Last night, when she had wrapped up Roddy's money in plain brown paper according to the blackmailer's ridiculous specifications, she had included a little something extra.

She had included a note saying that he'd simply have to ease up, that she wouldn't be able to make payments every two weeks like this. She couldn't afford it. Period.

She had no idea how he'd react. Yesterday, on the phone, it had required very little to antagonize him. But she had to take the chance. Her note was nothing but the simple truth. She could not afford this.

Besides, she had hopes that this might be the last payment she'd ever have to make. Mindy was coming for a weekend visit, and they'd finally have time alone to talk. Somehow, she'd make Mindy see that honesty and courage were their only real protection. They couldn't rewrite the past. And obviously they weren't going to be able to bury it.

When Tyler had shown up, Mallory had considered telling Mindy to stay away. But then she realized that Tyler's arrival made Mindy's decision that much more urgent. At any moment, the blackmailer might decide Tyler had deeper pockets and was the better customer for this information.

She gripped her package, which was starting to get soggy from the rain, and stepped onto the ferry, her stride much more confident, in spite of the rocking water, than the last time she made this miserable trip.

Funny how strong it made you feel to assert yourself a little.

She'd thought the ferry might be deserted, given the weather. But to her surprise it was crowded with row upon row of gray figures with ducked heads, anonymous bodies hunkered down inside hoods, under umbrellas, beneath the dripping rims of Gore-Tex rain hats.

She went to the front of the ferry and bent down to slide the package under the bench seat, following her instructions to the letter even though the seat was full. No one seemed to notice her. Even the person whose feet her package nearly touched didn't look up.

And that's when she got the idea.

A crazy idea. It made her heartbeat zigzag oddly with excitement, and she inhaled softly, tasting rain.

Maybe, in this kind of weather, she could blend into the crowd herself. Maybe she could pretend to exit the ferry, as instructed, but turn at the last minute and remain on board. Maybe she could watch the package quietly from the protection of her own hood…and eventually discover the identity of the blackmailer.

It was risky. It might even be downright dangerous. But once the idea presented itself, she couldn't seem to banish it. She wanted to know who was tormenting her like this. She wanted to know who would dare to threaten Mindy's future.

She wasn't sure exactly what she'd do with the information. But, as the blackmailer had so well illustrated, knowledge was power.

So she went through her paces. She moved toward the ramp again, pretending to leave the boat, but at the last minute she took a right turn and went through the outer walkway back toward the rows of benches.

As she wedged herself into a seat three rows back from her little package, but with a clear view of its sodden brown contours, the boat began to pull away from the dock. Too late to change her mind now. Her pulse must have been going about a hundred beats a minute. She tried to swallow, but her throat was bone-dry and wouldn't cooperate.

She glanced at the shining black raincoat of the man next to her and had the sudden, heart-stopping thought that she might have sat down right next to the blackmailer.

How on earth would she ever know?

Oh, God, she hadn't thought this through far enough. All along, for no good reason, she'd been assuming that the blackmailer must be someone she knew. Someone from Heyday, someone she'd actually recognize when she spotted him.

But what if he wasn't? What if he was a total stranger? Even if she saw him pick up the packet, how would that help her? She wasn't a professional spy. She didn't have a tiny camera in the pull tab of her jacket zipper. She couldn't transmit a grainy photo back to Double-O headquarters, where they'd computer-scan for known perverts and then send the ID to her through a radio hidden in her barrette.

And besides, at some point a lot of these riders were going to get off the ferry. At each destination the crowd would thin, until she would stick out here like a sore thumb. Unless the blackmailer planned to pick up his money very soon, she'd have to get off, too, just to keep from being spotted herself.

Another anonymous, cloaked man walked by. His path seemed headed straight for the money. Mallory held her breath until he turned left and sat down next to a woman who smiled up at him, then leaned her head gratefully against his shoulder.

False alarm. She noticed that her hands were shaking a little, so she slid them under her arms and tucked her chin toward her chest, making sure she could still see the packet of money.

No, she was definitely no James Bond. She was just a foolish bookstore owner who was suffering from sleep deprivation and stress and wasn't making good decisions. The best she could do now was get off at the very first stop and pray that the blackmailer didn't see her before she could escape.

"Well, my heavens! Mallory? Mallory Rackham?"

Her fingers clenched, and she looked up, startled and hot-cheeked from the sudden rush of adrenaline. The rain ran down her face as she stared helplessly at the rather large man standing in front of her.

Who was he? He looked familiar, but...

"It's Phil, Phil Earnshaw!" He reached out to squeeze her arm. "It's good to see you, Mallory, good to see you. Even if we are a pair of drowned rats out here!"

Of course. She couldn't forget that hearty voice, that overly friendly touch. It was Freddy's father, State Senator Phillip Earnshaw. They'd met only once, at Mindy and Freddy's engagement party, but for a career politician, once was apparently enough.

She managed something like a smile. But, God, of all the people to run into! And it certainly showed her the foolishness of believing a rain hood could render her completely invisible to everyone else, including the blackmailer.

"Hi," she said. "Yes, the weather's a mess, isn't it?" She was relieved to feel the boat slowing down for its first stop at the inner harbor.

She couldn't breathe properly. She had to get off.

"I want to tell you how much we're enjoying your lovely little sister. It's not an easy life, campaigning. She's young, I told Freddy that might be a problem, but she's doing real well. She's handling things like a trouper. And of course, she's pretty as a picture."

Mallory tried another smile, hoping he'd assume the rain was responsible for its unnatural quality. He had two or three men with him, all in elegant black coats with large, shiny black umbrellas shielding them—and him—from the rain.

She, on the other hand, probably really did look like a drowned rat.

Worst of all, he was so loud. He might as well have been shining a spotlight on her.

"Yes," she said valiantly, keeping her voice low. "Mindy is a wonderful person."

The boat was coming to a stop. She had no idea where they were, but it didn't matter. This was her exit.

But Phil Earnshaw was ready to move on anyhow. Politicians had to work the crowd. "Super to see you," he was saying again, this time patting her hard on the shoulder. "Just super."

Finally he and his entourage were gone, though several of the other passengers were still staring at her, wondering what that had been all about. With shaking fingers, she pulled the drawstring of her hood tighter and bent to pick up her purse.

And that's when she realized that the money was gone.

WHEN THE DOORBELL RANG, Mindy looked up at the clock guiltily. How could it be midnight already? She'd been sitting here with the sketch pad in her lap for the past four hours, and yet it felt like about forty-five minutes, at most.

She slipped the paper under the sofa cushion, cast a quick glance in the mirror and hurried to let Freddy in.

"Baby!" He swooped through the door, his arms full of white roses. He waved them at her with a flourish and then, depositing them on the table, he pulled her up against his chest. "We missed you tonight. Are you feeling any better?"

"Lots," she said, pressing her nose into his shirt and taking a deep breath. She loved the cologne he wore to parties. If only she didn't hate the *parties* so much. "Headache's all gone."

He kissed the top of her head. "I'm glad. Poor baby, I hated to think of you here all alone tonight, with no one to rub your head."

She shut her eyes, fighting back the guilt. He was too good—she didn't deserve him. There hadn't been any headache, of course. Every now and then, she just couldn't face one of the seemingly endless events on his social calendar.

Usually it happened when she was feeling tired, or insecure about her looks. If her face broke out, or if she had premenstrual bloating, or if she just couldn't afford anything new to wear, sometimes she told him she had a headache and stayed home. He thought she was devastated to miss the excitement, but she was secretly thrilled to have an entire evening to draw and watch TV and slouch around in an old T-shirt and socks.

Lately, though, she'd been letting herself do that too often. She'd have to watch out. Freddy was beginning to worry. As he left tonight, he'd said maybe she should go see a doctor, find out what was causing all the headaches.

He guided her to the sofa now and sat down, ready for a cuddle. But, as he sat, the sketch pad she'd hidden beneath the cushion crinkled noisily. He lifted slightly, felt around beneath his knees and pulled out the incriminating papers.

He frowned at her, half teasing, but half genuine disappointment. "Mindy," he said as he flipped through the pages. "You were supposed to be sleeping."

"I did sleep," she said. "But when I woke up, I needed something to do. I didn't draw for long, only after my headache was better." She looked up at him. "Don't be mad."

"Of course I'm not mad," he said quickly. He would have hated to think of himself as an overcontrolling male. "It's just that, if you weren't really sick, I wish you had come with me. I was the only man there without a date. It was pretty uncomfortable."

She took the sketch pad out of his hands and folded the top cover over. Her stomach tightened as she saw he really was upset. "I'm sorry," she said quietly.

He hadn't leaned back yet. He was watching her with a strange expression on his face. That look made her stomach tighten into such a small ball she felt a little nauseated.

"Mindy, I need you to tell me the truth about something," he said. "The honest truth, okay?"

She couldn't speak, so she nodded. But in her mind she crossed her fingers. She'd tell the truth, if she could. If it wasn't too dangerous.

"Do you really think you're going to like being a politician's wife? Do you think all the parties and dinners and fund-raisers and stuff are going to be too much for you?"

For one ecstatic second, she actually thought he was offering to give it all up. To become just sweet, comfortable Freddy—a businessman, maybe, or a tax attorney. To abandon the dream of being Mr. Frederick Earnshaw, up-and-coming politician, future governor, or senator….or maybe, though no one ever dared to say such audacious things, something even more glittering and powerful.

But then reality kicked in, and she understood what he was really asking.

He needed a partner, a second star to glitter faithfully beside him, or perhaps just a little behind. He needed energy and creativity and enthusiasm for this life. Could she be that partner, or had he fallen in love with the wrong woman? Had he put this beautiful diamond ring on the wrong finger?

Had he chosen a girl who would be nervous and tongue-tied, or, even worse, hiding at home with a headache?

Fear shot through her. "Of course it's not too much for me," she said, forcing herself to sound surprised and slightly amused. "I just had a headache, honey, that's all. And you know, I think you were right about the doctor. I was wondering if it might be eye strain. I might need glasses." She saw him knit his brow. "I mean, contacts. I might need to get contacts."

He grinned, and she saw that he had allowed her playful tone to push the unwelcome doubts away. He loved her, she knew that. He was probably just as unnerved by the thought of real trouble in their relationship as she was.

She tilted her head and gave him a teasing smile. "In fact. I think I'm hopelessly nearsighted. I can hardly even see you right now. Maybe you'd better come a little closer…."

She reached out and tugged on his bow tie, which unraveled under her fingers into a black silken ribbon. His breath came faster. He tilted toward her.

"I'd better not risk getting too close," he said, his whisper thick and playful. "If you ever get a look at what a homely dude I am, you might fall right out of love with me."

She laughed, because of course he was the most handsome man alive. He was gentle and good and so sexy she was already melting, just because he had smiled at her.

"All right, then," she said. "Just to be on the safe side, I'll shut my eyes."

She tilted her head back, exposing her throat. He loved to kiss her there first, and work his way down her body. He usually didn't kiss her on the lips until they were already making love, and she was on the edge, gasping for breath. Then he'd kiss her hard, catching those little cries between his teeth.

It was all so thrilling, so perfect. And so different from the only other experience she'd ever had.

She had thought joining the Heyday Eight would be wicked and fun, kind of rebellious and sexy and cool. She'd been so angry at her mother and Mallory, so ready to assert her independence.

In her mind, she hadn't ever taken it further than the moment when her client would gaze, admiringly open-mouthed, at her sexy animal-tamer costume.

But it wasn't fun. Instead, the experience had been...

It had been disgusting. And strangely pathetic. For both of them.

Dorian Swigert, that was his name, she'd never forget it. The name fit him. Odd and unattractive, full of ugly, bony angles.

For months afterward, the very idea of sex had made her gag. She was sure she'd never be able to see a naked man without remembering Dorian.

Without remembering a pale, freckled back with seeping red lines running across it. And the sweaty face of a stranger, a twisted stranger who wanted her to whip wounds into his skin, rub them hard, and then use her bloody hand to milk him to a noisy, disturbingly bestial climax.

When he left, she'd been sick in the hotel bathroom's plastic trash can. She had been as numb as a china doll for weeks, except when she tossed in her sleep and dreamed about blood and woke up roiling with nausea.

There had even come a time when she thought she couldn't go on.

But Freddy, like the answer to a prayer she hadn't believed she had the right to pray, had miraculously changed all that. With his warm arms and gentle lips, he had somehow managed to erase those pictures and make new, beautiful ones to take their place.

He had even quieted her dreams.

And that was why, she thought as she opened her arms and held him to her heart, she mustn't ever let him down again.

And why it was going to be so terribly hard to tell him the truth.

CHAPTER SIX

ALL SATURDAY MORNING, Mallory was a nervous wreck. She was counting the minutes until Mindy arrived, partly because she always loved her rare weekends with her little sister, and partly because this visit was so important. She'd have two short days to persuade Mindy that honesty, however painful, really was the best policy.

Plus, Mallory found herself eyeing the telephone the way she might watch a big, poisonous spider that was crouching on her counter. By now the blackmailer must know how disobedient Mallory had been. Not only had she tried to follow him, but she had also dared to dictate how often and how much he could require her to pay.

So how long could it be before the phone rang? And what form would his fury take this time?

Luckily, the bookstore was always hectic on Saturdays, which helped the hours pass more quickly.

It was Story Time over in Calliope Corner, the children's area. On her last visit home, Mindy had painted a darling mural of an ornate circus calliope on the walls, and Mallory had loaded the space with colorful pillows and stuffed tigers, lions, gorillas and monkeys.

The kids loved it. As an added attraction, Binky Potter, one of the seniors from the local high-school drama club, came in for two hours every Saturday to read aloud to the children.

That had been one of Mallory's best hires. Binky, who was gorgeous, always dressed up like a sparkling blue-sequined circus ballerina, and Mallory had noticed a trend of older brothers suddenly volunteering to bring their siblings in for story time.

Binky was also a darn good actor, terrific with accents and silly voices. Mallory knew she'd sell at least a dozen copies of whatever book Binky chose each week.

The rest of the store was hopping, too. If Mallory hadn't been so distracted, she would have been thrilled. If business kept up like this, she'd be able to pay Roddy back sooner than she'd thought.

The mayor of Heyday, Joe Dozier, didn't often grace her with his business, but today she couldn't seem.to get rid of him. Though Joe had plenty of money to spend, he wasn't her favorite person. He treated his wife badly, openly mocking her squeaky voice and mousy manner.

Plus, he had a mean look in his little eyes. She suddenly found herself trying to imagine how his voice would sound if it had been mechanically altered.

He was trying to pick out an antique book about the

circus to give a friend he wanted to impress, and he'd been combing through Mallory's special collection for two hours now. She couldn't just leave him here alone. He was heavy-handed and had already almost torn one of the old, fragile pages.

So, though she'd much rather be back in Calliope Corner, watching Binky act out *Madeline's Rescue,* she was forced to stay and listen to Joe criticize the books in a transparent effort to shame her into lowering the prices.

"Is this mildew? Oh, that's too bad," Joe was saying as he leafed through a lovely copy of *A Scotch Circus.* "You know what that will do to any other books on the same shelf."

Mallory didn't answer. Her vision was pretty good, and she saw no discoloration at all. And she wasn't lowering the price on that one, even if it was speckled brown clear through from endpaper to endpaper.

Stifling a yawn, she scanned the store, looking for Wally. Maybe she could get him to babysit Joe for a while.

Instead, she noticed Slip Stanton standing over by the magazines, talking to a couple of other men, one of whom was, she saw with dismay, Tyler Balfour.

Great. All her favorite people in the store at once. Seeing them together surprised her—Slip was hardly Tyler Balfour's type. But then she made the connection. Slip had just bought the Black and White Lounge from Tyler.

That made Slip the newest member of the Downtown Merchants Association. Which didn't make any of the old members very happy.

He seemed to feel her attention on him, and looked up with a smile. She was surprised to see that the gold tooth he'd always had in the front was gone. He must have realized that, while it might have looked appropriately roguish at the Absolutely Nowhere, his bar on the outskirts of Heyday, here in the chamber of commerce crowd it marked him as an outsider.

"Hey there, Mallory," he said, moving away from Tyler who, Mallory noticed, made no move to follow.

Slip was holding out several long white pieces of paper. "I'm giving away some free dinners at the Black and White. Just to the other merchants on the street. Want a couple?"

Mallory tried to look pleased, but everyone knew about the lounge's dreadful food. "Well," she said, "I usually work right through dinner."

He thrust them forward another couple of inches. "Take some anyhow. We're open late. We've completely overhauled the menu, and I gotta get the word out things have changed for the better."

Reluctantly she took them, scanning her mind for anyone she could give them to. Wally was always broke, always scrounging for a free meal. But he was only eighteen and wouldn't be able to order the stiff drinks necessary to help him choke down the nasty fare.

"Hey, your sister's coming to town today, isn't she?" Slip grinned and added another ticket to the stack.

"Bring her with you. If she's not too good for us here in Heyday, that is. Now that she's marrying into the big time."

His tone had an edge of bitterness, and Mallory wondered just how far this man's outsider complex might go. She tried out his voice in her mind, too. If he distorted it electronically, how would it sound?

Linda Tremel, who had been standing at the register looking at greeting cards and, obviously, eavesdropping suddenly made a rude noise. "She'd better *not* start thinking she's too good for Heyday! Just because you marry into the big time doesn't mean you get to stay there."

Linda jammed one of the cards back into its slot and slapped two more onto the counter. "It's not quite 'till death do us part' in their world. It's more like 'till boredom or a better bimbo do us part.'"

"So true." Slip winked at Linda. "And, as the ex Mrs. Austin Tremel, I guess you'd know."

Linda ignored him, except for a slight elevation of perfectly waxed eyebrows. She might not have Austin Tremel's social backing anymore, but she obviously still felt superior to Slip Stanton from the Absolutely Nowhere.

"Seriously," she said to Mallory in her husky voice. "These days most marriage vows are written in disappearing ink. You tell her I said be careful, okay?"

Mallory nodded. "Sure," she said calmly. "I'll tell her."

Some people in town hadn't forgiven Linda for

some nasty behavior in the first couple of years following her bitter divorce. Rumor had it she was an alcoholic and had sometimes warmed her cold bed with hapless teenage boys.

Rumors, of course, weren't always true. But Mallory, who knew that even good people might have a shameful secret or two, couldn't help feeling sorry for her.

Especially since, for the first time since her marriage, Linda was going to have to work for a living. Her new garden store would open in just a few days, and she was already getting a taste of the rigors of owning a small business.

Mallory hoped she could make a success of it. At least she'd picked a good market. Here in the Shenandoah Valley people loved their gardens and might be willing to spend more money on that than they ever did on books.

Mallory had just finished ringing up Linda's cards when, with a merry tinkling sound, the front door opened. Hopefully, she looked up, and smiled as she saw Mindy enter, like a breath of fresh air, in a glow of sunshine curls and a cloud of soft blue cotton.

Most of the men in the store stopped what they were doing and stared, even the ones who had been enjoying Binky Potter's *Madeline* performance.

Mallory knew what the men saw. Mindy was a beauty, young but ripe and subtly sexy. Hair that fell halfway down her back in glimmering waves. Round, large eyes as blue and sparkling as any of Binky Potter's sequins.

That's what the men saw, but in that first instant Mallory was looking for things that mattered more. Mindy had, thank heaven, put on at least another five pounds. A year ago, Mindy's bones had jabbed unnaturally at her too-pale skin, stretching it like broken twigs stuffed in a plastic bag.

And she was relieved to see that Mindy's eyes looked more normal. For the past few years, they had been feverishly bright in deep, haunted sockets.

Mallory knew that, after everything she'd been through, Mindy would never be exactly the same again. But Freddy Earnshaw must be very good for her. She was clearly getting stronger every day.

Mallory said a quick prayer that she was strong enough.

And that, when the time came, Freddy would be, too.

"Mallory!" Mindy spied her at the cash register and called out in a delighted, musical alto that made several of the customers instinctively smile. "Mallory, I've got a surprise! Look who came with me!"

She moved out of the doorway, and with a flourish ushered in a tall, blond, beautifully dressed man. Her fiancé, Freddy Earnshaw.

Freddy was smiling in a self-deprecating way that was so charming Mallory felt cynical to find herself imagining him rehearsing it in front of the mirror.

Mindy held his hand protectively, as if she had found a Norse god wandering loose on the highway and brought him home as a gift to the city. He was spectacularly good-looking, Mallory had to admit. Now the women were staring, too, smiling, thrilled at their luck.

Mallory wasn't thrilled. She had wanted Mindy to herself this weekend.

But worst of all, as she hugged her future brother-in-law and struggled to hide her dismay, she couldn't help wondering whether, somewhere in this crowded store, or out there on Hippodrome Circle, a black-mailer was staring at Freddy, too.

And was smiling, thrilled at his luck.

TYLER HADN'T BEEN SURPRISED to discover that Rackham Books was the warm, welcoming heartbeat of Heyday's downtown retail area. The Rackham family's last business, the Ringmaster Café, had been the same. Comfortably cozy, it had drawn people in, both locals and visitors passing through the little town whose eccentric circus legend guaranteed it at least an asterisk on every tourist map.

Once in, they had lingered, reluctant to return to the real world, letting Mallory and her mother pamper them with friendly service and fantastic coffee and pie.

Ironically, that was what had made it the perfect spot for the Heyday Eight. The atmosphere was so wholesome, so full of family charm. Who would ever have suspected those pretty little co-ed customers of propositioning the lonely salesmen traveling to Richmond, or the tired truckers a thousand miles from home?

Watching Mallory now, Tyler saw that, even after all her losses, even after the shame of seeing her café's picture in a dozen newspapers and the tragedy of nearly losing her mother, she still had the same magic.

All morning long, people had entered Rackham Books through the musical door, but they didn't ever seem to leave. They browsed through the neatly ordered bookshelves, chatted with other customers, listened to the ballerina read stories to the children. Sometimes they took books to the armchair niches Mallory had created between stacks, and sometimes took them out the side door to the reading garden.

But Tyler knew that what they were really waiting for was a chance to talk to Mallory. They asked her for book recommendations and updated her on everything from their surgeries to their nasturtiums. The little kids gave her hand-drawn pictures of their new kittens, and the older kids confided about their rotten report cards.

And, amazingly, she seemed to care. Tyler, who hung back by the magazines, which were centrally located and gave him a panoramic view of the human circus, was amazed. Tyler had no idea what his own secretary's birthday was, though she'd worked for him for five years, but Mallory knew that little Erica Gordon's puppy's birthday was coming up in three weeks, and that Harry Wooten's fifteenth anniversary had been celebrated at Bennini's last night.

Apparently the only person in the shop she *didn't* like was Tyler.

And yet, even he was allowed to linger quite a while. She had eyed him coldly several times, but he'd been there nearly an hour before she finally got fed up.

It was right after Mindy and her glossy fiancé left to get some lunch at the diner down the street. Mallory had seen them off at the door, and then, squaring her shoulders, she'd made a beeline for Tyler, who was all alone by the magazines.

"Finding everything all right, Tyler?" She made the classic shopkeeper's line sound poisonous. Her smile wasn't a millimeter smaller than it had been for the other customers, but it was as cold as if she'd just dug it out of the polar ice cap.

"I wasn't really looking for anything special," he said pleasantly. "Just browsing, getting acquainted with the shop. You seem to be the center of social activity for the town." He smiled. "As always."

She bristled, of course, though he actually hadn't meant to be sarcastic.

"Oh, yes," she said. "We try to provide plenty of excitement for visiting investigative journalists. Have you found the bookies in the bathroom yet? The still behind the Dumpster? The drug deals go down in the poetry section every Wednesday at eight."

"Mallory." He reached out to touch her arm. "I know how angry you are. It was rotten luck that the Heyday Eight chose to work out of your café. But be fair. I couldn't sit on a story that big just because it would embarrass you."

"*Embarrass* me?" She flushed, but she kept her voice low and half turned away from him, pretending to straighten the fashion magazines. "It nearly destroyed me. It did destroy the café. It did destroy my mother."

"I know," he said. "I'm sorry."

Her hands stilled, and he could tell she was working to keep her emotions in check.

"Sorry doesn't change anything, Tyler," she said, her head still bent over the magazines. "Sorry is just about the most pointless word in the dictionary."

He nodded. "Yes. But even so I am sorry. I would have liked to spare you. I wish you could believe that. I wish we could be friends again."

Finally she turned around. Her face was set in lines so stiff it shocked him. He'd seen her aching with pain when her husband had hurt her, and boiling with fury when Tyler had betrayed her. But he'd never seen her like this, frozen hard with contempt.

"And do you know what *I* wish, Tyler? I wish that, whatever scandal you're trying to dig up this time, you'd do it somewhere else. I wish you wouldn't insult me by thinking I'm dumb enough to fall for your innocent *let me be your friend* charade a second time. I wish you would get out of my store."

He opened his mouth but then shut it again without speaking. He decided to let her have the moment. He let her pivot on her heel, satisfied that she'd told him off for good this time.

She needed, at least this once, to have the last word. So he didn't say what he could have said.

He didn't say, *Technically, Mallory, this store is mine.*

"DUDE, HAVE A LITTLE FAITH in me, why don't you? I won't run off with the bank deposit." Wally looked down at the cash drawer and whistled. "Although, for once we've got enough in here to actually tempt me."

Mallory had to laugh. He was right. It had been an exhausting day, but it certainly had been lucrative. She didn't ordinarily let anyone else close up for her, even when the register was half-empty. If Wally picked tonight to suddenly turn larcenous, he could really do some damage.

But she wanted so much to join Mindy and Freddy for dinner. She'd hardly seen them all day. Freddy had never been to Heyday before, and he had expected Mindy to show him the sights. The bookstore hadn't amused him for more than about ten minutes; apparently he wasn't much of a reader. Mindy, who seemed tuned into his every mood, had picked up the signals immediately and begun racking her brain for more exciting adventures.

Heyday was a little short on those, but she'd done her best. The Riverside Park neighborhood, with houses old and splendid enough to impress even a senator's son. The circus museum, where you could learn everything you ever wanted to know about zebras—and then some.

The college, which looked quite attractive in the spring. The newly renovated park, with the hilarious statue of St. Kieran McClintock riding a stubby, cross-eyed zebra.

The three of them had arranged to meet for a late dinner, after Mallory closed up shop at eight-thirty. But Mindy had called at six, reporting that they'd run out of things to do, and Freddy was hungry. Was there any chance Mallory could get free and join them now?

"Okay," Mallory said, and she took a deep breath. "You know how to run through the credit cards?" Wally nodded. "You won't forget to lock the back door?" Wally shook his head. "You will remember to turn off—"

"Boss." Wally looked pained. "I'm not a moron. I've seen you close up a million times. I'll do everything I should do, and nothing I shouldn't do. I promise."

And he would, she knew that. In spite of his piercings and his red-and-green hair, Wally was smart as a whip, and actually one of the last great innocent teenagers. He kissed his mother when she dropped him off in the afternoons, for heaven's sake. He loved comic books and classic movies and milk, and he didn't care who knew it.

So why was she so nervous? Why did she have this niggling feeling that, if she left the store, something bad might happen?

Perhaps it was just that, surprisingly, the blackmailer hadn't called today. She wasn't stupid enough to think he had decided to play nice. She knew he'd do something to make her sorry. She just had no idea what.

Or maybe it was the confrontation she'd had with Tyler this morning. She'd tried to ignore him, but the sight of him over there, with that detached, analytical look on his face, evaluating the store, the customers and even Mallory herself, had finally driven her nuts.

It reminded her too much of how he used to sit in the café, at the back booth, the one nearest the counter where she was working. He had watched people then, too, with that same blandly curious expression. But when he had talked to her, after everyone else was gone, he had seemed to lose a little of the detachment, and she had foolishly believed that they were…friends.

And she'd needed a friend so badly right then.

It had felt good to confront him directly this morning. She would have liked to be even more direct. When he dared to speak of being friends, she would have liked to slap the word right off his mouth.

She couldn't do that, of course. Even if they'd been alone in the shop she wouldn't have. Her mother would have been ashamed of her for even thinking about something so uncivilized.

So she had settled for telling him to get out.

However, she knew that, like the blackmailer, Tyler wasn't going to take orders from her for long. She didn't know why he'd bothered to spend so much time in her shop, but she knew that he must want something.

And when Tyler Balfour wanted a thing, he tended to get it.

The front doorbell rang again. Ordinarily the dinner hour was pretty quiet, so Mallory and Wally both looked up curiously.

It was a courier, a young man about Wally's age, bringing in a large, quite lovely bouquet of flowers. White roses, white carnations, baby's breath, and a big white satin bow in the center.

For a second, Mallory thought someone must have been confused about Mindy's wedding date. The bouquet looked positively bridal, all that white.

But then she looked at the card. It was addressed to her.

A trickle of discomfort made its way down her spine, as light and disagreeable as a bead of perspiration. She looked at the courier.

"They're beautiful," she said. "Who sent them?"

The boy looked annoyed, as if she were pretty stupid to think he actually knew or cared about her dumb old flowers.

"I don't know," he said, setting them down on the register counter. He gave her a slightly sarcastic smile. "Guess you'll have to check the card."

And then he turned around, mission accomplished, and exited the store.

"Dude, what an attitude," Wally said, with the delight of a superior employee. "If I treated your customers that way, you'd fire me. Wouldn't you?"

But Mallory only half heard him. She had opened the card, and the words she saw typed there made her blood rush in her ears.

Can't wait to meet your sister's fiancé, it read. We have so much to talk about.

And it was signed with a name she'd heard only once, in Mindy's trembling, tearful, tragic voice. A name that, even so, Mallory would never forget.

Dorian Swigert.

CHAPTER SEVEN

MALLORY OPENED THE DOOR to her apartment over the bookstore with a sense of tired relief. It was almost ten, and she knew Mindy was pretty exhausted, too. After helping Freddy check into his hotel, she and Mindy had made a visit to the Chronic Care Center. By then the place was empty except for sleeping patients and soft-footed, hushed-voiced nurses.

Mallory knew it hadn't been easy for her little sister. She hadn't seen their mother in almost two months now. And, as Mallory had feared, Mindy had started off the visit by crying. The minute she sat down and tried to say hi, her voice broke and she began to sob softly, putting her hands over her face.

It took about ten minutes, but finally Mindy began to root around in her purse for a tissue. And then, to Mallory's delight, she seemed to pull herself together, and spent the rest of their visit chatting pleasantly, telling their mother all about her job and the wedding plans.

"You did great tonight," Mallory said as they began unfolding the sleeper sofa in the living room.

"Not really. I'd sworn I wasn't going to cry, but right off the bat I fell apart. I'm sorry."

"Hey." Mallory picked up a pillow and tossed it to her little sister playfully. "Mom wouldn't know it was you if you didn't cry a little. It's tradition."

Mindy stuck out her tongue, but it was a sign of how much she had matured that she didn't seem to mind the teasing. Once, the simplest criticism would have set off a storm of fury, ending in slamming doors and shouted recriminations.

"It's true," she said, shaking her head. "I've been a pain in the neck. But things are going to be different now, I promise." She looked at Mallory over the pillow as she shook it into its case. "So...what do you think of Freddy? Now that you've had some time together without all the other people around?"

Mallory smiled. "I adore him, of course. How could I not love him when he's so crazy about you?"

It was mostly true. For all his fantastic looks, Freddy was a touch too conservative for Mallory's taste, too conscious of his own image. But she wasn't the one who had to live with that. Mindy, who catered to his every whim, certainly didn't seem to have any reservations. And Mindy's happiness was all that mattered here.

Still...looking at her sister now, with her once-wild hair carefully flat-ironed and tied back with a pretty blue ribbon, with her demure dress and her matching sweetheart-pink lip-gloss and fingernail polish, Mallory had to wonder.

This new, straitlaced, mild-mannered Mindy was the polar opposite of the rebellious teenager she'd been, with deliberately tangled bedroom hair and black leather skirts up to here.

Could this Alice in Wonderland creation actually be the real Mindy? Wasn't it more likely a temporary overreaction against all the drama and ugliness of the past few years? Wasn't it more likely that the *real* Mindy lay somewhere in between the two?

And if that were true, how would Freddy feel about the real Mindy when she finally found the courage to emerge?

Just then Mindy's cell phone began to ring. She rushed over to her small blue envelope purse, which exactly matched her dress. She scrounged around for the little silver phone with such urgency she might have been trying to locate a ticking bomb.

"Hi, honey," she said when she found it. Mallory knew instantly, from the warm, satisfied tone, that it was Freddy. That smile of Madonna bliss could not have been conjured by anyone else.

"Oh—" The smile began to fade slowly. "Oh, Freddy, no. Oh, I'm sorry. No, really, I don't think that's a—" She glanced at Mallory, who frowned quizzically.

What? Was something wrong?

Mindy waved her hand, assuring her that everything was fine. But then she lowered her voice and, giving Mallory an apologetic smile, moved into the kitchen and shut the door behind her.

After that, Mallory heard only murmurs. But her protective instincts, her big-sister antennae, registered a distinctly unhappy sound. She stared at the kitchen door. It was ridiculous how quickly her stomach tightened when she thought something might be wrong with Mindy.

Finally Mindy came back into the room. Her face had lost some of its radiance. She looked tense but still, thank goodness, under control.

"It was Freddy," she said unnecessarily, not meeting Mallory's eyes.

"Is something wrong?"

"Not really." Mindy returned her cell phone to her purse, arranging everything neatly before she sat on the edge of the fold-out bed and looked at Mallory.

"He just wanted me to come over and stay there tonight. I told him of course I wanted to be here with you."

Mallory frowned. Earlier Mindy had let it slip that Freddy was concerned about how it would "look" if Mindy spent the night with him before they were married.

"I thought you said he didn't— He was concerned about—"

Mindy lifted one shoulder, and the gesture was strangely sad. "He still is. He just thinks he's found a way to sneak me in."

Mallory hardly knew what to say. Though the hypocrisy of it infuriated her, she knew she didn't have the right to lash out at the man Mindy loved.

So she didn't say anything.

"It's not that I don't want to be with him," Mindy said. She looked down and toyed with the edge of the blanket. "I do. I always do. But not like that. I don't want to sneak up there in the dark, as if I'm ashamed of what we're doing."

She lifted her face to Mallory. "One of the reasons I love him so much is that, when we…when we're together, he makes me feel good. He makes me feel clean." Her voice was strained and miserable. "If I have to sneak up there, it will change everything. Don't you see that?"

"Of course," Mallory said vehemently. She realized her hands were fisted in her lap. "Of course I do."

"Then why doesn't *he?*"

"I'm sure he does." Mallory tried to be fair, though she wanted to strangle the man for making Mindy so unhappy. But she couldn't go through life exterminating everyone who upset her little sister. Part of Mindy's new maturity had come from handling things on her own, and she'd handle this, too.

"Maybe he's just a little disappointed right now. I'm sure he misses you."

Mindy looked on the verge of tears again. "I don't want to let him down. I want him to be happy. But this is wrong. If you have to hide what you're doing, you probably shouldn't be doing it. I certainly learned that the hard way."

She was threading her fingers together and kneading her palms. Stress was like a throbbing aura around her and, sensing the intensity, Mallory's heart dropped.

Why was Mindy so insecure that she didn't dare tell her fiancé that he'd have to sleep alone for one night? Was sex so very important in this relationship?

"Mindy, I hate to bring this up right now, but maybe we should talk about how you're going to break the news about your past. And when. I honestly think it needs to be soon."

Mindy looked stricken. "How soon?"

"As soon as possible."

Mallory hated to be rough, but the past couple of days had been extremely unsettling. Mindy didn't have any idea there was a blackmailer, of course, but the blackmailer wasn't the only problem.

Until today, Mallory hadn't seen enough of Freddy to form her own opinion, and she'd let Mindy's assurances console her. But today she'd seen a man who walked, talked and smiled like a politician. Not just a politician's son. A man who expected someday to hold office himself. He didn't just meet people; he greeted them. He didn't just socialize; he campaigned.

And look at Mindy. She'd practically turned herself into Freddy's geisha. All day long she'd flattered him, clung to his arm, paraded the high points of Heyday out for his inspection. And now he wanted her to sneak into that hotel and let herself be hustled out in the dawn like dirty linen.

Thank God she had enough self-respect to draw the line at that.

Still, though the relationship wasn't as solid as Mallory had been led to believe, it was apparently crucial to Mindy's happiness. It was such a tricky balance. How was she going to make Mindy look at this situation squarely without sending her back into an emotional tailspin?

"I know I have to tell him," Mindy said miserably. "But I can't do it now. Not *here.* I have to choose the perfect time. We've both been so stressed-out, with the wedding preparations and every—"

Mallory touched her arm.

"Mindy, think a minute. We have to face reality. Freddy obviously is very concerned with his reputation, with what the world thinks of him. How can you be sure that, once he knows about your involvement with the Heyday Eight, there will even still *be* a wedding?"

Mindy recoiled. Her eyes widened, as if Mallory had slapped her.

At first she didn't answer. Resisting the effort to jump in and take the words back, Mallory let the silence go on. This was a very dangerous situation, especially now that the blackmailer had sent the flowers, a bold in-your-face reminder that he knew incriminating details, like Dorian Swigert's name, and he was ready to use them if necessary.

"I know," Mindy said finally. "I've thought of that. That's one of the reasons it's so difficult. But I have faith in him, Mal. He loves me, I know he does. I just have to find the right time to tell him."

Her cell phone began to ring again, and Mindy leaped up to retrieve it.

"It's Freddy." She hugged the phone briefly. "He's probably calling to say he's sorry," she said, giving Mallory a teary smile over her shoulder. "See? He's really a sweetheart. He never stays mad for long."

She must have seen the skepticism on Mallory's face, because she paused, the phone still singing in her hand.

"Please trust me, Mal. I'm not as brave as you are, but I'm trying. I just need a little more time."

TYLER ATE DINNER that night with Dilday Merle, to discuss details and plans for trying to identify the blackmailer. There wasn't much to go on, just Dilday's instinct that it must be a local, someone who knew him and understood his vulnerability and his finances.

It was frustrating. Blackmail was an odd crime. Often it was clumsy and heavy-handed, easy to thwart. But now and then it was brilliantly simple, like this one. When you were up against that kind of blackmailer, you had to hope the luck fell your way.

Tyler got back to his apartment about eleven, early for someone accustomed to D.C. hours, but apparently way past the official Heyday bedtime. Everything was dark and quiet on Mallory's side of the building, so he fixed a drink and decided to sit a while on his balcony, which overlooked Hippodrome Circle.

Not much to see, but he appreciated the crisp spring breeze, the pointy crescent moon and the peace of the park laid out beside him, where now and then a bird would abruptly coo, just once, as if talking in its sleep.

Beneath him, as the street stretched out on either side, the stores were all closed, their pretty bay windows glowing softly under muted night lights. Heyday looked less silly at night, he thought. He almost understood why people might live in a place like this, where the rhythms were so regular and in tune with the natural world.

Not that he could stand it for long. A week or two, maybe. Like a vacation. After that, he'd be itching for the unpredictable excitement of D.C.

Out of the corner of his eyes, something caught his attention, a subtle movement that didn't seem to fit the swaying tree shadows and rippling moonlight. He stared into the park across the street, where the incongruous shadow had shifted. He waited, but everything was still.

Maybe he'd imagined it. It might have been a larger tree catching a gusting breeze. Or maybe an animal? Perhaps his noises had spooked a raccoon or even a deer, and now it crouched in the brush, afraid of the human who should be asleep but wasn't.

Maybe, but it had seemed bigger than that. As big as a man. A man standing at the edge of the park, looking across the street toward Mallory's store.

Suddenly he heard a muffled thump. Felt it, actually. Under his feet, the floor moved just slightly. He frowned. Something was happening in the bookstore itself.

He glanced one more time toward the park, which was still completely silent. If someone had been there a minute ago, that person was gone now.

Tyler left his apartment quickly, moved without noise down the outside staircase. At the side entrance to the bookstore, he used his landlord's key, which he'd been given yesterday by detail-obsessed Elton Fletcher. Closing the door behind him, he slipped silently into the shop.

The main store was all soft, bluish darkness, lit only by the moonlight that streamed in through the bay windows at the front. Everything seemed different, transformed by the night. The bookcases stood like hulking sentinels, and the armchairs squatted, like fat toads, in the spaces between. The books themselves seemed to have disappeared into the shadows.

As his eyes adjusted to the gloom, he saw that the main area was completely empty. Certainly no one was fiddling with the cash register, which he could see clearly near the front bay.

And then he heard another noise, much more subtle this time. He tilted his head, listening as he scanned for movement or light.

The back room…

This morning, he'd seen Mallory go in there several times, consulting files or talking on the phone. The door was shut now, but a thin white line was painted in light on the floor beneath it. Someone was in there.

He moved toward the door, dodging CD cabinets and spinning racks of bookmarks, cards and gift certificates. Making a mental note of the heavy brass book-ends displayed on the back wall—just in case he needed a weapon—he put his hand on the knob, twisted silently and yanked it open.

Mallory's head jerked up. "Tyler!"

Mallory? He remained in the doorway, waiting for the adrenaline to die down. He was glad he wasn't hoisting a bookend. He would have looked even more ridiculous than he undoubtedly did right now.

"Tyler, what on earth are you doing here?"

She hadn't ever been good at hiding her emotions. He saw her go from fear to relief in a nanosecond. But immediately after the relief came something that looked a lot like nervous guilt.

That was odd. She was in her own shop, on her own turf. What could she possibly be up to that she'd need to feel guilty about?

She clearly hadn't been expecting anyone to come in. She was wearing a pair of cotton blue-and-green-plaid pajama pants and a skimpy blue T-shirt—no underclothes. He looked down, and saw that her feet were bare.

So what was she doing?

"I was on the balcony. I heard a noise in here, and I thought I'd better make sure everything's okay. It's pretty late. I assumed you'd be asleep, like the rest of the town."

He was casually moving into the office as he spoke. She, however, seemed almost paralyzed, her hands awkwardly wrapped around something white.

When he got close enough, he saw to his surprise that she was holding a chrysanthemum. Or rather, not holding it but mangling it, the stem in one hand and the blossom crushed almost beyond recognition in the palm of the other.

At her elbow stood the half-empty glass vase the flower must have come in. And littered on the desk around her were the bits and pieces of at least a dozen other flowers. The air smelled like a perfume counter, all crushed roses and shredded sweet things.

No point trying to pretend he didn't see it. And even less point trying to act as if mutilating a fresh bouquet of flowers was normal.

He smiled, glancing at the mess on the desk. "Which one was the culprit? The flowers, or the guy who sent them?"

She was recovering. She put the chrysanthemum down slowly and brushed her hands together to whisk free the remaining petals. The gesture released a fresh puff of perfume into the air.

"Did you need anything else, Tyler? It was thoughtful of you to check on me, but, as you can see, I'm fine."

He smiled again. "Is that what you call it? Some people would call it displaced aggression. See, it works like this. The civilized world won't allow you to chop off the head of the guy who sent you these, so you sacrifice the flowers in his place."

She began collecting some of the pieces and dropping them into the trash can beside the desk. "Well, if that's what I'm doing, maybe you'd better let me get back to it. Before I decide to displace it somewhere *else*."

He chuckled, but he didn't move. He had not forgotten about the shadow in the park, and he had no intention of leaving her in here alone.

Besides, this display of anger really made him curious. Who could have sent these poor, doomed flowers? Her ex-husband, maybe? Or was there a new lover in the picture? He'd seen her kissing that guy at the golf club, but he'd assumed there was no real heat, on account of the skirt.

Maybe he'd misjudged. Maybe, for some women, men in skirts were kind of a turn-on.

As she stood there glaring at him, he discovered that, for some men, a woman in soft cotton pajama pants *definitely* was a turn-on.

She must have been trying to sleep before she came downstairs, because her hair was a mess. She used to wear it super short, but it was growing out, and curls were tumbling everywhere, tickling at her chin, her ears, her eyelashes.

He pictured her in bed, tossing and turning, creating that disarray. His whole body tensed, a feeling he remembered all too well.

She had always affected him this way, damn it. He remembered the first time he saw her. She'd been wearing her silly Ringmaster Café uniform, which was all black and white with a mannish bow tie. He'd thought she was sexy as hell, and he had, for just a moment, considered breaking his firm rule against one-night stands with total strangers.

Then he saw the ring on her finger, and the fantasies screeched to a halt. The rule against sex with *married* women was one he never messed with.

It hadn't been easy. Everything about her had turned him on. Sometimes, when he sat in the café late at night, going over his notes from the day's interviews, he'd been so distracted he couldn't think straight.

When she poured him water from a sweating silver pitcher, apologizing as the cool drops splashed on his fingers, he'd nearly gone crazy. When she bent down to pick up a straw wrapper, or leaned over to wipe the counter, her breasts pressing against the Formica, he'd had to look the other way.

"So—" He glanced at the flowers. "Are they from your husband?"

He didn't know why he asked. She wouldn't think this was any of his business and undoubtedly would refuse to answer.

She cocked her head and smiled. "Of course not," she said, surprising him. "How big a fool do you think I am?"

"I don't think you're a fool at all. Frankly, I thought *he* was."

A fool, or *worse.* Sometimes, at the café, Tyler had seen her pick up her cell phone when she thought no one was watching. She'd dial a number, wait, then hang up with a tight frown between red-rimmed eyes. He knew she'd been calling her husband, because afterward she'd roll her wedding ring roughly around and around on her finger, as if she'd like to take it off and toss it into the deep fryer.

That combination of fear and fury, of helpless pain and indignant pride, had been enough to drive Tyler mad. He had wanted to go over and kiss her until she did it, until the little gold band was bubbling and melting alongside the French fries.

Or else he'd wanted to go beat the tar out of the bastard who made her eyes so sad.

Stay out of it, stay out of it, he'd tell himself. But even while the warnings were playing in his head, he'd call her over for a refill of coffee, and then he'd start a conversation. He'd try to make her think of something else. He'd try to make her laugh.

And sometimes he did.

"I've always wanted to ask you." He decided to press his luck, sensing something a little softer in her tonight, as though the starchy indignation she'd felt toward him today might have passed. Maybe she appreciated that he had been worried about her just now. Or perhaps her annoyance had merely been chased away by more important problems. "Why on earth did you put up with it?"

"With what?" She frowned. "With Dan?"

He nodded. "You were married, what, something like six years? He didn't deserve six months."

She shrugged. "I hoped I could make it work, I guess. You can't just throw away your wedding vows the minute your new husband disappoints you."

"The hell you can't. People do it every day."

"Well, I can't." She was looking at her hands, rubbing at the palms as if something sticky had remained from the flowers. "It was a tough time for our family. My mother was working so hard to keep the business going, to make it support both Mindy and me. Mindy was having problems, and I—"

She swallowed. "Oh, well. It's over now. He's getting remarried. He actually even invi—"

Suddenly she glanced up, moving her shoulders as if to shake off a trance.

"No wonder you're such a good investigative reporter," she said, her voice cool and amused. "You have a way of making people open up to you, even when they've made a solemn vow they absolutely will not ever do any such thing."

He gazed at her beautiful, vulnerable face and wondered what she'd been going to say. He wondered what she'd do if he reached out and brushed away the white specks of pollen that had settled on her cheek.

"Did you make a vow like that, Mallory? Did you vow you'll never open up to me again?"

"Not exactly," she said, meeting his gaze without wavering and smiling just a little. "Actually, I vowed that, if you ever set foot in Heyday again, I'd claw your lying eyes out."

CHAPTER EIGHT

LINDA TREMEL'S garden store, The Welcome Mat, had been built on the very spot where the Ringmaster Café used to stand, back before it was burned down by an angry and unstable Imogene Jacobson.

Mallory had wondered if it would hurt to attend Linda's grand opening. Would it bring back painful memories of their own opening celebration? Her mother had been so proud, and rightly so. It had been a risky venture, and she had pulled it off so well. Mallory could still see her, exhausted but happy, greeting all her friends, who thronged the place to support her efforts.

But that was the great thing about Heyday. They stuck by one another, no matter what. So Mallory knew she couldn't let her own disappointments keep her from helping Linda Tremel celebrate her own success.

Once she got there, she was glad she'd come. The Welcome Mat was one of the most charming shops downtown Heyday had ever seen. Austin, Linda's ex-husband, must have helped bankroll the venture. Mallory knew the huge expense of ordering enough merchandise to stock a store. Linda had spent a fortune.

She stocked everything frivolous and delightful to make a garden into a fairyland. Wind chimes shaped like tulips and sunflowers; Italian planters carved into garlands of ivy; white arbors and trellises strung with climbing roses; bird feeders in every shape, from a thatched English cottage to the Taj Mahal; multicolored gazing balls, wall fountains and CDs that brought you bluebird sounds all year long.

And of course she had the zebra corner, which she had cleverly named "The Savannah" and filled with a tumble of grassy plants and a "watering hole" made from an in-ground vinyl pond.

"Amazing." Lara Gilbert, Bryce McClintock's fiancée, was already in "The Savannah" when Mallory showed up. She was inspecting an outdoor water faucet topped by a brass zebra head. "Who knew there were this many zebra yard thingies on the planet?"

Mallory looked at the dozens of items scattered around. Cast-iron zebras to stand in your vegetable patch, a weather vane with a zebra on top instead of a rooster, a zebra-head doorknocker, a welcome mat painted with cavorting zebras.

"I knew," Mallory said with a sigh. "You wouldn't believe what I get offered at the bookstore. Zebra stationery, bookmarks, paperweights, bookends, stuffed toys, coloring books. There's even a CD of zebra sounds. It reminds me of my grandfather gargling."

Lara laughed and put the faucet back on its shelf.

"I was going to buy something for Bryce for the frat house, but I think I'd better look in another section. He hates zebras."

"I don't hate them." Bryce stuck his head around the corner. "I'm terrified of them. My worst nightmares always feature zebras."

At the sight of him, Lara's face lit up. She and Bryce were to be married in June, and Mallory had never seen two people more in love.

"Hey, there, Mal." Bryce leaned over and gave Mallory a kiss, too. When Bryce first came to town, Kieran and Claire had tried to fix him up with Mallory. But it hadn't taken root. He was already crazy for Lara, though he had been in complete, stubborn, typically McClintock denial.

But he'd become a good friend. That was the story of Mallory's life since her divorce. Lots of friends, no lovers. She worked hard to keep it that way. She wasn't ready for a lover. She wasn't sure if she ever would be.

She noticed that in his left hand Bryce was holding a ceramic statue of a frog. Unfortunately, the statue was in two pieces, head separated from the body.

"Oops," Mallory said with a smile. "You broke something already?"

Bryce held out his other hand. "Two of them, actually. At least we'll have a matched set."

The second little green frog was broken, too. Its arms were detached and lying loose in Bryce's palm.

Lara blushed. "Well, we didn't mean to. There's this

little alcove over there, and we just thought we could…you know, a little privacy and—"

She looked over at Bryce, who was grinning rakishly at her, refusing to help out. "Anyhow, I bumped into this shelf on the wall, and the whole thing fell down. Dozens of frogs. We were lucky only two of them broke."

Mallory shook her head, laughing. She didn't know why they had bothered to hide in the alcove. Everyone in town knew Bryce and Lara couldn't keep their hands off each other. Aurora York openly said she hoped they'd hurry up and get married so they could start taking each other for granted like decent folk.

A minute or two later, Claire McClintock joined them, which meant Kieran couldn't be far behind. So far, Claire and Kieran were proving the exception to Aurora's philosophy of marriage. Though they'd exchanged vows last summer, they were almost as sickeningly in love as Bryce and Lara.

Claire, who carried baby Stephanie over her shoulder, stood close to Mallory, rippling her fingers through a silver zebra wind chime.

"You okay?" She smiled at Mallory. "Not too many…uncomfortable memories?"

Mallory had wondered who would bring it up first. She should have known it would be Claire, who was sensitive but believed in discussing problems openly. Her brother had died about five years ago, and refusing to work through her grief had almost killed her, too.

"I'm okay," Mallory said. "It's a little sad, of course. But Linda's changed it so completely. There's hardly anything left to remind me."

Kieran showed up then, burying his face in his wife's neck so that he could kiss Claire and Stephanie at the same time. After a few minutes of small talk, the foursome moved outside, to the small Victorian garden Linda had set up to show off her merchandise.

Though they urged Mallory to come with them, she held back. Most of the time she didn't mind being unattached, but around those couples it felt like a sin not to be in love.

Besides, she was going to have to pick out something to buy quickly and get back to the bookstore. Wally was holding the fort, but she knew he had homework and couldn't stay forever.

She picked up a small pair of pruning scissors. These would be good for her balcony philodendron. The rest of this stuff was for people with houses, with green lawns and brick patios, with elm trees and swimming pools and gazebos out back.

Mallory didn't have any of that, not anymore. Her mother had sold the family home to start the café. And, though Mallory and Dan had owned a house, she'd discovered that it wasn't possible to "split" the house in a divorce. You could only split the proceeds.

With her share, she'd started Rackham Books. With his, Dan had bought a big, new house in Grupton. Probably he'd felt rich, with all the money he was saving on prostitutes, now that the Heyday Eight were out of business.

But listen to her. She sounded bitter. And she wasn't, really she wasn't.

Well, not much, anyhow.

To her surprise, she saw Tyler Balfour over by the water features, chatting with Slip Stanton. As she watched them out of the corner of her eye, she wondered what they were talking about. Tyler hadn't come to a garden shop grand opening because he was eager to buy some wind chimes. Besides, he had his sharp-eyed reporter face on, that hyperfocused look she could easily imagine on the face of a miner panning for gold.

He was sifting through Slip's conversation, looking for any valuable nuggets.

She wondered if he suspected that Slip's hotel and bar, the Absolutely Nowhere, might have been an assignation spot for the Heyday Eight. If so, for once the great Tyler Balfour was barking up the wrong tree. The police had thought of that, too, but no connection had ever surfaced.

As if he could feel her gaze, Tyler glanced up and gave her a quizzical look. *Darn.* Now he'd think she wanted to talk to him. She answered it with a chilly courtesy-only smile that offered no encouragement, then turned away.

When she felt someone come up very close, at first she assumed it was Tyler and tried to pretend she hadn't noticed. How many times did she have to tell this man she wasn't interested in his friendship? His friendship always came with strings attached.

But then she heard a deep, husky, yet clearly female voice. "So it's you. I knew you'd be here."

Mallory turned with a shock, the skin along her shoulders breaking out in a sudden rash of shivering bumps. It was Imogene Jacobson, the woman who had torched the Ringmaster Café.

Imogene, who was supposed to be in an institution. Wasn't she?

"Yes, I'm back," Imogene said, her handsome face altered by emotion into something ugly and almost frightening. A forty-year-old former nurse, she had for years been growing more and more eccentric, more and more paranoid and delusional. Even before the fire, she'd quarreled with almost everybody in town, from the grocer to the mayor.

Most people, when they learned about Sander Jacobson's involvement with the Heyday Eight, had said they didn't blame him.

"Did you think they'd keep me locked up forever? While you and your family see what other lives you can ruin? While you hunt for other marriages you can destroy?"

"Imogene, I—"

"I'm Mrs. Jacobson to you," the woman said, holding up a finger that shook with rage. "I'm the wife of a prominent lawyer whose family has practiced for three generations here in Heyday. And you. You're just a whore. You, and your mother, and your trashy little sister."

Mallory had to fight the urge to slap the woman. *Her*

mother? This woman would dare to say such things about Elizabeth Rackham, after what she had done to her?

Though a million furious insults bubbled toward her lips, Mallory tried to remind herself that Imogene Jacobson was mentally unstable. She'd spent two years in an institution instead of going to jail for her crime. How on earth had she convinced anyone that she was sane enough to be released?

Mallory saw Tyler coming toward her. He gestured for her to back away, which she did, as far as the crowded tables of merchandise would allow.

He put his hand on Imogene's arm.

"Mrs. Jacobson," he said. "You're not supposed to be bothering the Rackhams. I think you'd better leave."

Imogene turned to him. "Who are you?" Her eyes narrowed. "Oh, that's right. The reporter." She exhaled with a rasping sound. "You can't tell me what to do. You're as bad as she is. You destroy people. And then, because you're just a vulture, you pick over the bones to make your stories."

"I'm sorry you think so, Mrs. Jacobson," Tyler said equably. "But the fact remains that you're not supposed to come within fifteen hundred yards of the Rackham family. I think you'd better leave."

"You can't make me leave." To Mallory's horror, Imogene jerked her arm free so roughly she set a dozen wind chimes pinging and clanging with fear.

The commotion attracted plenty of attention.

Within a minute, both Kieran and Bryce, who knew all about the restraining order, were at Tyler's side.

"Come on, Mrs. Jacobson," Kieran said. "Come on, now. You don't want to make a scene."

"Kieran, thank heaven," Imogene said. Even lunatics, Mallory noticed as if from a great distance, worshipped Kieran. "Please tell *that man*—" she glared at Tyler "—that I have just as much right to be here as *she* does."

Kieran murmured something soothing. Just behind him, Bryce had his cell phone to his ear. Mallory couldn't hear his low, measured words, but she was sure he was calling the police.

After a couple of seconds, he flipped it shut and turned to Tyler, motioning him closer.

"Her husband is on his way, and the police won't be far behind," Bryce said quietly. "Can you get Mallory safely out of here?"

Tyler nodded. He already had his arm around Mallory's shoulders. She was very much afraid that they were shaking.

"I don't want to run away," she said stubbornly, even though she knew she sounded a little like Imogene Jacobson, which horrified her. But it was true. She wasn't the one under a restraining order. According to the law, it was Imogene who should leave. "I don't have anything to be ashamed of."

"I know," Tyler said. He ducked down to look straight into her eyes with a bracing smile. "But there's no way to win a fight with a crazy woman, you know."

"It's true," Bryce said with his own devilish grin. "I've tried a million times. It simply doesn't work."

In spite of herself, she smiled. Nodding his approval, Tyler began guiding her toward the exit. And, because the trembling had made its way to her legs, she let him.

Bryce went with them as far as the door. At the last minute, Tyler smiled and put his hand on Bryce's shoulder.

"Thanks," he said.

They both looked back toward Imogene, who was now almost calm, slightly tearful, unburdening her woes to Kieran, yet another victim of his trademark charm.

Bryce laughed slightly.

"I believe we should all thank St. Kieran," he said. "But hey. What else is family for?"

"WHAT ON EARTH is going on in here?"

Tyler, who was standing on a ladder just inside the front door of Rackham Books, looked over at Mallory, though he didn't have to see her face to know how shocked she was. Her voice said it all.

And he knew why. Her store opened in one hour, and right now it looked as if a bomb had gone off in here.

"We're installing a security system," he said. "I know it looks bad right now, but they've promised me everything will be finished by ten. Down here, at least."

"Down *here,* at least?" She repeated the words with ominous clarity.

She still stood by the side door, with her keys and purse and satchel dangling from her hands. She slowly scanned the rest of the store. He knew she could see at least three men working, and there were two more outside, where she couldn't see.

"Down here, at least? What do you mean by that? Where else are you planning to…install things?"

"The whole building," Tyler said, handing down a thin cable to the man below him, who was tacking the wire to the baseboards. "The shop, as you can see, and then we'll do both apartments. This is Jerry, from Chilton Security Systems. Jerry, this is Mallory Rackham."

Jerry looked up, his mouth full of brads, and waved politely.

Mallory tried to smile, but it didn't quite work. She gestured toward the back office. "Tyler, may I talk to you alone for a minute?"

He'd known this was coming. He'd even prepared the Chilton men for a fairly cool reception, though he'd assured them it was in the lease that he did have the right to make adjustments to the building as he deemed fit, with or without notifying the tenant.

As Tyler climbed down the ladder, Jerry looked up at him with a sympathetic expression.

"If I'm not out in five minutes," Tyler said, tucking his polo shirt neatly into his belt, "send help."

"No way," Jerry said, grinning. "I'm married, and

I know that look. If you're not out in five minutes, no power on earth can save you."

At first, it seemed that Jerry was right. When Tyler joined her in the narrow office, Mallory was standing behind her desk, looking like a generalissimo preparing to attack. He shut the door and hoped for the best.

For a few seconds she fiddled with some papers, stiff fingered, as if she needed time to compose her thoughts. Then she looked up, her eyes shadowed and her mouth tense. She looked as if she hadn't slept all night.

"Don't you think you might have discussed this with me first?"

"I would have," he said politely, "except you made it pretty clear you didn't want to talk to me. I called twice last night, and once this morning, but you didn't answer."

She didn't have a response for that one. What could she say? She'd been pretty strung out yesterday, when Imogene Jacobson had accosted her at the garden store. By the time he got her back to the apartment, she'd rallied a little and obviously regretted the show of weakness. She'd thanked him at the door but declined to invite him in, and then refused to answer the telephone for the rest of the night.

Which had been fine with him, really. He'd gone back to the garden store, hoping to find Imogene still there. She was a talker, and she'd make a great chapter in his book. But she'd been taken down to police headquarters. By the time the cops were through with her, she'd either be back in the loony bin or so scared she'd never open up to Tyler on the record.

So, for the time being, he'd had to settle for talking to Linda Tremel. He'd already identified Linda as a potential suspect. She had a husky voice, which might sound masculine if altered, but more importantly she had that bitterness, that impotent anger against a world that hadn't treated her fairly, that so many black-mailers possessed.

She was a talker, too. Even when he told her why he was there, she hardly drew a breath. If was as if she'd waited her whole life for a chance to tattle on her neighbors.

She seemed to think that, because of the Heyday Eight story, he was primarily interested in the sex lives of small-town America. Problem was, most of her gossip was so petty that she ended up saying more about herself than she did about the poor people of Heyday. For instance, she hinted that Mallory Rackham harbored a hopeless passion for Bryce McClintock, which Tyler knew to be pure baloney.

When he got back to the apartment, he'd shredded his notes and tossed them in the trash.

"Look, Mallory," he said now. "What is your problem with this? Surely, after yesterday, you agree that we need a little more than a dime-store dead bolt to protect this place. Heyday may be ninety percent heaven on earth, but that other ten percent, into which Imogene Jacobson falls, is seriously screwed up."

She bit her lower lip. "Are you saying you really think Imogene might—"

"I'm saying she already burned down one business of yours. She's still pretty pissed off. Why take chances?"

"I—" She took a deep breath, but didn't finish her sentence. She hadn't relaxed a single millimeter. She absolutely hated the idea of the security system, and for the life of him Tyler couldn't figure out exactly why. Surely it wasn't a power thing? Surely she didn't mind that Tyler owned the building and planned to assert his right to protect it?

Something wasn't right here. He hadn't exactly expected her to kiss his ring in gratitude, but he hadn't expected this level of resistance, either.

"Mallory, I don't think you get it. Personally, I don't give a damn if she burns the place to the ground. I wish she'd burn every building I inherited so I can get the hell out of Heyday." He frowned. "This is for you, to protect you. Don't you understand that?"

"I understand it," she said slowly. She looked at him with dark eyes. "I just don't believe it."

"What?" He had been leaning against the door, his hands in his pockets, but now he straightened and gave her a hard glare. "Why the hell not?"

"Because in my experience, you don't do things for other people. You do them for yourself, to get stories. For all I know, those men are really just installing bugs and spy cameras and tape recorders."

Spy cameras? He almost laughed, but somehow it wasn't very funny.

"For crying out loud." Now he really was ticked off. This state-of-the-art security system was costing him thousands. And he had to crawl around helping install it, just to get it up in time to let her open for business as usual at ten.

"You're paranoid, Mallory, did you know that? You think I'd break the law to find out who you talk to on the phone or what kind of bubble bath you use? What kind of secrets could you possibly have that—"

And then it hit him.

Good Lord.

She did have a secret.

She was staring at him, but she wasn't really seeing him. Her face was white, and so were her knuckles. She must not have unclenched her fists since she'd seen his crew in her store, installing wires.

"Mallory." He leaned toward her. He reached for her hands, instinctively thinking he might be able to rub some life back into them. "Mallory, listen—"

But just then the telephone rang. She turned her wide, unseeing eyes toward it, but she didn't answer it. It rang again. And again, loud in the little office.

Finally it stopped. And in a second or two, Wally, who must have just arrived, stuck his multicolored head through the office door.

"Sorry to interrupt, boss, but this one's for you." Wally rolled his eyes. "Lucky you. It's Darth Vader again."

Darth Vader? While Mallory tried to compose her face, tried to take a deep breath, tried to force herself to reach for the phone, Tyler's mind was moving quickly.

Darth Vader. A man in a black mask. A man whose identity was unknown, though his evil agenda was recognized by everyone who met him.

A man with an electronically distorted voice.

"Mallory," he said.

But she cut him off.

With a voice that sounded a little like a robot itself, she said, "I'm sorry, Tyler. You'll have to excuse me. I need to take this call."

CHAPTER NINE

WHEN HER ALARM WENT OFF at six Friday morning, Mallory squinted toward the window, feeling sure it must be a mistake. Her bedroom was so dark, how could it be time to get up?

She groaned at the sight of the glass panes, which looked as if they were melting with rain. Another gloomy day? Most Virginia springs were rainy, swelling the rivers and urging millions of wildflowers up out of the mud. Ordinarily she didn't mind—it was good for business. It made people want to stay in and read a good book.

But this was too much.

Besides, she was tired, so tired. Her body ached all over, as if she might be coming down with something. The area behind her eyes felt tight and pounded in time with her pulse. She didn't see how she could face another long, gray drive to the ferry.

Damn the blackmailer.

She'd made the money drop only twice so far, but the ordeal was so stressful she already hated the very sight of the ferry. She'd never realized how emotionally exhausting it was to be frightened and furious at the same time.

As she sat up, she felt a little dizzy. She pressed her thumbs to the inside corners of her eyes. Her face was hot.

Even at the best of times she couldn't afford to be sick, since it would mean she had to hire someone to watch the store. And she especially couldn't afford it now, with the blackmailer sucking money out of her like a leech.

She rarely ever caught anything. So what was this? Was the stress starting to get to her? Surely this coward who hid behind a telephone and a voice distorter couldn't have defeated her, not after all she'd been through.

Through all the ordeals of the past three years, she'd remained tough. She hadn't fallen apart when she found out about Dan, or when the café burned down, or even when her mother had collapsed in the kitchen that terrible night.

And yet the other day, when Imogene Jacobson had accosted her at Linda's store, she'd thought for a minute she might faint. It was almost as if, ever since the blackmailer had first called, Mallory hadn't been breathing properly. It was like wearing a corset of fear, and the laces just kept pulling tighter and tighter.

And yesterday, when Tyler had reached out for her hand, with that strangely compassionate look on his face, she'd almost fallen for it. That's how weak and mixed up she'd become. She'd almost told him everything.

Thank God she'd caught herself in time. She could handle this alone. But if she ever did get so desperate that she needed help, she would turn to Roddy or Kieran or Bryce. Maybe even the police.

She would never, never turn to *Tyler.* Anyone who was fool enough to take the comforting hand Tyler Balfour offered would be smart to check out what his other hand was doing.

Chances are it would be scribbling down every word you said.

All the better to quote you with, my dear.

FROM THE SHELTER OF HIS CAR, Tyler watched as Mallory stood in the pouring rain to buy a ticket for the 11:00 a.m. Green Diamond Ferry. He knew what she'd do next. She'd get on early. She'd slide a small brown packet of unmarked twenty-dollar bills under one of the seats. And then she'd get off again and drive home.

He knew, because it was almost exactly the same scenario Dilday Merle had described to him. The only difference was that Dilday had been told to use the Richmond city bus.

The basic theory was the same. Put the money on a crowded moving vehicle that was scheduled to make many stops in quick succession. The victim would have no idea where or when the blackmailer would board the vehicle to pick up the money. Thus, the blackmailer assumed, there was almost no use even trying to catch him.

The guy was pretty clever, Tyler would give him

that. For his very first payment, Dilday Merle had hired a private detective to stay on the bus and snap a photograph of the person who finally picked up the packet. But the blackmailer must have recognized a sting, because that day no one picked it up at all. The next week, the blackmailer had called Dilday and told him that for his little trick he'd have to pay double.

Dilday could take risks like that. He had the advantage of knowing he was innocent.

But what about Mallory? What sin was she paying for? And was she innocent, like Dilday…or was she guilty?

He watched her as she huddled under her umbrella, waiting for the ferry to finish docking. Her face was just a pale oval inside the hood of her raincoat. He thought he'd never seen anyone look so miserable.

As soon as she stepped onto the ferry, he got out of his car. If he was right, she wouldn't be gone long, and he wanted to be sure to catch her on the way out. Years ago, a policeman he'd interviewed had told him that the secret to getting a confession wasn't thumbscrews or truth serum. It was surgically applied shock.

Catch 'em when they're nervous, the seventy-year-old decorated cop had said, *and catch 'em by surprise.*

Tyler had used it a hundred times, and it hadn't failed him yet. Even if he didn't get his confession in words, he got it in wide eyes, pale cheeks and stumbling, unprepared responses.

But when Mallory saw him, her reaction was more

dramatic than anything he'd seen in ten years of journalism.

She couldn't go white, because she was already whiter than a sheet of fine paper. She didn't rush into ridiculous explanations, because she clearly couldn't speak. She merely made a choking sound, stumbled on the slick exit ramp, then blindly reached for something to steady herself on.

Tyler put out his arm. He had the feeling she took it without registering exactly what it was.

The rain was falling even harder now. Without thinking, he pulled her under the protection of his umbrella. As he wrapped his arms around her, the shell of the umbrella rode so low its metal points pressed into their shoulders, shutting them off from the rest of the crowd.

She didn't protest, though the embrace brought their bodies into full, intimate contact for the first time in all these years. He was shocked by how delicate, fine boned and perfectly female she felt...and by the primitive surging of a protective instinct in his own chest.

Apparently shock worked both ways.

Damn it. This was dumb.

But he had wanted to do this for so long, since the first time he saw her wipe away angry tears over her husband's neglect. This ache had begun three years ago, and he realized that, though he'd ignored it, it had never quite gone away.

"How did you know where I was?" Her voice was muffled, her lips against his raincoat.

"I followed you," he said. "I knew something was wrong when you got that call yesterday. I—" He paused. "I was concerned."

She didn't answer. She probably didn't believe him. He was a little surprised himself, but it was true. His first thought had been that he needed to know the truth. If she was in some kind of trouble, she might need help.

His second thought had been the story. The book.

She had no way of knowing how amazing it was. Personal first? Professional second? That hadn't happened to him in a decade.

"We need to talk," he said.

Finally she lifted her head. "I think I need something to eat first. I don't feel…quite right."

She wasn't kidding. She looked as if she might be on the verge of passing out. He tilted the umbrella and glanced around the inner harbor. The rain had washed away most of the tourists, and they ought to be able to find a restaurant without a waiting list.

But this area, however quaint, was too close to the scene of the crime, both figuratively and literally. She'd never relax enough to talk openly as long as she feared the blackmailer might be watching her from the next table over.

"I saw a little place a couple of miles back," Tyler said. "Let's take my car."

That got a small reaction. She frowned. "My car…"

"We'll get it later. I'm not sure you're up to driving."

With a sigh, she nodded.

They didn't say much on the way to the restaurant, which turned out to be a tiny diner with five booths covered in sparkling blue plastic, one Formica counter and a huge jukebox.

They were alone, except for the waitress, who was reading a paperback novel, and a burly biker-type at the bar, who kept playing "Wind Beneath My Wings" over and over again while he nursed a Diet Coke.

Tyler got coffee, and all Mallory decided she could handle was some dry toast. When she'd picked at enough of it to bring some color back into her cheeks, he asked her the question that had been driving him insane the past twenty-four hours.

"Do you feel up to talking about it?"

She shrugged. "Do I have any choice?"

He ignored that. She could always simply stonewall him, but he saw no need to remind her of that.

"Is it the Eight?" He spoke in low tones, though he was pretty sure the biker hadn't even noticed their arrival. "Is that what he's got on you?"

Mallory shut her eyes briefly and set down the piece of toast she'd been toying with. When she opened them again, they were shining in the overly harsh diner lights.

"Yes," she said without inflection. "It's the Eight."

He felt an odd sinking sensation to hear her confirm it.

Why, he wondered? Surely he hadn't been irrationally hoping that the two blackmail schemes weren't related?

He hadn't been that naive since he believed in the tooth fairy.

He tried to keep on his reporter's face, his reporter's voice. This wasn't personal, though after holding her in his arms it was difficult to remember that.

"Okay." He took a sip of coffee. "What about the Eight, exactly? Surely you aren't trying to tell me you were—one of them?"

She smiled thinly. "You would think that was terrible, wouldn't you? Inexcusable. You'd think it was disgusting."

"No," he said. "I'd think it was a lie."

She flushed, which on her pale cheeks looked dramatic and oddly unhealthy. "Okay. If you know so much about it, then why don't you tell me? What do you think the truth is?"

He'd been mulling this over for nearly twenty-four hours, ever since he discovered she was getting the Darth Vader calls, too. He had eliminated the possibility of Mallory's personal involvement immediately. She'd been about three years too old and hadn't been a co-ed at Moresville College anyhow. Plus, she was just too innocent. Not virginal, nothing that primitive. Rather, it was a sort of emotional innocence. She hadn't been a hooker. For one thing, she had suffered too much over her capsized marriage, tried too hard to keep it afloat.

In the end, he had narrowed it down to two possibilities.

"All right," he said. "The way I figure it, the blackmailer could know that you and your mother were abetting the girls, that you knew what they were up to when they met at your café. The police checked that out, of course, and found nothing. But it wouldn't be the first time they misjudged."

"It would mean that you misjudged, too."

He laughed. "It wouldn't be my first time, either. But there's another possibility, and I actually prefer this one."

The tension around her eyes tightened. Though his first hypothesis hadn't touched a raw spot, she was clearly more afraid of what he might say next.

"The other possibility," he said, watching her carefully, "is that your sister *did* become a member of the Eight."

And there it was, the trademark collapse of the perfectly hit target. He'd seen it so many times on the faces of people who had carried a painful secret for too long. Anger that anyone dared breach the fortress, fear at what exposure would bring and, paradoxically, relief that the burden no longer was theirs alone.

The miserable stew of emotions almost always ended in tears. Mallory was fighting them hard, but the red rims and sparkling lashes told him she would soon go the way of all the others.

"Look, Mallory," he said quickly. Surprisingly, he didn't want her to fall apart, even though, in his experience, the tide of tears frequently swept out the most intimate revelations. She'd despise herself for it later. "I know you hate me right now. I know you think this is the end of the world. But it isn't."

"Maybe not yours," she said, her voice thick and tight. "And not mine. But it may well be the end of Mindy's."

"No," he said softly. "Not even hers."

She wouldn't look at him. She turned her face and seemed to be studying the fringed jacket of the biker at the counter. The man was hunched over his grilled-cheese sandwich now, holding his Diet Coke like a beer and singing along with his song in an off-key but heartfelt baritone.

Tyler indulged himself in a long contemplation of her profile, the way he used to do when she was working at the café, and he was just sitting in the corner booth, waiting and watching. She had such a small, fragile face, really. A short, well-defined nose and full lips that seemed overlarge above her pointed, feminine chin. Even from the side you could tell her eyes were a clear, crystal blue that seemed to reflect all the light in the room, like very clean water.

When she looked at you straight on, with that undaunted gaze, she made you forget the fragility. But from the side, she was very young and very vulnerable. The rain had stuck several strands of hair to her cheek. She looked like a little girl who needed to go inside and let her mama clean her up.

"I didn't know about it at first," she said, without turning back to face him. "When you were there, when your story first ran. I didn't have any idea that Mindy was…"

He waited, but she never finished the sentence. "When did you find out?"

"About two months later. Things were tough—your story made a lot of people suspicious of us, and business was bad. I'd just gotten divorced and moved home. Then Mindy tried—she tried to commit suicide."

Her voice was fairly steady, but Tyler heard the hollow tone, and he knew how terrible that must have been. A time of horrors. No wonder she hated him. He must have seemed like the instrument of Armageddon.

"I don't think she really meant to succeed. We found her in time, thank God. But while she was in the hospital, I went into her room. I found it then. I don't know why she kept it."

Tyler hesitated. "She had one of the whips?"

Mallory shut her eyes and nodded. "I knew, then, of course. I knew what it meant."

Thanks to Tyler's stories, which had laid out the details of the Heyday Eight's strict club rules, *everyone* knew what the whip meant.

Because Heyday was a town born from a circus escapade, and was ripe with circus themes, the Heyday Eight decided to bill themselves as animal tamers. Each initiate was given a black plastic whip, the kind sold at every annual Heyday Ringmaster Parade. The men who bought their services understood that, because they were *bad, bad men,* a light whipping would have to be endured before they got the sex they had paid for. For some of them, the whipping was enough, and they went away mildly sore but completely satisfied.

As each girl entertained more customers, bringing money into the club's coffers, colored ribbons were threaded into her whip, creating a cat-o'-nine-tails effect.

White meant she'd slept with only one customer. Pink meant five; green meant ten. At twenty-five, the girls got gold ribbons, and had a tiny whip tattooed on the small of their backs.

When any member had serviced fifty men, she was promised a tiger brooch, solid gold with diamond eyes. Only one girl, the leader, Greta Swinburne, wore the little gold tiger. Somehow she made it look as bewitching as the Holy Grail. Everyone in the Eight yearned for one of their own.

And, weirdly, she had been so proud of it that she'd been glad to show it to Tyler. It had made a wonderful series. No one had been surprised when he won the Pulitzer.

"What color was the whip?" He asked the question without inflection, as he always did. But he felt abnormally tentative, as if, instead of conducting an interview, he were probing a bullet wound, trying to find the festering metal.

"White." Mallory looked at him over her lifted chin. "Just once, that's all, with a man named Dorian Swigert. But it was enough to nearly kill her."

Once. That must be why he hadn't been able to unearth her name. Greta Swinburne had been about to graduate. Mindy must have been her replacement. Once the eight girls had been caught, they obviously had conspired to keep Mindy's name clear.

Interesting. He wouldn't have thought there would be such honor among…animal tamers.

"Well, now you know." Mallory's voice was harsh. "Now you've got your scoop. Are you happy?"

He frowned. "I'm not a daily journalist anymore, Mallory. I'm not on anyone's payroll. I don't need *scoops*."

She laughed, or tried to. "Are you saying you won't use this information? If not in tomorrow's newspaper, then at least in your wonderful book?"

He didn't answer for a long minute. He knew what she wanted to hear. But could he promise that he'd never reveal her sister's involvement? What if it became necessary to expose the blackmailer?

And she was right. What about his book? He'd contracted to tell the full, honest story of the Heyday Eight. Could he withhold Mindy's name and maintain any authorial integrity at all?

"I'll try not to," he said. "That's all I can promise right now. If I can possibly keep her secret, I will."

Finally the tears began to spill. She picked up her napkin and lowered her head, covering her face with the cheap white paper.

"Mallory." He reached out and touched her arm. To his shock, it was burning. Her fever must be well over a hundred.

"Mallory, you're sick," he said. "We have to get you home."

Tyler had, in his urgency, spoken too loudly. The

biker had noticed them. He was still sitting by the jukebox, but he was scowling toward their booth. He pointed one triangle of grilled cheese at Tyler firmly.

"Hey, you. Don't you go making that lady cry." The biker's eyes were as red as Mallory's. He must have had some recent personal experience with crying. "You tell her you're sorry, you hear? Right now. You tell her you're goddamn sorry you made her cry."

Tyler didn't bother to respond. He stood, moved to Mallory's side of the booth, and gently pulled her up, into the crook of his arm.

But as he guided her out to the car, a little voice inside him was saying the same thing over and over.

I am, it said. *I'm sorry.*

CHAPTER TEN

THANKS TO Tyler's vigilant care, her fever went down in about twenty-four hours. After that, Mallory actually enjoyed her minivacation in bed.

Tyler had insisted on staying in her apartment, sleeping on the sofa, and at first she had been just too tired to argue. Then she began to like having someone around.

He didn't hover. She often heard his laptop clicking away, and he held muffled conversations on his cell phone. Obviously he couldn't suspend his own life, but somehow he seemed to be nearby whenever she needed aspirin or a drink of cool water.

Even better, he had mobilized her part-time workers, Wally and Lara Gilbert's mother, Karla, to keep the bookstore covered. What shifts they couldn't handle, he took himself.

She could hardly believe it. Karla and Wally—that was fine. But whenever she imagined Tyler standing behind her cash register, it seemed like a fever-induced hallucination.

Tyler? Tyler selling *Roar, Little Rhino* and *The Colic*

Chronicles to Mary Beth Singer, who was due in three days and was convinced that everyone wanted regular updates on precisely how many centimeters she was dilated?

Tyler selling *Alien Probes: Truth or Fiction?* to Mack Beanstaff, a retired air force major who firmly believed there was a patch of Heyday out by the abandoned railroad tracks that should be named Martian Interplanetary Airport?

If laughter was really the best medicine, no wonder Mallory was getting better fast.

The store closed early on Sunday, so Mallory was hoping she'd see Tyler soon. At 6:05 p.m. on the dot, she heard his code knock on the front door of the apartment. Eager for company after a dull day watching nature shows on TV, she rolled over and touched the alarm-release button. Then she heard his key in the door.

She lay back on the pillows with a tired smile, trying to figure out exactly how she'd gone from wanting to kill him to giving him a key to her apartment.

Four days ago, even this temporary truce would have seemed impossible. And yet somehow they'd drifted so easily back into the rhythms of quiet friendship they'd established three years ago. He was such good company—smart, witty, with a knack for soft silences in which it seemed their minds were doing the talking.

She tried not to remember how badly that earlier "friendship" had ended. Maybe he was using her.

Maybe he just wanted more information for his book. Well, fine. She wanted something, too. She was tired. And she was tired of being alone with her fears. Just until she got well, she wanted relief from the stress of the past few weeks.

By unspoken agreement, they'd avoided talking about Mindy or the Heyday Eight or his book. What was there to say, anyhow? He had discovered her one big secret, and, in a move that shocked Mallory, he had said he wouldn't expose it unless he absolutely had to.

Now all she could do was wait and see whether he would keep that promise.

In the meantime, it was lovely to be pampered. All pampering in the Rackham household had always been showered on poor, unhappy Mindy. Sensible, competent Mallory had been expected to soldier on like one of the adults.

As Tyler passed the door to the bedroom, she caught the aroma of Aurora York's chicken soup. "Hi," she said. "Something sure smells good."

"Aurora sent dinner," he said over his shoulder as he went toward the kitchen. "You feel up to some?"

"I think so." For the first time, she did feel a little hungry. She'd eaten nothing all day Friday except those crumbs of dry toast at the diner. On Saturday Tyler had insisted she take a few spoonfuls of broth and drink a few swallows of clear soda, but mostly she'd slept. Today her systems seemed a little more alive.

After a very few minutes, he came in with a tray.

She propped up her pillows and scooted over to make room for him to sit on the edge of the bed.

He put the tray down across her legs, then reached out and felt her forehead with the back of his hand.

"Good," he said. "Still normal." He chose a sandwich off the pile, arranged himself at the foot of the bed and smiled. "So did you get plenty of sleep?"

"Too much. I feel lazy. I haven't taken two whole days off since I was sixteen."

"Then you're overdue," he said. "Did you watch some TV?"

"Four nature shows in a row. I learned some amazing stuff. Want to know why wildebeests have overdeveloped forequarters?"

He grimaced. "No. Want to know why Verna Myers believes knapweed is good for running sores?"

"No!" She shut her eyes and shook her head. "I'm so sorry. I know the customers must all be driving you crazy."

"Actually, they're kind of interesting. In Washington, everyone wants to look and sound and act like everyone else. Around here, it's a badge of honor to invent a brand-new psychiatric disorder. I'll probably be bored when I go back."

"Have you decided when that'll be?" She didn't look at him. She stirred her soup, releasing the warm, salty scent and breathing it in. She wasn't sure what answer she hoped he'd give.

"Not yet. The property situation is even more tangled than I realized. And as for the book—" He chuckled. "As you can imagine, I'm having a little trouble getting some of the interviews I need."

She smiled wryly. "Have you tried bringing them chicken soup?"

"I could bring these people bars of pure gold bouillon, and they'd still refuse to open the door. But that's okay. That's why it's called *investigative* journalism."

Her smile deepened. "Is that what it's called? I thought I remembered hearing...something different."

"Hey, now. If we're going to exchange insults, I could tell you what people are saying about *you*."

She looked up quickly.

"Well, not *people,* exactly," he amended with a grin. "Linda Tremel."

"What is Linda saying about me?"

"She told me, purely off the record, that you and Bryce McClintock once had a thing. Apparently you're brokenhearted now that he's engaged to Lara."

"Oh, for heaven's sake."

Tyler raised his eyebrows. "Not true?"

"Definitely not true." She sipped her ginger ale. "Not that Bryce isn't fantastic. McClintock men are just plain—"

She stopped, wishing she could dive into this bowl of soup and drown. How could she have forgotten, even for a second, that Tyler was a McClintock, too?

"Go on." He grinned. "McClintock men are just plain what?"

She gave him a dirty look. "Well, for one thing, they're all just plain too conceited to live."

He chuckled, but she knew she hadn't fooled him. He'd have to be blind not to know how devastatingly good-looking he was, with that rugged McClintock jaw topped by the most sensual pair of lips she'd ever seen. And those blue eyes…

He also knew she was attracted to him. She'd never been very good at hiding it—not three years ago, and not today.

He was still looking at her, with a heated gaze that made her think her fever might be coming back. Flustered, she went for another spoonful of soup and, of course, dribbled it onto her chin like a baby.

He leaned over, picked up her napkin and rubbed the warm liquid away. She clenched her fingers hard around the spoon, trying not to react.

But the flush she felt in the pit of her stomach must have radiated out, all the way to her cheeks. He tilted his head and brushed the tips of his fingers across the burning skin under her eyes.

For a long minute he didn't speak. He just looked at her, a frown between his brows.

"Damn it, Mallory," he said finally. He let his fingers drift to her hairline, just above her ear. "For ten years I've had an immutable rule against mixing my job and my personal life. You almost made me forget that once before."

She didn't pull away, although shivers trickled down like a silver star-fall from his fingertips. She didn't want him to know how vulnerable she still was to his touch.

He was looking at her lips. "I'm dangerously close to forgetting it now, too."

She lifted her chin. "Well, you might be," she said. "But *I'm* not."

He didn't drop his hand, didn't pull away, as she'd assumed he would. Instead, for a moment she thought he might try to prove that she was lying.

And she *was* lying. She was close, couldn't be closer, to forgetting all the hard lessons he'd taught her three years ago. She was close to forgetting his book and the blackmailer and everything that existed even two inches beyond these crisp, blue-flowered sheets.

He leaned in, and she wondered whether, if he lowered his lips to hers, she'd be able to turn away. She remembered that, in their only kiss, his lips had been firm and warm. She remembered that he had tasted so familiar, like blueberries and coffee—and yet so strange, too, like potent, nameless spices they didn't have in places like Heyday.

Against her will, she'd dreamed of that kiss. She wondered what it would be like today. Would it still blend the tastes of gentle berries and exotic mysteries? Or would it be bitter now, laced with the knowledge of deceit?

At the last minute, he stopped. He drew back slowly. Tilting his head, he met her unflinching eyes, and let his fingers fall to the downy blue comforter.

"All right, then," he said pleasantly. "I guess one of us needs to be sensible."

He stood, and the mattress shifted subtly, causing

her soup to quiver. He went over to the sliding glass doors that led out onto the balcony and stared at the last of the pink-and-silver sunset clouds, which were disappearing behind the treetops. It would be dark soon.

After a minute or two, he cast a quick glance over his shoulder. "Did I ever tell you about how, ten years ago, my journalistic career almost came to an ugly and embarrassing end?"

She couldn't decide whether he was just trying to cushion the conversational transition, or whether he really had something he wanted to tell her. His voice was normal, casual even, but his body was oddly tense.

"No, you didn't," she said. "What happened?"

He took one last look along the street, then reached out and pulled the drapes, closing them off from prying eyes. It was a big-city gesture, a big-city awareness that, as it grew dark outside, their lighted window would be as clear to passersby as a stage under the spotlights.

Here, in Heyday, she rarely thought about drawing the curtains unless she was changing clothes or sleeping. Here in Heyday the only eyes out in the darkness would belong to your friends and neighbors.

Or your blackmailer.

She realized that the line between Heyday and the "big city" wasn't as distinct as she'd thought.

He came back into the room and sat down. But this time, instead of the bed, he took the armchair in the corner. It wasn't a large bedroom, so the difference shouldn't have been as great as she felt it to be.

"I was twenty-two," he went on. "I was just out of J school, and I'd landed the job of my dreams at a Washington-area paper. Not *the* Washington paper, you understand, but still. I was on top of the world. I was going to be a star, and I wasn't going to waste any time."

She had to smile. He might call himself Balfour, but he was a McClintock through and through. They never settled for second best. Apparently it had little to do with Anderson's upbringing. Confidence, force, ambition were encoded in the genes, just like the virility and charm.

"And then?"

He shook his head wryly. "And then I made one of the dumbest mistakes on the books. I got mixed up with an older woman."

Women. That was a McClintock specialty, too.

She moved the tray off her legs and sat up straighter. This was a story she wanted to hear.

"Is that particularly dumb?" She crossed her legs and propped her pillow behind her back. "I'd think a lot of twenty-two-year-olds do it."

"Yes, but this older woman wasn't just your garden-variety lonely housewife searching for someone to *understand* her. This woman was the ex-wife of a local politico. Not national, but high profile. Plenty big enough. She came to me out of the blue. She said she had a story for me. A story that would put my byline on the front page and make me a household name."

"Wow. You must have been thrilled."

"Oh, yeah, I was thrilled, all right." He laughed. "She held out that carrot, and I ran after it with my tongue hanging out. I was so damn full of myself. I thought I was some really hot-shot investigative journalist. And yet I never even asked myself the most important question of all."

"Which was?"

"Why me?" He raised his eyebrows. "Washington was full of journalists, real ones. Men and women who already *were* household names. Why me?"

Mallory, looking at him sitting there, all grace and gilded lamplight on rugged features, thought there was a simple answer to that question, but she didn't say it out loud.

"She said she'd seen my stories and thought I was a wonderful writer. What a joke. I hadn't snagged any good assignments at all. A few deadly dull zoning-board workshops and a couple of fluff pieces about a Pre-Raphaelite sketch that turned up in a yard sale. I was nobody."

"So why *do* you think she picked you?"

He rested his head against the back of the armchair. From that angle, the lamplight made his smile look particularly sardonic.

"She was looking for the dumbest sucker on the block. She wanted a new alimony arrangement, and she needed someone to do a hatchet job on her husband. All trumped-up charges. He was cruel, he was violent, he took drugs, he abused her, he killed her cat. God, it was enough to choke a horse, but I was such a hungry, ambitious idiot. And of course, she was persuasive. She had this sexy-as-hell red-velvet dressing gown."

Mallory didn't say anything. He was telling the story with a lightly sarcastic melodrama, but she wondered whether there might be a touch of true bitterness beneath it all. And yet why should there be? Surely he didn't mind so terribly much that someone had exploited his youth and naiveté. Even the great Tyler Balfour could be forgiven for being foolish at twenty-two.

"She flattered me until I was so bloated with my own importance I couldn't tie my shoes." His smile seemed to find the young Tyler ridiculous. "In her tight red party dresses, she took me around and introduced me to powerful people I hadn't ever met. And in the red-velvet gown, she introduced me to bedroom tricks I'd never imagined. Naturally, I fell head over heels in love with her."

"Oh," Mallory said. She pleated the sheet with her fingertips and wondered what the right thing to say was.

"I didn't sleep for six months, working my regular job during the day, and at night secretly drying her tears, worshipping at her red-velvet breast and gathering my story. Then I proudly turned it in."

"Oh, dear."

"Yep. I could hardly wait to see my name on the front page. But, thank God, that's where I finally got lucky. My editor knew the lady and her husband only by reputation, but apparently that was enough. He recognized it for the total crap it was."

"What did he do?"

Tyler's smile finally reached his eyes. He made a sound that was clearly a chuckle.

"He printed out my story, walked over to my desk right in front of everyone and dumped the whole thing into my trash can. He said I could either be that rich bitch's pet Chihuahua or I could work for that newspaper, and he didn't much care which, given what an unmitigated moron I seemed to be. He gave me thirty seconds to choose."

He was laughing openly now, and the sound was infectious. She put her hands over her face and let out a gasp that was half moan, half chuckle. She could just picture it.

"Oh, Tyler," she said. "How terrible."

"Yeah, it was probably the most embarrassing thirty seconds of my life. Some of the other reporters knew her and thought she was pretty hot, so they were calling out raunchy suggestions from all over the room. Lots of dog metaphors. The worst thing was that, judging from some of their comments, I could tell one or two of them had spent a good bit of time in her bedroom, too. But at least they hadn't been stupid enough to write the story."

Mallory smiled. "Well, at least that probably cured you of being in love."

"You'd think so, wouldn't you?" Tyler shook his head ruefully. "But to tell you the truth I thought about her for years. Every time I saw a woman in a red dress." He raised one eyebrow. "Or a Chihuahua."

They sat there in silence for a few moments, smiling at the poor kid who had been so dumb. Mallory had a few choice thoughts about the lady in the red dress, too.

"Funny," he said. "I haven't told that story in ten years. Not since I sobered up the next day. I fear I told most of D.C.'s bar scene about it that night."

She looked at him. She could believe that. The story humanized him, made him seem real and vulnerable. He wouldn't like that. He worked so hard at not being human.

"So why did you tell me? Did you want me to understand why you try not to get personally involved with the people in your stories? I knew that already."

"No." He seemed to be studying her, as if he wasn't quite sure of his reasons himself. "I think I told you because you wouldn't let me kiss you."

"What?"

"Just now. You reminded me of her, if only because you are so different. She was quite comfortable using sex to manipulate the story, to try to get me to write what she wanted me to write. Doing that wouldn't ever have occurred to you, would it?"

"No," she said, folding the sheet and comforter around her lap neatly and resting her hands in her lap. "It wouldn't occur to most of the women in the world, either. And if you think it would, you've been hanging around in the wrong places, with the wrong people."

"Yes," he said slowly, giving her a look she couldn't quite interpret. "I'm beginning to think you may be right."

TYLER WONDERED if he was losing his mind.

He stood at the front reception desk of the Heyday Chronic Care Center, looking for someone who might care that, due to a power surge, Elizabeth Rackham's television was broadcasting snow instead of classical music.

He'd just spent about twenty minutes in Mallory's mother's room, feeling like both a fool and an interloper. He didn't belong there. He didn't know what to say to the beautiful, sad-faced woman who lay lost in her coma.

He shouldn't have come. He had met Elizabeth when he was in town three years ago, and probably she hated him just as much as everyone else did. If she had realized who was sitting by her bed, she undoubtedly would have kicked him out on his ear.

But he hadn't come to please Elizabeth. He'd come to please Mallory.

Mallory, stricken to realize that her mother had gone forty-eight hours without a visit, had begun to talk about getting dressed and coming down here. She wasn't well enough for that, and he'd tried hard to stop her.

Then he made the mistake of saying that, if Elizabeth really was in a deep coma, she could have no idea whether she had visitors or not.

Mallory, who had been laughing with him over the old Sonja Jean Mattingly red-dress story just moments before, had turned indignant immediately. Of course her mother knew whether she had company. Of course she knew whether people cared enough to visit.

Tyler realized he was in danger of squandering any goodwill he might have earned by tending Mallory through the flu.

Why he should give a damn about that he wasn't sure. But he did. He wanted her to stop hating him, to stop thinking of him as an unfeeling bastard who had a computer keyboard where his heart should be.

The fact that it just might be true—somehow only made things worse.

So he'd taken another tack. He'd warned her that she couldn't import her flu germs to a nursing facility, where people were weak and vulnerable. She couldn't risk giving her illness to her mother.

At first he'd thought that keeping her safely at home was enough. But when she had lain back, white-faced and disappointed, against her pillow, he had felt a twist of something that felt strangely like guilt.

And so, instead of returning to his own apartment, where he had at least half-a-dozen interviews that needed to be transcribed, he'd trotted down the stairs, climbed into his car and driven to the care center.

And spent the most uncomfortable twenty minutes of his life. What on earth could he say? But just sitting there felt like cheating. Mallory had described how much her mother "loved" chatty, upbeat visits.

So he'd talked about the weather, which was the perfect flowery Shenandoah spring…he'd omitted the gray, nasty rain. He'd talked about Mallory's bookstore…he'd omitted the fact that most of the customers were kooks.

What next? He had to be careful. Nothing about Mindy. Or the book.

But what else could he talk about? Could he say, well, I have to tell you, your daughter is driving me crazy. I'm writing a story about all of you, and that puts her strictly off-limits. But my hands itch from wanting to bury themselves into her hair, and I dream things I'll never admit to anyone.

Of course he couldn't say any of that. He'd eventually found himself talking to Elizabeth Rackham about his problems liquidating the hideous buildings he'd inherited from Anderson. He talked about the leaping zebra house, which, he'd discovered was quite lovely inside, the kind of house he'd want to live in if he ever settled down. Which he had no plans of doing, of course.

He quickly changed subjects. He told her about the stupid carnival-colored diner, and the boxy tract plots in Yarrow Estates, and how he wished he'd inherited something simple and easy to unload.

Like diamonds. Or Krugerrands.

"What exactly are you doing here, young man?"

He looked up to see Aurora York coming through the double glass doors. She was one of Heyday's most interesting characters. She was a bossy, over-the-top eccentric, but she had a no-nonsense mind he couldn't help admiring. Like that wild Mrs. Milligan from the property offices, most of Aurora's quirks seemed deliberate, not the result of true weirdness.

Plus, she'd endeared herself to Tyler at the bookstore this afternoon by shutting up that whacko Major Beanstaff, who seemed disturbingly interested in alien probes. Aurora had entered the alcove where Beanstaff had Tyler cornered and said loudly, "For God's sake, Mack, give it a rest. Aliens may find your colon fascinating, but I guarantee you the rest of us are sick to death of it."

"Hi, Aurora," Tyler said. He leaned over and gave her a kiss on the cheek. She seemed to like it, though she harrumphed and reached up to adjust the angle of her feathered hat. Tonight the feather was as orange as a pumpkin, and almost as big. "Thanks for the soup. Mallory loved it."

"Of course she loved it. I make a damn fine chicken soup." She frowned at him. "But you haven't answered my question. What are you doing here? Visiting Elizabeth? I know you've inherited the McClintock ego, but surely even you don't think you're good enough to squeeze information out of a woman in a coma."

He smiled. "No. It's just that Mallory's been worrying about leaving her mother alone too long. I thought maybe I could fill the gap."

"Very interesting." The intense look Aurora directed at him proved she was telling the truth. "I thought you were Super Journalist. I thought you'd taken vows of complete detachment. And yet, here you are, in one day playing doctor, bookseller and a little Florence Nightingale on the side. Isn't this coming dangerously close to…getting involved?"

"Journalists do all kinds of things, Aurora. We're just regular people."

She snorted her skepticism. "There's nothing regular about any of the McClintocks. They do things differently. Or rather, they overdo them, with that fierce McClintock passion."

"I'm not really a McClintock," he said, smiling, although he was getting a little sick of repeating that line. "I was raised a Balfour. And I'm afraid an excess of passion is something Balfours have never been accused of."

"Not a McClintock!" She laughed out loud. "Baloney. Besides, passion shows up in strange ways. Take Kieran, for instance. Until he found Claire, he channeled his McClintock passion into being virtuous. Before Lara, Bryce channeled his into being mad. You have decided to bury yours under a mountain of indifference. But that doesn't mean it's not there."

Arguing was pointless. She had her mind made up. He opened his mouth to say good-night, but then, to his surprise, she reached out and tucked her hand under his arm.

"Come buy me a candy bar, son. As long as you're pretending to be human today, I'd like to tell you some things about your father."

Oh, brother, it didn't get much worse than this. Actually, she hadn't been far off in her evaluation of him. He didn't give a damn about most people, including— perhaps especially—Anderson McClintock. Tyler was a professional observer. From inside his sealed bubble of objectivity, he watched people, analyzed them and recorded their behavior.

He'd spent ten years making sure the bubble was airtight. He'd always suspected that even one little crack was enough to screw things up. It started with a trickle, but before long the messy, destructive outside world would just come flooding in.

"Mallory will be waiting," he said, aware that he was making excuses, and also aware that he was fighting a losing battle. They were already walking down the dimly lit corridor toward the snack room. "Since she's been sick, I've been checking in on her before she goes to sleep."

"She can wait," Aurora said testily. "I want to get to know you better. I'd like to find out what you plan to do with all that passion once it busts free."

Suddenly she stopped in her tracks. "Wait a minute. Have you two already started having sex?"

He had to laugh. Her mental connections were about as subtle as a sledgehammer.

"No," he said, chuckling. "Even if I *had* inherited the McClintock ego, I draw the line at seducing a woman delirious with fever."

"Okay, never mind." Aurora took his arm again. "In that case, she can wait."

CHAPTER ELEVEN

"SWEETHEART," Freddy said as Mindy led him toward the Home and Hearth Shoppe, "I'm sure I'll love whatever dishes you picked out. I don't need to look at them, honestly."

Mindy hugged his arm and kept walking. "I know, but I'll feel better once you see them. We've got a few minutes before I have to be back to work, and it's right here, so…"

She wasn't sure why she was so uncomfortable about this fairly inconsequential decision. After all, Freddy's mother, Sarah Earnshaw, had spent the entire afternoon this past Saturday helping her pick it out.

Sarah had insisted that the decision was entirely up to Mindy. But she had hinted and nudged until Mindy had somehow been left with only one choice: an intensely formal gold-and-black-trimmed set of ivory bone china.

To be honest, Mindy had thought the dishes looked slightly funereal. But when she'd dared to admire a livelier pattern, Sarah had laughed merrily, as if Mindy had surely been kidding. "Just imagine how those tacky flowers would clash with your food," she'd said with a grimace.

So gold and black and ivory it was. Mindy, who had grown up with simple department-store stoneware, wouldn't have dreamed of going against Sarah's exquisite taste. The thought of playing hostess for all the political dinners Freddy would require was intimidating enough. Mindy couldn't face that future if she knew the guests would be whispering about her tacky china.

"Oh, yeah, very nice," Freddy said when she pointed it out to him. "Really. It's perfect."

To his credit, he made an effort to look interested. He even picked up a butter plate and turned it over to read the back. There were no prices on anything in this store, but Mindy had seen a brochure on her new china pattern, and she knew it cost a fortune.

It almost embarrassed her to list it on the gift registry. The Earnshaws' powerful friends might not bat an eye, but Mindy knew that her co-workers would all have to pitch in together just to buy one place setting.

"Hey, look, there's Bill," Freddy said abruptly. He set the butter plate down, paying little attention to the elegant arrangement. "I'll be right back, Mindy, okay?"

She nodded, though Freddy was already gone. She should have known he'd run into someone he knew, even here. He always did.

She was probably in for a wait. Oh, well. She ran

her fingers idly across the cool, slick surface of her new china, wondering why it made her so uncomfortable.

It wasn't as if the Earnshaws were the first rich people she'd ever met. Heyday might be small, but its tucked-away charm attracted plenty of wealthy people. The McClintocks, for instance.

And Roddy Hartland.

Now that she thought about it, it was probably the awareness of what Roddy would say that made her so queasy about this china. Roddy had more money than even the Earnshaws, but she'd never seen him spend it on stuff like this. He threw wild parties and took exotic trips and bought X-ray machines for the local clinic. He did have a big, fancy house with its own tennis court, but he played on that court with everyone from Kieran McClintock to Jim Stiller, the guy who changed the oil in Roddy's car.

To Mindy, Roddy had always been a surrogate big brother, so his opinion mattered. And he didn't pull any punches. When she was a rebellious sixteen, he'd been the first to tell her she was a jerk for tormenting her mom. When she was twenty, he'd laughed her out of getting a tattoo and run her secret pack of cigarettes through his garbage disposal.

And, recently, when he'd heard she was getting married, he'd told her flat out that she was making a mistake. "Come on, squirt," he'd said. "Don't be a dork. You can't be happy with a stick like that."

That had hurt her feelings. The last time she went

home to Heyday, she hadn't even gone by Roddy's house to say hello.

But now, standing here in this perfumed, snooty home store, she found herself wondering what Roddy would say if he knew she planned to eat off dinner dishes that cost more than most people earned in a day.

She could hear him now. "If plates cost more, do they make the food taste better?"

Glancing down at her watch, she realized it was getting late. Darn it. Freddy might have all day to schmooze with potential voters, but she had to be back in ten minutes or get docked a full hour. She needed every penny to pay off the turquoise bikini...and a few other indulgences.

Where was he? She looked around the store, over the tops of gold-leaf chocolate pots and through the cut-glass goblets lined up on shelves like so many crystal soldiers.

Good, he was still nearby, next to the door.

But who was that man he was talking to? Did she know him?

An extremely thin, tall, man.

Suddenly she felt dizzy. Her pulse beat against her temples, and her vision flickered strangely. She squinted, praying she was mistaken.

She wasn't. The man standing next to Freddy was...

It couldn't be...

But it was. It was Dorian Swigert. She thought

she'd probably recognize that skinny, elongated back anywhere on earth.

Oh, God, oh, God. What did he want with Freddy? What was he saying to Freddy?

She tried to breathe, but her lungs might as well have been made of cement. Only half-conscious of the gesture, she pressed the palm of her hand against her skirt and wiped it, as if she felt something sticky there, something bloody and disgusting and hot.

Oh, God. She needed more oxygen, or she would faint.

But then the man turned. And the face….the face was completely different.

Her knees trembled slightly as she sucked in her first real breath. It wasn't Dorian. She'd just imagined that it was. This was someone else, some other friendly, smiling, *normal* face. Someone named Bill. Someone quite safe.

The men shook hands, and then Freddy hurried back over to Mindy. He put his arm around her and planted an apologetic kiss behind her ear.

"Sorry, sweetheart," he said. "I haven't seen Bill since my senior year at Annapolis. He's a great guy. I think I'll add him to the invitation list."

At first she didn't understand. She was focused on trying to take deep breaths, forcing clear, fresh air into the corners of her agitated mind.

"The *wedding* invitation list?" She shook her head. "Your mother said five hundred is the absolute outer limit, and we're already there."

Freddy sighed. "We *were* there, yesterday. But this morning Inigo White got arrested. Security fraud, poor devil. He won't be getting an invitation now."

"He won't?" Mallory hadn't ever liked Inigo White, the pompous CEO of a plastics company, but something about the easy way his name had been x-ed off the list surprised her.

"Of course not." Freddy looked confused. He probably wondered why she cared. "There will be a full SEC investigation. Dad can't afford to be tainted by all that right now, just a few months from the election."

"But…I thought Inigo was one of your dad's best friends."

"He was. I mean, he is. It's just that right now—" He put his arm around her and gave her a hug. "Oh, don't worry about it, sweetie. Inigo understands. Come on, let's go. I refuse to spend my last precious minutes with you discussing the Securities and Exchange Commission."

She let him lead her out of the crowded little store. She was glad to have his arm around her, because her legs were still a little wobbly, and there were pieces of precariously perched, disastrously fragile glass and china everywhere. It felt like maneuvering through an obstacle course, where the least mistake would result in immeasurable loss.

When they were outside in the full warmth of the spring sun, she felt that she could breathe again. Out here, there was plenty of room, and the air smelled of blue violets.

"Freddy." She turned to him with an impulsive urgency. "Is it that easy, really, to eliminate people from your life? Suppose I—"

She took another breath. "Suppose I was the one who'd been arrested. Would you have to x me off your list, too?"

Freddy looked at her blankly for a second, and then, laughing, he picked her up and twirled her around in a quick circle.

"I don't mean to hurt your feelings, sweetheart," he said. "But I don't think the Securities and Exchange Commission has ever even heard of you."

When he put her down again, he kept her tucked up close to the breast of his navy blazer. The scent of his aftershave mingled with the scent of violets, and she thought how very much she loved him. She rested her cheek against him and wondered why this was the only place in the world she felt truly safe.

But still the thoughts wouldn't go away.

After a couple of seconds, she lifted her head and looked up at him. "You know what I mean. Suppose you found out I had done something awful, something that could embarrass your father. Something that could embarrass *you*. What would happen then?"

He smiled quizzically, as if he weren't sure whether she was pulling his leg. But the smile didn't quite match the furrows that had appeared between his brows, or the flicker of something dark and wary she saw in his eyes.

In an instant, though, all that had disappeared. He was her Freddy again.

"What a nut you are," he said, chuckling. "I adore you."

"I love you, too," she said. "But that's not an answer."

He sobered, and he took her face between his hands. The expression in his eyes almost brought tears to her own.

"I love you, Mindy Rackham," he said. "There is nothing I could *find out* about you that would ever change my mind. I know you too well. You're good and beautiful, and I'm the luckiest man on earth. Is that answer enough for you?"

She nodded slowly. What was the use in pushing? She already had her answer. Not in his words, he always said the right words. She saw it in that momentary frightened flash behind his eyes.

It had told her two terrible things.

The first thing was this: If Freddy found out about the Heyday Eight, their relationship would be over.

And the second followed with a cruel and inescapable logic.

She was never going to be able to tell him.

MALLORY LET the phone ring so long it annoyed the honey-toned Telephone Goddess.

"The person you are calling is not answering," the recorded voice pointed out, as if Mallory might be a little slow. "Please hang up."

Mallory clicked the end button, lamenting the days when you could slam the receiver down with a satisfying thump. But *why* wasn't the person answering? Why didn't the know-it-all voice tell her that?

Mallory knew she was overreacting. She was edgy today, because she was going to have to go to Dan's wedding. But darn it, Mindy should have been home. It was Saturday morning, and Mindy always lay around in bed late on the weekends.

At least the young Mindy used to do that. Mallory reminded herself that Mindy was an adult now. Maybe she'd gone out to breakfast with Freddy, who was probably an early riser. A-personalities usually were.

Whatever the reason, Mallory knew it was crazy to let an unanswered call upset her so much. She had no earthly reason to believe anything bad had happened to Mindy.

But it would be a long time before she could forget that one terrible day two years ago, that day when an unanswered phone really *had* been the precursor of something dreadful.

Mallory had been at the café that morning, calling home, furious with Mindy for refusing to answer the telephone. Mindy was always trying to avoid being tagged for chores, but this time Mallory really needed her. The deep fryer had gone out, and she needed the electrician's private cell number, which was at home on the foyer table.

She knew Mindy was there, but no matter how many times she'd called, she'd had the same result. Just the repetitive, echoing buzz, over and over. Furious, she'd closed the café, put out the hanging sign that said, Back

In Twenty Minutes, and driven home, muttering under her breath that when she got hold of that little slacker, she'd—

She'd found Mindy in the bathroom, slumped against the sink, ribbons of red blood forming a lacy network over her hands and onto the checkerboard tiles.

Shaking off the vision, which was still as horribly vivid as it had been on that day, Mallory picked up the phone and dialed Mindy's number one more time.

Again no answer.

Luckily, at that moment Tyler's knock sounded at the door. Mallory glanced at herself in the mirror. The face that looked back at her was somber, still wrestling with old ghosts, so she pinched her cheeks and tried on a smile.

That helped. She pushed her anxieties to the back of her mind. She had to stay focused today. If she was going to attend this wedding, she needed to hold her head up and look confident.

And it shouldn't be that hard. She wore a sky-blue dress that fit just right, and, though she hadn't had time for a haircut, she'd tamed her shaggy curls with a blue hair ribbon. If she smiled, she actually looked pretty good.

She picked up her purse and opened the door.

"Hi," she said. "I'm ready."

Tyler tilted his head, surveying her. "Nice. Very nice." He grinned. "Maybe too nice. You don't by any chance have a secret agenda? We're not trying to bust up this wedding, are we?"

She flushed. "Don't be silly. I'd like to save the poor kid from Dan's clutches, but not enough to offer myself in her place. I served my time in that jail already."

But as they walked down the stairs to his waiting car, she had to admit she'd felt a lovely wriggle of pleasure at the look on his face. And she realized suddenly that the tight blue dress wasn't all about showing Dan Platt what he was missing. It was all about lighting that fire in Tyler Balfour's eyes.

She leaned her head back against his leather seat with a sigh. *God, Mallory. Aren't you ever going to learn?*

Tyler wasn't her boyfriend. He wasn't even a real friend, although he'd been very good to her this past week, and she appreciated that.

But the generosity wasn't a gift. It was a loan. He was going to want something in return. She tried to make herself remember that. He was just putting goodwill in the bank, so that when the time came, he'd have the right to make a withdrawal.

It was a half-hour trip to Grupton, where Dan now lived, and the perfect weather after all those days of rain made driving a joy. And being physically well, after spending the past week recovering from the flu, was heavenly.

After about fifteen minutes, Mallory realized she felt almost buoyant. She could even laugh at her earlier overwrought worries about Mindy, who was undoubtedly out doing nothing more dangerous than shopping for clothes she couldn't quite afford.

Not even Mindy could manufacture a crisis on a day like this.

Above them, the sky was like a bolt of blue cotton embroidered with knobby white clouds. On either side of the car, fields of periwinkle, phlox and chicory swept past in blurred rainbows of pink and purple.

Mallory smiled and breathed deeply. This was exactly what she needed. A day out of the house, out of the store…enjoying the beauty of a Shenandoah Valley spring morning.

"I really appreciate your coming along," she said after a few moments of comfortable silence. "I could have done it alone, but it would have been awkward. I won't know much of anyone there but Dan, and if I remember correctly the groom is usually pretty busy."

"Especially *that* groom," Tyler said, smiling but keeping his attention on the road. "He'll probably be busy putting the make on the maid of honor."

"Oh, come on," she said. "He's not that bad. We were having problems before the Heyday Eight, you know. I wasn't exactly the model wife. I was disappointed in him, and not very…warm. You can't blame him for everything."

Tyler laughed. "Sure I can."

"Tyler—"

"I mean it. He was a bozo to let you get away. He must have been blind, deaf and dumb. Especially dumb."

Finally she laughed, too. Even after all these years, it felt good to hear Tyler stick up for her. It had meant even more back during those lonely days, when she'd had no idea where her husband was or even if she still wanted him to be her husband.

"Even so, you don't really think Dan could be the blackmailer, do you?" She glanced over at him. "Just because he's incapable of fidelity doesn't mean he's capable of extortion."

"No, not really. I've done a background check on him, and he's stayed clean since his episode with the Eight." He shifted, putting one arm up on the seat back. "I don't know him well, but I'm not sure Dan's got the right personality quirks. Our blackmailer has serious self-esteem issues. He needs to feel powerful, in control. As I remember him, Dan Platt is just emotionally stunted, in love with himself, and always looking for the next ego fix."

"Wow." She shook her head at how well Tyler had nailed it. "Makes me seem pretty stupid for marrying him, doesn't it?"

"I don't think so. When you got married, he was what…twenty? Maybe he acted a little young for his age, but that would just make him seem lighthearted and fun."

"Right again," she said. "Dan was always the life of the party. Everybody loved him."

"Sure. A twenty-year-old man who acts eighteen isn't going to raise any red flags. A thirty-year-old man with the emotional needs of a teenager isn't quite as cute."

No, it wasn't. She could certainly vouch for that.

She wished she could have five minutes alone with Jeannie Soon-To-Be Platt. But, sheepishly, she remembered the minutes her mother had spent gently trying to coax Mallory into reconsidering her own engagement to Dan. That had gone nowhere.

Apparently Dan Platt was a lesson every woman had to learn for herself.

Once they reached Grupton, it took another five minutes to find the Ye Royal English Wedding Garden, which Jeannie and Dan had chosen for their ceremony.

Mallory spotted it from a block away. In keeping with the pink-flowered wedding invitations, the gardens were a jumble of everything pink. Ribbons, bows, bells, flowers, streamers. Even the carpet, which led to the rose-covered trellis where Jeannie and Dan would exchange their vows, was pink.

Mallory started to say it reminded her of a *Cat in the Hat* book she'd read as a child, where naughty little creatures explode pink all over the house and snow. But she stopped herself. She didn't want to sound petty. Pink was perfectly fine. Pink was very pretty.

They hadn't hurried, and consequently they arrived just in time to take the last two pink-cushioned folding chairs.

Dan was already standing under the pink trellis, quite handsome in a black tux with a pink-ruffled shirt. He winked at Mallory when he saw her come in, a breach of good taste she pretended not to notice.

Taped music filled the air, and then a stream of six

teenage bridesmaids filed in and lined up to the side, as fuscia and frothy as strawberry ice cream floats.

And then the bride herself, starry-eyed, nineteen-year-old Jeannie. Pink from head to toe. Even her veil.

Mallory heard Tyler clear his throat, but she didn't dare look at him. She had no intention of laughing at this poor girl. Weddings were personal. Mallory knew she'd probably wince if she watched her own wedding videos now. That hairdo, for instance, had definitely been questionable.

Of course, she *couldn't* watch the videos, because she'd burned them all the day Dan was arrested for soliciting a prostitute, right there in her café, in booth eleven. The bum had never even paid for that sandwich and fries.

Somehow Mallory made it through the ceremony, although when they came to the vows, which the couple had written themselves, she had to fake a cough herself, just to cover a helpless sputter.

Jeannie had apparently found a sale on similes. She likened their love to angel wings, and bridges over troubled waters, and rain on the desert, and fire in the winter, and meat when you're hungry, and fertilizer on the flowers.

"Now that one," Tyler whispered when she got to the fertilizer part, "I can actually believe."

Mallory squeezed his hand, warning him to hush. He subsided obediently, but he threaded his fingers through hers comfortably and didn't let go.

When the groom had kissed the bride, the guests

moved to the pink-satin-draped tables and toasted the new Mr. and Mrs. Dan Platt with, of course, bubbly pink champagne.

The whole experience could have been much worse, Mallory thought, especially since every single guest obviously knew she was the infamous ex. Several people said they admired how civilized the divorce must have been.

Yeah, right. But wasn't that the impression she'd been determined to project? She could have pleaded an earlier engagement and skipped the wedding. No one would have blamed her. But she had decided she couldn't bear to have Dan feeling smug, believing she was still too emotionally torn up to face the sight of him marrying another woman.

It helped that she'd brought along such a handsome, attentive date. When she walked by, people whispered behind their champagne flutes, but they weren't gossiping about her. Their curious gazes were always on Tyler.

He was a natural socializer, mingling easily with total strangers. Ten seconds after introducing himself, he'd have any group of people laughing like old friends. He even eased her through the meeting with Dan's parents, who had blamed Mallory for Dan's downfall.

But the nicest part was how Tyler kept one arm always around her waist, as if he adored her, as if they were infatuated lovers, as if they were Bryce and Lara, or Kieran and Claire. Standing inside the charmed embrace, Mallory realized for the first time just how sweet such a partnership might feel.

Once, out of the corner of her eye, she even saw Dan scowling in Tyler's direction. She smiled to herself, surprised at how little she cared. When Tyler had offered to accompany her here, she'd thought it might be gratifying to make Dan just a little jealous.

But, now that it had happened, she found that she didn't really give a damn. Dan seemed like a stranger, and not an attractive one at that. Though he was only thirty, his drinking and womanizing were catching up with him, his character stamping itself hard on his once-charming face. When he stood next to Jeannie, he looked old enough to be her father.

Finally it was time to cut the cake. Relieved, Mallory realized that soon she and Tyler could leave without being rude. She was already tired. Maybe she should have stopped at one glass of champagne. Obviously she hadn't yet recovered one hundred percent of her strength.

Five more minutes, a piece of cake, and then she'd give Tyler a sign.

As the photographer knelt before the wedding couple, ready to capture the moment, Dan carved out two pieces of cake and handed one to Jeannie. Smiling, they twined their forearms, posing for the traditional shot.

Jeannie touched her piece of cake lightly to Dan's lips, laughing a little when a few crumbs spilled down into the ruffles of his fancy shirt. Mallory remembered doing the exact same thing nearly ten years ago. She wondered if she'd looked as young and innocent as Jeannie. As full of hope.

Now it was Dan's turn. He moved the cake toward his bride's smiling, half-opened mouth. And then, without any warning, just as it touched her lips, he shoved it forward, smashing it into her teeth.

Everyone laughed and clapped as the poor girl recoiled, choking slightly, her makeup now smeared with pink icing and crumbles of cake. Dan laughed loudest of all, as if he'd done something very original and witty.

Mallory felt herself going oddly numb. She looked at Jeannie, who was struggling to laugh, to pretend she thought it was funny. But Mallory knew that, in her heart, Jeannie was stunned…and wounded, pricked with a sudden, troubling fear of her new husband.

Mallory wasn't guessing about these complex emotions. She *knew*. She remembered feeling that way herself. But when?

"Let's go," she said to Tyler suddenly. He didn't look surprised. Maybe he understood.

But what was she remembering? The cake episode at her own wedding had been uneventful. And through the years, Dan hadn't ever hit her, or been physically abusive. All the way home, a quiet ride with little conversation, the memory eluded her. She really had overdone the champagne. Her thoughts seemed fuzzy.

It wasn't until they were almost home, when Tyler was parking his car in the access lot behind the bookshop building, that it finally came back to her.

One night, after they'd been married about a year, Dan had arrived to pick her up at the café. They'd had lots of "campers," customers who hung around for hours without ordering anything new, and it had taken forever to coax them all into going home. She'd kept Dan waiting nearly twenty minutes.

He'd been annoyed. He thought she'd been insensitive to waste his time like that. But instead of simply saying so, as a mature man might have done, he'd taken his pound of flesh another way.

He'd waited until she'd opened the door of the car and begun to step in. Then he had hit the gas, causing the car to lurch away from her. Just a couple of feet, but enough to make her nearly lose her balance.

He'd done it twice, then three times, until finally he had collapsed against the wheel in raucous laughter, apparently finding it hilarious that she had continued to fall for it.

She remembered how she'd tried to laugh, too. She had to accept that it was just a joke. If she'd let herself see it for what it really was—the power trip of a petty sadist—she might never have been able to go home with him at all.

She remembered, too, the strange tenderness he'd shown her in bed that night, the fake concern for the bruises on her shin. The confusing seduction that had followed too smoothly after the nasty teasing.

"Tyler," she said suddenly. She reached out and touched his arm.

He turned off the motor and looked over at her. "I

thought you were sleeping." His voice was low. "How are you holding up?"

"I'm fine. There's—there's something I have to tell you." She kept her hand on his arm. "It's something I should have told you years ago."

"Mallory, you don't have to tell me anything."

"Yes, I do. It's important. It's about Dan."

He frowned. "I don't think I want to talk about Dan."

"Not Dan, exactly. Dan and me. It's just that in my heart I've always blamed you for exposing Dan's cheating. Even though I knew it was Dan's fault, I blamed you for the breakup of our marriage. I kept telling myself that somehow we might have made it work if you hadn't come along and ruined everything."

"I know," he said. "I wondered if you'd ever forgive me."

"But don't you see? That's what I've finally come to understand. That marriage was a horror, from beginning to end. I don't need to forgive you. I need to *thank* you."

He stared down at her for a long minute. A muscle in his forearm twitched under her hand. "Mallory, I—"

He bit off whatever he'd been going to say. Instead, he took her hand and pulled her toward him. She *had* drunk too much champagne, she realized suddenly. The movement made her feel dizzy, and the car smelled of pink roses, as if they'd carried the perfume of the gardens all the way home.

"You don't need to thank me," he said, his voice oddly harsh. "As you've always pointed out, I didn't do it to save you from Dan. I did it for myself, for my story."

"But you did save me," she said. She was losing her train of thought. Being this close to him was unsettling. He had unknotted his tie, and she could see the pulse beating in the curve of his throat. "You helped me find my way free. It was a very—"

"Damn it, listen to me. I'm telling you the cold, hard truth."

He sounded angry, which surprised her. She hadn't meant to upset him. She'd merely wanted him to know that this one sin, at least, no longer needed to trouble his conscience, just in case he had one.

"All right," she said softly. "I believe you."

"Good." He took her chin between his fingers. "Because I'm going to kiss you, Mallory. And you're going to let me. And I don't want it to have anything to do with gratitude. I want it to be about now. About *us*. Do you understand?"

"Yes," she said. But it wasn't true. She hadn't ever been so confused in her life. She didn't understand him, and she certainly didn't understand herself.

All she knew was that she wanted this kiss so much it frightened her. And yet, somewhere deep inside, she knew that kissing Tyler Balfour was a very dangerous thing to do.

She nodded again, accepting the risk. And then, slowly, he lowered his head to hers. He brushed the edge of his mouth against her cheek first, taking his time. Shivering, she put her hands on his chest.

And then their lips met. She made a soft sound, as an aching heat spread through her. *Tyler's kiss.* Finally, it was real. These lips, these arms…all real. No longer a dream, a memory, a half-forgotten craving in the night.

But if that long-ago kiss had been a gentle thing, a gift offered to soothe an aching heart, this one was a fiery taking. His lips were fierce, and hers fell open under the heat. With a groan, he went deeper, the probing hard and sure.

It sent a streak of lightning shivering through her spine. Immediately he slid his hands down her back, all the way to the lightning point, massaging the small aching hollows on either side of her spine, as if he knew the pain that coiled there.

"I want you, Mallory," he said, moving his lips to the crook of her neck so that she felt the words as much as heard them. "I want to make love to you until there's nothing real in this world but you and me."

Nothing but the two of them. Oh, she thought, it was already true. She no longer knew whether it was day or night, whether he was good or bad, whether she was wise or foolish. She knew only that his hands were searching but they couldn't find what they needed, that her dress was in the way, and his shirt, too, and the cold, thrusting parts of this confining car.

"Come," she said, fumbling behind her for the handle of the door. "We can go upstairs."

But when she opened the door, it met resistance. She pushed harder, and someone cried out in wounded indignation.

"Dang, Mallory," Wally said. "Try not to kill me, okay?"

She looked up at the boy, at his red-and-green hair haloed by the bright afternoon sun. She felt oddly disoriented. Was it really still broad daylight?

His face was cast in shadows, and he looked like a total stranger. She couldn't, for one clouded moment, remember what on earth he could be doing here.

"So you *are* already back. Aurora said she saw you drive up, but the windows were so fogged I wasn't sure." He rubbed his kneecap. "Some thanks I get. I came all the way out to the parking lot, just to let you know you've got a phone call."

"I can't take any calls right now," she said, half surprised that she could form a coherent sentence. Beside her, Tyler was waiting silently, obviously giving her the chance to decide how to handle this. "Unless it's Mindy. I'm not working today, Wally. I'm—"

"Yeah, well I'm just following orders. You said you always wanted to know when Darth Vader calls, remember?"

She clenched her hand around the handle. "You're saying this is—"

"Yeah. It's your buddy Darth." Wally held out the little white cordless phone smugly. "And to tell you the truth, boss, Mr. Vader here sounds kinda pissed."

CHAPTER TWELVE

TYLER KNEW that when Mallory took the roam phone from Wally and brought it into her office, she was probably just making sure the kid couldn't eavesdrop on her conversation with the blackmailer.

But Tyler was glad she did. As soon as they shut the door behind them, he held out his hand. "You answer the desk phone," he said. "Let me listen on this one."

Mallory clutched the telephone up against her chest instinctively, as though his suggestion were some kind of personal violation.

"No," she said. "Why?"

"I interviewed a lot of people about this story, Mallory," he said as patiently as he could. "I might recognize something. A tone. A phrase. Something."

"I—" She seemed to be searching for a good reason to deny his request, but coming up blank.

"I already know Mindy's secret, remember?" He hesitated. "Unless of course you're hiding something else."

"Of course not." She frowned. "It's just that—"

"Mallory, give me the telephone. I don't think this guy is exactly going to appreciate being kept on hold."

She still didn't like it, he could see that in her face. But she wasn't stupid. She handed over the telephone, gave him a minute to get ready, and then indicated that she was going to pick up her phone.

They clicked on simultaneously.

Mallory took a breath. "This is Mallory Rackham."

Tyler had to admire her self-control. She still looked slightly unfocused from the three glasses of champagne, and significantly mussed from kissing him. Plus, she was probably scared to death to hear what the black-mailer had to say. And yet she sounded crisp and natural.

"Hello, Mallory," the weird voice said slowly. "I guess you know what this call means. It's time."

God, the guy really did sound like Darth Vader. Tyler pressed the phone to his ear, determined not to miss a syllable. He'd planned to get Mallory to install a recorder on her phone, but she'd assured him the blackmailer wouldn't call until next Thursday. That was the pattern. Every two weeks, on Thursday, he called to set up a Friday drop.

This was only Saturday. That piqued Tyler's curiosity. Any break from the pattern meant something. What it meant, and how important it might be, Tyler couldn't tell yet.

"It's *not* time. It's early," Mallory said calmly, without aggression, just stating a fact. "I can't afford this every week. It's difficult enough getting it every two weeks."

"But you always manage, don't you? And now

you'll be a good girl and manage one more. I want it tomorrow. Same time, same place."

Staring at Mallory, Tyler shook his head firmly. Her eyes widened, but amazingly she didn't balk.

"I can't," she said without a hitch. "I don't have it. I can't get it."

In the pause that followed, Tyler thought he heard people talking in the background, from the blackmailer's end. Lots of people, like a party.

Maybe it was just the television?

Still…he wondered. Was it possible he had misjudged Dan Platt? Dan was at a party right now. Tyler had seen the look Dan gave Mallory when he'd seen the two of them holding hands at the wedding. Dan Platt might not love Mallory anymore, but he obviously still hated the idea of anyone else touching her. Could he be making this call from his own wedding reception?

It seemed far-fetched. But Tyler had seen people do weirder things.

"All right," the voice said. "You can have until Monday. The Green Diamond. Monday at eleven."

Mallory glanced at Tyler, who shook his head again. He needed more time, more words. Maybe if they riled the guy up a little, he'd say something impulsive. Something peculiar to his own speech patterns.

She frowned hard this time. But Tyler didn't back down. Squaring her shoulders as if preparing to take a blow, she inhaled another deep breath.

"Monday is still too soon. The banks are closed tomorrow. I can't get the money."

The electronic voice exploded in high-pitched whine and static, as if the man had cursed so loudly the equipment couldn't handle it.

"What the goddamn hell is the matter with you people? Do you think I'm somebody you can play with? You'll put the goddamn money on that goddamn boat at eleven o'clock Monday—or someone else will. Freddy the Fiancé is a rich boy. I bet he'd be glad to pay."

"No." Mallory's voice trembled. "Please."

The man chuckled, and the eerie electronic sound sent a disagreeable crawling sensation down Tyler's backbone. This guy loved knowing he had frightened her. Tyler had to tighten his jaw to keep from telling the bastard to take his threats and go straight to hell.

"Or I might decide to sell it to the newspapers," the voice went on slyly. "Not your buddy Balfour, of course. The only thing he's investigating these days is how to get inside your pretty panties. Do you still have Mindy's whip? I'll bet that would turn him on big-time."

Mallory flushed, and her hand tightened around the phone. Tyler held her eyes steadily and shook his head again. *Don't let him get to you,* he telegraphed. *Let him rant. He might let something slip.*

She swallowed hard, but she nodded.

Tyler gave her a smile. He was proud of her. This was hard, but it was helping. He'd already learned a couple of interesting things about their blackmailer.

One—though his schemes seemed fairly well

planned, he wasn't as intelligent and self-controlled as Tyler had originally thought. Ranting was stupid, and this guy couldn't stop himself. People like that usually lived in the lower social branches, unable to discipline themselves to achieve anything higher.

Therefore, goofy Roddy Hartland, who liked to wear a skirt, could probably be eliminated. Hartland was eccentric, but his eccentricities were completely under his control. *Too bad.* Ever since Tyler had seen Roddy kiss Mallory at the country club, he'd sort of liked the idea of exposing the offbeat millionaire as a blackmailer.

The second thing Tyler had learned was that this wasn't just about money, and it wasn't even really about Mindy. This blackmailer had a chip on his shoulder about Mallory personally. That might mean he was local. Tyler would have to ask her if she'd had any persistent, unwelcome suitors in the past few years.

With her looks, the list would probably be a mile long. But at least this personal element meant that Tyler probably could cross Dorian Swigert, Mindy's one client, off the list. Dorian lived in Seattle. He'd been in Heyday only three days, three years ago. He'd never met Mallory at all.

Best of all, something in the blackmailer's phrasing sounded familiar. "What the goddamn hell" wasn't exactly a unique phrase, but it rang a bell deep in Tyler's subconscious. Someone connected with the Heyday Eight had used it. He'd have to go through all his taped interviews again.

Suddenly, though, the man on the phone seemed to realize he was talking too much. The electronic voice grew clipped and final.

"No more crap," he said. "Just be on that ferry, you frigid bitch. Or I guarantee you'll regret it."

Mallory looked at Tyler. He nodded. The blackmailer had pulled himself together again, and stalling wouldn't help. He was ready to hang up.

"I'll try," she said quietly. And sure enough, the phone immediately went dead.

Tyler clicked off his phone. Mallory lowered hers more carefully, as if she moved in a trance. He could imagine how bruised she felt. This had been almost as brutal as a physical attack.

Tyler's hands made involuntary fists. God, how he was going to enjoy putting this guy behind bars where he belonged.

"Okay," he said, making sure he sounded calm and matter-of-fact. "At least we have a time and place. Let's get him, Mallory. Let's bring in the police and catch this sick bastard."

She sank into her desk chair slowly. She was still staring at the telephone. "No," she said. "I followed your orders while he was on the phone. But I'm not taking orders anymore. I'm going to pay, assuming I can find the money."

He could hardly believe his ears. "We can put an undercover policeman on the ferry. They can get this guy and lock him up."

She transferred her focus to him. She looked a little glazed but determined. "Even if you do, he still can talk. Mindy needs more time. She is going to tell Freddy, very soon. She just has to find the right moment."

He couldn't help it. He laughed. "The right moment? You mean when hell freezes over?"

She turned her face away without answering, hurt, and perhaps angry, too. Damn it. He should have been more diplomatic, but this was so willfully stupid he could hardly believe it.

Frustrated, he moved closer to the desk.

"Mallory, look, be realistic. Mindy may be deluding herself that Freddy can somehow get past the fact that his fiancée used to be a prostitute, but you know better than that."

She snapped back, glaring. "She wasn't a prostitute. Don't call her that."

"Call it whatever you want. It's going to be fatal. You've met Freddy. You've met his family. They'll drop her like a stick of dynamite."

Her face was tense and completely closed in. She didn't even look like the same woman he'd held in his arms just fifteen minutes ago.

"You don't know that," she said. "Don't judge everyone by your own standards, Tyler. Freddy loves Mindy."

"I'm sure he does. But he loves power more. I've lived in Washington my whole life. I know politicians. She's dreaming, and she's going to wake up with a crash. Every day you wait just makes it harder."

"I don't really believe this is yours to decide, Tyler." She seemed to be finding her focus. She put her hands on the desk, palms down, and speared him with a tough glance. "I've promised Mindy time, and I'm going to give it to her. I'll pay this guy once more, and then we'll see what happens."

"You'll go broke, that's what will happen. And a criminal will go free."

She raised her eyebrows. "You're not in charge of ridding the world of criminals, Tyler. You're a journalist, not a policeman."

He shook his head. This was beyond dumb. "You know, I could just go to the police without your permission."

She blanched, but she remained stiff and erect in her chair. "You promised you wouldn't do that unless you absolutely had to. Was that just another of your bald-faced lies?"

He cursed. Of course it hadn't been a lie, but—

What the hell could he say that would persuade her? He had obviously overestimated the progress he'd made over the past week. He'd thought he could override her objections whenever he decided the time was right. But her determination to protect Mindy was stronger than anything he had in his arsenal.

"Damn it, Mallory. I thought we were past all this. I thought we were—" He stopped himself. He'd been about to say "friends." He remembered how she had reacted the last time he used that word. "Just a few minutes ago we were—"

"Yes. We were. Probably it was the champagne. Believe me, I regret it already." She narrowed her eyes. "But what does that have to do with this? Did you think a few kisses would give you the right to boss me around? Was it your way of guaranteeing I'd be putty in your hands?"

"You know it wasn't any—" he began harshly. But her face was so blank, so unyielding, that suddenly he was angry, too.

"Oh, to hell with it," he said. He'd been a fool to think they could ever overcome the past. She might briefly forget. She might be seduced by champagne and wedding bells and a soft spring sky. But the past was always lurking just beneath it all, ready to rise up and create an insurmountable wall between them.

He moved toward the door, but at the last minute he turned back. He shoved his hands into his pockets.

"Before you do anything, think about this. How do you know this guy won't turn violent? How do you know he won't be waiting there when you get on the ferry? How do you know he won't hurt you?"

She gave him the coldest smile he'd ever seen. "I guess I don't. But that, too, is my problem, not yours." Her voice was utterly flat. "Besides, would that really be so terrible? Think what an exciting chapter it would make for your book."

"OH, MY LORD," Bryce McClintock said that Monday afternoon, as he strolled into Dilday Merle's office on the Moresville College campus and saw Tyler sitting there. "Don't tell me the old fox has snagged you, too."

Tyler looked up. "Snagged me for what?"

Dilday, sitting on the other side of the desk, cleared his throat, a distinctly grumpy sound. "No, I have not *snagged* him, and I didn't snag you, either, Bryce. You took this teaching position of your own volition."

"The hell I did." Bryce grinned at Tyler. "I'm warning you. This is how it starts. He looks innocent, but he's diabolical. When you leave this room, you'll be on his payroll, and you won't have a clue how it happened."

Dilday tapped his zebra letter opener on the desk. "McClintock, did you want something? I have to assume your classroom is on fire, considering how you burst in here without even the slightest hint of warning."

Bryce sighed. "No. So far I've managed to refrain from setting anything on fire. Tomorrow, of course, is another day."

Dilday growled. *"McClintock."*

Tyler loved to hear the old man take that tone. It was pure power.

Even Bryce snapped to attention. "Yes, sir! I'm sorry I didn't knock. Angie isn't out there, and I didn't realize you were in conference. Lara told me yesterday to ask you to dinner tonight, and I forgot. She'll kill me if you don't come."

"Oh, I'm sure." Dilday rolled his eyes. "That delightful woman worships every follicle on your arrogant McClintock head." He turned to Tyler. "It's clearly a form of mental illness. She could have married a king."

Bryce lifted one eyebrow. "Not if I got hold of him first. There wouldn't be enough left of him to marry."

Tyler laughed, but Dilday waved his hands, as if shooing away a bee. "Get out of here, and take all that testosterone with you. Tell Lara I'll be there at eight."

As Bryce opened the door to leave, he looked at Tyler. "Why don't you come along, too? Bring Mallory. Lara would be thrilled."

Tyler hesitated. Though he'd turned down several of these invitations, this one was tempting. Though they hadn't exactly become close, he liked Bryce, who was smart and acerbic enough to be interesting.

And of course Lara was a living dream.

But the temptation was more than that. During the past two nights, when Tyler had been back in his own apartment, he'd been restless. He might call it lonesome, except that he was used to being alone. Thrived on it, in fact.

Maybe he just needed time to adjust. He'd spent the whole past week on Mallory's couch, listening to every movement, evaluating every sniffle or sigh to see if she needed anything.

And, of course, he knew that today she had made the money drop on the ferry. She hadn't sent any word to him about how things had gone, and he had a feeling she wasn't planning to. He wondered why he had hoped. Surely he knew by now that good stories didn't just fall into your waiting hands like ripe apples. You had to go after them.

It annoyed him to discover how reluctant he was to get aggressive here. The minute he saw Mallory's car ease into a spot on Hippodrome Circle—right after breathing a sigh of relief—he should have made a bee-line to the bookstore. He should have confronted her. He should have asked those difficult questions that he knew so well how to ask.

But since he wasn't going to do that, maybe it would be better to have dinner with Bryce and Lara than to sit around all evening like a stooge, waiting for Mallory's knock on the door.

"Would Lara still be thrilled if I came alone?" Tyler smiled. "At the moment, bringing Mallory might be difficult. She isn't speaking to me."

"Really?" Bryce laughed. "Sorry about that. Mal always has been a feisty one, I hear. But you *have* to come. Lara's linguini can make a man forget a world of troubles."

"Good, fine, great," Dilday interjected impatiently. "Our dinner plans are settled. And now, Mr. McClintock, could I possibly persuade you to leave us in peace?"

Bryce, who obviously had caught on that no one was going to offer any explanation for Tyler's presence in Dilday's office, cast one last curious glance at the two of them. And then, with his usual sardonic grin, he was gone.

Dilday chuckled under his breath. "Those McClintock genes certainly do pack a punch. Three different mothers, three different childhoods. And yet you boys are as alike as triplets."

"Do you really think so?" Tyler looked at the other man, genuinely surprised. He didn't even think Kieran and Bryce were much alike. And he…well, he was a different breed entirely. "In what way?"

"In every way." Dilday shrugged. "I'll admit you look different. Kieran looks like his mother, who was very fair and very beautiful. You and Bryce, you take after Anderson. He was a handsome old coot, which got him into plenty of trouble, as you well know."

Tyler smiled. "Yes. I've heard a lot about that since I got to Heyday."

"But that's just surface. Under the skin you're all McClintocks, all bigger than life, all tougher than nails. But then the right woman comes along, and poof! You're so addled you can't even think straight. Just like your daddy."

"I'm not sure you can lump me in that group," Tyler said lightly, hoping he could hide the fact that for some reason this conversation made him uncomfortable. "I'm afraid I haven't had the pleasure of meeting the 'right' woman yet."

Dilday's wild white eyebrows rose up. "Maybe not. But you've certainly already had your brush with the *wrong* one."

For a minute, Tyler thought Dilday was referring to Mallory. But then he realized what the old man really meant.

"That was ten years ago. How on earth did you find out about that?"

Dilday took off his black glasses and began cleaning them on his sleeve. "I did my homework," he said. "Surely you don't think I would have solicited your help without first finding out what kind of man you are."

"I guess not." Tyler smiled. He shifted on the chair, eager to change the subject. "But I've taken enough of your time already. I came here because I want to ask your help with something. I'm afraid the blackmailer may be getting edgy. I want to go with you to your next drop and see if I can spot the guy. I know it's a risk. He might spot me, instead, and take it out on you. But I'm not sure he's going to get caught any other way. He's just smart enough, and he's damn lucky."

Dilday put his glasses back on. He blinked twice as his eyes adjusted, and then he focused his intelligent gaze on Tyler. "I'd like to help you, but I can't."

"I understand your reluctance," Tyler said. And he did understand it. But he had to overcome it.

His best source, the one he'd been counting on to help identify the blackmailer, was Greta Swinburne, the former leader of the Eight. But Greta, who had married and started a new life, had been avoiding his calls. She said her husband had forbidden her to talk to Tyler.

He could strong-arm her, of course, but that wasn't really his style. And she wasn't exactly the subtle type, so it was hard to reach her any other way. Still, the idea of intimidating her, threatening her, however indirectly, didn't sit well.

But if he couldn't get Greta, Mallory and Dilday were the only leads he had. If he lost Dilday...

There was only Mallory.

He knew he had to avoid that, at all costs.

"As I said, I know it's a risk. He might get mad enough to do what he's threatened, write that anonymous letter accusing you of consorting with the Eight. But I honestly think I can avoid—"

"No, no," Dilday broke in. To Tyler's surprise, the old man was smiling sheepishly. "You don't understand. I can't help you because I'm certain I won't be hearing from him again. He called a couple of nights ago, and...well, I guess he caught me at a bad moment."

Tyler felt a sinking sensation. "What did you do?"

Dilday adjusted his neat plaid bow tie with a gesture of unmistakable pride. "Well, let's see. First, I told the son of a bitch he wasn't getting another dime from me."

"But what about his threats?"

Dilday grinned. "I told him to go ahead and write his letter. I told him that, at my age, it's actually flattering to be accused of being kinky and oversexed. Then I told him to go to hell. And I'm not one hundred percent sure about this part, as I was fairly wrought up, but I think I may have suggested what he should do when he got there."

For a minute Tyler couldn't even speak.

"I'm sorry, Tyler," Dilday said earnestly. "I know I asked you to catch him for me, and now we probably never will. But I couldn't help it. It felt so damn good."

Tyler smiled. "Good for you," he said.

And he meant it. One part of his mind was applauding. The old guy really was amazing.

But the other part was thinking of Mallory. He knew now why the blackmailer had sounded so furious when he'd talked to her. He'd just lost control of Dilday, which a personality like his simply couldn't endure. Outwitted by a seventy-year-old man? No wonder the blackmailer had needed to lash out at someone. At Mallory.

The real question was how far would he go to regain his sense of importance and power?

WHEN TYLER LEFT Dilday's office, he sat in his car, right there in the parking lot, and dialed Greta Swinburne one more time. She answered warily, obviously knowing from her caller ID that it was Tyler.

"I have to talk to you," he said.

"No. Look, I've already told you everything. My husband doesn't want me talking to reporters. Can't you just leave me alone?"

"I wish I could." He was sorry, but if it was a choice between hurting Greta and hurting Mallory, he'd choose Greta anytime. For one thing, Mallory was innocent.

For another...

"There's too much at stake," he said. "You can pick

the day, and the place. But this time if you don't show up, I'll have to come to your house."

A long silence. He ordinarily could read silences pretty well, and could predict whether they would end in a yes or a no. But this one was too ambivalent. He didn't know what Greta would eventually say, because Greta herself didn't know.

Finally, he heard her sigh. It was the sigh of surrender.

"Friday," she said. "Four o'clock. Same place we met last time. City Hall, in Grupton."

Then she hung up.

And as he sat there, in his car, lurking in the shadow of the leafy maple trees, with his cell phone in his hand, he realized that he'd become a blackmailer himself.

CHAPTER THIRTEEN

THE BEAUTIFUL WEATHER LASTED only a few days. By midweek, black clouds marched in from the west and squatted over Heyday, like a grumbling, heavy-booted army setting up camp.

And they seemed to have no intention of marching away anytime soon.

Business was terrible. For the first time in a year, the Bobbies didn't show up for their Thursday night book-club meeting. The circus historian who had a book signing scheduled for Friday afternoon phoned first thing in the morning to cancel. People called to put books on hold but then never showed up to get them, undoubtedly daunted by the sight of choking, bubbling gutters and flooding roadside ditches.

By four o'clock on Friday, when a thunderstorm began waging war on Heyday with booming cannons and jagged spears of lightning, Mallory had been all alone in the bookstore for hours.

She could have used the money, but maybe it was just as well no customers showed up. Monday afternoon, as soon as she got back from making the payment, she had called Mindy. After a strange conversation, in which Mindy seemed strangely reluctant to commit, her sister finally agreed to tell Freddy everything by the end of this week.

Mallory had been on tenterhooks ever since. So a little quiet time was very welcome right now. Her customers expected her to chat and charm, but until she heard from Mindy, she was hardly able to think. Charm was out of the question.

Besides, she loved her store when it was empty, and all hers. She curled up in the comfortable seat in her front bay window and watched the ragged clouds, which had an odd greenish tint, racing across the low-hanging sky.

The street was deserted. The wind and rain owned the park today. The raindrops romped and splashed in the puddles. The wind rode the swings like invisible children and whipped the treetops in a mile-high game of tag.

She kept her phone on the cushion next to her. She hadn't strayed more than ten feet from a telephone for days now. But so far, no call from Mindy.

The whole thing was driving her crazy.

Suddenly the front door burst open, and the little bells trembled as the wind came rushing in. Mallory swung her feet down from the window seat and hurried around the corner, slipping her phone into her pocket. Who would be out in such a storm?

To her surprise, it was Aurora York, as disheveled and upset as Mallory had ever seen her.

"I thought that was you in that window! Get somewhere safe, girl! Haven't you been listening to the weather report?"

Mallory couldn't tell what color Aurora's signature feather had been when she got dressed this morning. Right now it was limp and the color of old asphalt.

"No, I haven't," Mallory answered. "You're soaked, Aurora. Let me get you a towel."

"No time for that," Aurora said. "There's a tornado warning. One already touched down in Grupton. They say it's headed this way. The spotters say it may be a multiple-vortex tornado. It has a two-mile rotating column!"

"Oh, dear." Mallory tried to sound supportive, but she wondered whether Aurora might be making a mountain out of a molehill. Aurora tended to watch the news stations compulsively, and frequently let the newscasters wind her up pretty tightly about things that didn't even remotely affect Heyday, like botulism lurking in California's canned goods, or a sinkhole swallowing a motel in Florida.

"Multiple-vortex tornado." "Two-mile rotating column." Those weren't her words. She must have been listening to the radio in her car and panicked.

"I'm sorry about Grupton," Mallory said, reaching behind the checkout counter and grabbing the roll of paper towels. She pulled off half a dozen and handed them to Aurora to mop her face. "Still, there's no reason to be too worried, is there? Tornadoes affect a pretty small area. Unless it spins right down Hippo-

drome Circle, it'll come and go without our realizing it."

She wasn't quite as confident as she tried to sound,
of course. She knew that tornadoes were unpredictable
and quite deadly. But Aurora looked absolutely ashen,
and Mallory felt sure calming down would be good for
her.

And probably it was the truth. The odds of a tornado hitting downtown Heyday were slim. Thankfully, Heyday got very few. They were many miles
outside the official "tornado alley."

The last one to hit within the city limits had been
four years ago, when a small funnel cloud ripped a
path through a dairy farm at the southeast edge of
town. The damage had been minimal—one barn down,
two cows injured and, what upset the city leaders most,
about a thousand gallons of manure lifted and splat-
tered on the rooftops of the good people of Heyday.
Even that wasn't all bad. Once they washed the odor
away, they noticed that their flowers had never
bloomed better.

"Two people in Grupton are already dead." Aurora
sat down in one of Mallory's armchairs, obviously exhausted. Mallory wondered if she'd been running from
shop to shop warning people. "The spotters say—"

But before she could finish her sentence, a roaring
sound, the kind you might hear if you stood close to a
big, beautiful waterfall, filled the room.

Mallory didn't think. She just acted. She'd never
been in a tornado before, but she'd read enough stories

about its thundering power. Without a word, she grabbed Aurora's hand and pulled her toward the checkout counter, which was large and sturdy, the biggest piece of furniture in the room.

Aurora didn't need to have things spelled out. She ducked under the counter, moving pretty quickly for a seventy-year-old woman who complained of wretched arthritis. There wasn't room for both of them, so as soon as she was sure Aurora was secure, Mallory ran back to her office. It had one window, which wasn't ideal, but it also had a large desk.

Within seconds the rushing waterfall had turned into a roaring, deafening freight train. Pressure built in Mallory's ears, and she could see the office window reverberating, shivering, as if it were made of flexible material, not firm glass at all.

Suddenly a bright light flared just outside the window, blue-white against the stormy darkness. Out in the store, Mallory heard something heavy fall, and the smashing of glass. Something hit the desk above her and rattled to the floor.

The lights flickered and went out.

She prayed for Aurora, but there was nothing else she could do. They were like two islands, adrift in this roaring, pulsing darkness.

It probably didn't last more than a minute, at most. But it felt like an eternity. Finally the freight train began to scream off into the distance, and a trembling silence returned to the store.

She climbed out carefully. What little light came in

through the windows was that green-black storm light, and it didn't help much. Stepping over things she couldn't quite identify, she made her way out into the store.

"Aurora?"

She got no answer. There was more light out here, because of the bay window, which now had a large tree branch thrusting through it. The splintered, leafy ends spread over the window seat where, just minutes ago, Mallory had been sitting.

She turned away from that and scanned the room. At least two of the heavy book stacks had toppled over. One of them had fallen across the counter.

"Aurora!" Forgetting caution, she stumbled across scattered merchandise, slipping on the glossy covers of magazines and colliding with spinner racks that now lay broken, on their sides. "Aurora, are you all right?"

Only an ominous silence answered her.

Mallory wasn't strong enough to move the bookcase alone. She climbed on one free edge of the counter and tried to find Aurora. But the open side of the counter, a narrow area that backed up to a wall, was now piled with books.

She reached her hand in and felt around until she touched Aurora's shoulder. But Aurora seemed unaware of Mallory's hand. The frail shoulder didn't move at all.

Mallory straightened, trying to think, trying to stay calm. She needed help. She touched her pocket. The phone was still there, thank God.

But when she clicked the button, nothing happened. Either the lines were down or the power outage had disabled the telephone. Her own cell phone was upstairs. She didn't know what she'd find up there, and besides, there wasn't time.

She made her way to the front door, which at some point had blown open. Aurora must not have shut it firmly, caught up in her urgent need to warn Mallory. The carpet in front of it was soaking wet, littered with twigs and leaves, pieces of paper, and some wet pink goop that looked suspiciously like the insulation from someone's roof.

Mallory rushed past it all, out into the rain. She had to find someone to help her.

At first she saw no people, only a confusion of *things*. Mixed-up things, broken things, things so mangled she couldn't identify them.

Trees were down all over the park, the pines snapped in half, the oaks yanked up by the root-ball, huge circles of earth and grass lifting with them like bright green skirts. On the sidewalk in front of her shop, one of the park's baby swings lay in pieces, the chains tangled in the leather seat. A chair from the diner sat in the middle of the street, looking startled, as if it had no idea how it got there.

"Mallory!"

She turned eagerly toward the sound of the voice. "I need help," she called, though she couldn't tell yet who it was. "In here. It's Aurora. I think she's hurt."

The man's pace quickened, and he started loping toward her. It was Kieran. *Thank heaven.* Kieran would know what to do.

"I told her to get under my counter," Mallory explained as they hurried back into the store. "But then a bookcase fell right on top of it, and I can't move it by myself. She's—" She said another prayer. "She doesn't seem to be conscious."

"We'll get her," Kieran said steadily. He touched her shoulder. "She'll be okay."

He took one edge of the bookcase, and within ten seconds he had hoisted it to its normal position.

"Don't bother trying to clear away the books," Kieran said when Mallory started trying to gain access from the back. "I'm just going to shove the counter away from this side."

He moved the heavy maple-and-granite counter as easily as if it had been made of cardboard. As soon as he did, Aurora's body tumbled free.

"No," Mallory cried softly. She ran to Aurora and knelt beside her. Kieran was there, too. He'd already lifted Aurora's head and taken off her bedraggled hat. "She's breathing," he told Mallory, smiling bracingly.

He had his cell phone in one hand and was already punching in 911.

"Come on, Aurora," he said when he'd finished talking to the emergency operator. He touched the old woman's lined face and wiped some dirt from her forehead. "Talk to me, you old tyrant."

Mallory held her breath. *Come on, Aurora,* she echoed. *Talk to us.*

Finally, when it had gone on so long Mallory's lungs ached and screamed for oxygen, Aurora began to stir. She made a muffled noise and shifted her head, frowning.

She looked at Kieran and blinked several times. "Well," she said finally. "It's a good thing you're the saint. If I'd opened my eyes and seen that devil Bryce leering down at me, I would have thought I'd died and gone to hell."

Mallory began to breathe again. She heard herself laughing from sheer relief.

Kieran grinned. "Nice to see you, too, Aurora," he said. "I knew it would take more than a little old tornado to knock you down."

Aurora made a *harrumphing* sound and closed her eyes again.

Suddenly there was noise at the doorway. "Kieran! Have you seen Mallory?"

Mallory's heart began to race. It was Tyler. His voice sounded tight, anxious. She stood quickly, realizing he must not be able to see her squatting off to the side, beyond Kieran and Aurora.

Her hand flew to her mouth. Oh, God, he looked terrible. His shirt was practically torn from his body. His torso was covered in mud, and under the mud were streaks of blood. Without thinking, she rushed over to him and grabbed hold of his hands.

"Tyler! Are you all right? What happened?"

"Mallory." He didn't ask permission. He just wrapped his arms around her and held her close. "Thank God."

Bryce's dry voice suddenly spoke over her shoulder. "Uh, I'm sorry to be a buzz kill here, brother dear, but have you forgotten that we were actually on our way to the hospital?"

She glanced up. Bryce looked almost as bad as Tyler. He was muddy and disheveled, and he held his left arm up across his heart, supporting it at the elbow.

Tyler didn't release her, and she didn't ask him to. She spoke from the shelter of his strong, muddy arms. "Bryce! Are you okay?"

"Well, I'm alive," he said. "Thanks to Tyler. I was driving along, minding my own business, when out of nowhere this monster wind comes at me and slides my car into the ditch. The impact messed up my arm, and then I couldn't get the damn door open. I figure I was about five minutes from drowning when Tyler broke the window and dragged me out."

She looked at Tyler. "He's exaggerating," Tyler said with a smile. "He was already halfway out when I got there."

"Anyhow," Bryce went on. "Tyler here could use about a hundred stitches, I think, and I damn sure need to have this arm set. But do we go straight to the hospital, like normal people? No. First we've got to stop off and check on *you*."

Kieran, who was helping Aurora to her feet, began to grin. He arched an eyebrow.

"Well, what were you doing driving around when we were under a tornado warning, Bryce? One will get you ten you were on your way to the ranch to check on Lara."

Bryce scowled. "Oh, yeah, like you wouldn't do the same for Claire, if she—"

"Oh, for heaven's sake," Aurora bellowed. She shrugged off Kieran's steadying hand and shoved her wet hat onto her slightly tilted wig. "Look at you. *The heroes of Heyday,* my left foot! If you boys are arguing about which of you is stupider when it comes to women, I can tell you there's not a skinny millimeter's worth of difference. You're all nuts."

Tyler chuckled softly. Mallory felt his chest move beneath her cheek. But still he didn't let go of her.

"Now, if you lovebirds and lunatics will be so kind as to step out of my way," Aurora said, waving her hand regally as she began to hobble forward, "I believe my ambulance has arrived."

IT WAS ALMOST TWO in the morning.

Mallory leaned against her balcony railing, letting the cool breeze blow over her. Maybe it could wash away the stress of this incredible day. She had never been so tired in her life. She wasn't sure she could even summon up the energy to go back inside and go to bed.

After hurrying to the Chronic Care Center to be sure her mother was all right, Mallory had spent the past eight hours helping her fellow shopkeepers board up broken windows, salvage whatever merchandise wasn't destroyed and vacuum water from sodden carpets. They had done as much as they could for her.

Then, when they'd accomplished all they could on Hippodrome Circle, they had driven to the hardest hit neighborhoods and helped there, too. Tarpaulins over gaping holes in roofs, chainsaws on trees that blocked the streets.

It was a sad sight, all that destruction. But thankfully no one in town had been killed, or even seriously injured. The X-rays showed that Bryce's arm was indeed broken, but as soon as they set it, he joined the cleanup crew and did more with one hand than some men could do with two.

Tyler's cuts turned out to be fairly superficial. The hospital washed and dressed them, but no stitches were required. He, too, had returned to wield a chainsaw by battery-operated torchlights and haul massive sections of tree trunks to the flatbeds of waiting pickup trucks.

In fact, he worked so hard and fit in so seamlessly that no one would have guessed he didn't belong in Heyday.

There had been no time for the two of them to talk in private. And she'd been glad of that. After their impulsive embrace when they'd first found each other, a strange shyness had set in. She was self-conscious, aware that those few moments had revealed a lot…to both of them.

And she wasn't sure she was ready to explore those revelations yet.

Her emotions were so conflicted. The last time she'd seen him, last Saturday, when the blackmailer had called, she'd been so angry. She'd resented his interference, his authoritative tone, the hateful things he'd said about Mindy. She'd felt used, exploited, as if every generous gesture he'd made over the past week had just been a cold-blooded scheme to butter her up.

To soften her up so that, when the time was right, he could get a good story, or a good roll in the hay. Or both.

But did she still believe that?

Had she ever really believed it?

When she'd seen him today, she had run to him without thinking. At that moment, her anger and her suspicions hadn't even existed. She had welcomed his strong arms around her. She had found a profound relief as she rested there, as if she were a storm-tossed boat and she had finally made it to harbor.

And, though she was almost ashamed to admit it, she had also felt an awakening. No matter how inappropriate the timing was, with mud and blood and broken bones all around them, she felt it. A stirring of something sexual between them that wouldn't die, no matter how many storms blew through, no matter how many times they quarreled, no matter how many years they were apart.

But what did that mean? Did it mean that he *wasn't* planning to exploit her? Or did it just mean that she was so attracted to him that she had ceased to care what his motives were?

She closed her eyes, unable to support the mental struggle anymore, and leaned over the balcony, putting her face into the wind. Fingers of cool air feathered her hair and plucked at the shoulder straps of her thin nightgown. It felt probing and sensual. She had a sudden urge to take the gown off and bare herself to the night.

It would be crazy.

But she felt a little crazy tonight. Maybe nearly dying did that to people.

Though the electricity was still out and the streetlights were dark, the tornado had blown away the last of the bad weather, and moonbeams lay liquid on the damply shining park. She could see the fallen tree trunks, but even they had a certain strange sensuality, as if they were bodies lying there, basking in the moonlight.

She heard a soft footstep. She drew into the shadows. Tyler had come out onto his balcony, too.

She should slip back inside. She was barefoot, and her doors were already open. He'd never hear her, never know she'd been out here just inches away from him in the moonlight, with only a wrought-iron rail between them.

But she didn't. She kept telling herself to, but she didn't.

He bent forward, the mirror image of what she'd done just minutes ago. With no power, it was stuffy in the apartment, and he probably craved the cool breezes.

His chest was bare and caught the moonlight. Over his heart a white bandage glowed.

She caught her breath. He was a gorgeous man. *All* man, with smooth, perfectly proportioned muscles and long, powerful arms. The moon caught one side of his profile, outlining it in shades of silver and black. It eliminated all color, all nuance, all expression. It stripped him down to the bare, male essentials.

He had never looked more like a McClintock.

She ought to go inside. But…

"Tyler," she said softly.

He turned, and the movement threw his face into shadows. She couldn't tell whether he was surprised. Perhaps he'd known all along that she was there.

"Hi," he said. "You can't sleep, either?"

She shook her head. "No. It's hard to relax."

He didn't say anything to that. He just looked at her, his eyes the only gleaming spots of light in a face made of shadows.

"I—" She stopped. She wasn't sure what to talk about. Everything she considered sounded fake, when what she really wanted to say was *I can't stop thinking about how it would feel to have your arms around me right now.*

"I heard the tornado destroyed a couple of the properties your father left you," she said. "I'm sorry."

"It's okay." He shrugged, which made moonlight move like silk across his shoulder. "Actually, the tornado did me a favor. The land is easier to sell when it's undeveloped anyhow."

"Oh, yes, that's right. I remember. You did say that before."

God, didn't she have a single interesting sentence in her head? He was probably wondering how he could escape without being rude. She sounded like a fool.

But then, why shouldn't she? She *was* a fool.

Because, in spite of a thousand powerful reasons why it would never work, why it could only end in heartbreak, she had done the most foolish thing she could ever do.

She had fallen in love with Tyler Balfour.

CHAPTER FOURTEEN

HE OUGHT to go inside.

If he stayed out here, they would end up making love.

He could see the yearning on her beautiful face. He could see, in every self-conscious movement of her perfect body, that restless need. She wanted to be touched. She wanted to feel alive after this terrible day spent facing the possibility of death.

But...he tried to be honest with himself. That wasn't completely true. While today's fear and exhaustion had certainly raised the stakes, the desire that arced between them hadn't been born in the tornado. It had begun three years ago, over a piece of blueberry pie. It had simmered for years, and if he didn't go inside right now it was going to end here on this balcony, in a storm of passion that would put the tornado to shame.

His body was already hard, ready for her. He turned back toward the street. He didn't dare move out of the shadows, or she would know everything.

She was stumbling over her words, trying to start a

normal conversation. She was miserable. Oh, God, he should go inside and put them both out of their misery.

But he couldn't. He wasn't strong enough.

Suddenly she gave up the charade. She stopped talking, mid-sentence, made a soft, helpless sound, and walked slowly over to the railing between the two balconies.

"Tyler," she said. She stopped at the edge, but he could feel her there. He could smell her bath soap and her shampoo. She was so close now that he could have reached out and touched her. So close that, when the breeze blew her gown through the bars of the railing, the cool fabric licked at his feet.

"Tyler, look at me."

He turned his head slowly. He bit back a groan. The moon spotlighted her, as if offering her up to him. He could see each strand of golden, curling hair, aglow with moonbeams. He could see the outline of her legs under her nightgown. He could see the soft, pale curves and dusky tips of her breasts barely concealed by the flimsy cotton.

He gripped the cold iron and tried to hold on.

"I don't want to be alone." Her voice was very soft. "Will you stay with me tonight?"

"Mallory." He closed his eyes and tried one last time to fight the building heat in his body. But he was drowning in it. It was pulling him down, with its heavy, throbbing, molten weight. "I'm sorry. I can't be with you like that tonight. I'm not that strong."

She put her hand on his arm. "I'm not asking you to be strong."

He opened his eyes and instantly he knew he was lost. Her lips were parted, the inside edges shining like dew in the moonlight. Her eyes were starry with need.

He shook his head once, and then he bent over and, after scooping her into his arms, swept her over the ridiculous wrought-iron barrier. She wrapped her arms around his neck and kissed his chest where the glass had cut him. It was pain and pleasure all at once, and he tilted back his head, letting it go through him.

He eased her slowly to the ground, groaning as her body slid across the part of him that was already hard and aching. She made a small sound, too, and he knew that she was ready for him.

She looked down at the sleeping bag and pillow he'd brought out onto the balcony, and then, with surprise on her face, she looked back at him.

"The security system went out with the power," he said. "I was going to sleep out here so that, if anyone tried to get in, I would be more likely to hear."

She smiled. He wondered if she didn't believe him.

"It's true," he said simply. "I promise you I wasn't planning. I didn't know that this would happen."

She smiled again, a strangely sad smile, he thought. Taking his hand, she placed it on her collarbone, just above her breasts. A pulse beat quickly at the bottom of her throat.

"I knew," she said. "Not that it would be tonight. But I knew that someday, somehow, this would happen."

She looked so beautiful there. He would have liked to make love to her in the full, streaming beams of the silver moon, but he knew it wasn't wise. The street seemed deserted, but, if someone stood quietly in the shadows, they would never know.

So he pulled her back, deeper into their own shadows, where the sleeping bag lay, spread out and waiting. But was even this much exposure wise? He glanced toward the interior of his apartment. It would be safer there.

"Out here," she said, obviously aware of his thoughts. "Please. I can…I won't make noise. No one will ever know."

He smiled. "No noise at all? Are you so sure about that?"

She nodded. "Test me," she said, her eyes shining.

And so he did. He took the straps of her gown and slid them over her shoulders, baring her high, round breasts.

She gasped as the cool air found her, and he covered her with the warmth of his hands. He stroked slowly, building heat, and then he bent his head and put his lips against her skin. She reached up and held on to his wrists, as if she might need to stop him if the intensity overwhelmed her.

But she was true to her word. Though he could tell she struggled, she never once whimpered or let a single moan escape.

He pushed the gown farther, past the gentle slope of her hips, until it fell to the balcony floor with a rustling whisper, like a leaf falling from a tree.

She was so perfect, so much more beautiful than he'd ever imagined, all smooth, enticing curves and dark, tempting hollows. He removed his own clothes, somehow forced patience into his throbbing body and lowered her to the sleeping bag.

He knelt in front of her. She reached up to touch him, but he pressed her back against the pillow. He shook his head. *Not yet.*

She nodded and let her hand fall to the side. While she watched him, he stroked her stomach slowly, over and over, letting his fingers go a little lower each time. Within seconds, the muscles of her abdomen were trembling and she was breathing a light, fast rhythm that told him she was on the edge.

It would have been so easy just to drive into her then, to take what they both needed. But he didn't want it to be easy. He wanted it to be long and slow and hard to endure.

He wanted it to be hard to forget.

He opened her gently, and lay the tip of his finger against her. She lifted her hips, asking for more in the only way she could, since he had denied her words.

He gave her a little, enough to make her writhe and lace her fingers through the wrought iron behind her head for strength. But he wouldn't give her all of it.

Not yet.

When she subsided, and he could tell the heat had receded enough, he started again. And then again.

But he couldn't go on forever. Each time he brought her to the edge, he went there with her. Before long, his body was nothing but pain, nothing but thrust and need. As if he had finally pushed himself beyond his own control, he moved forward and entered her fast, without warning.

She cried out, shocked, her body buckling, her hands reaching up to grab his shoulders. She tossed her head, racked instantly with involuntary, pulsing shudders.

His own climax followed quickly, a helpless release that was both fierce and joyous, both breathlessly violent and blissfully easy.

He didn't understand it. He'd never felt anything quite like it before.

It frightened him a little. Because, as he sank down beside her and pulled her limp body up to his, he recognized one thing. This moment would, as he'd hoped, be hard to forget.

But it would also be hard to live without.

WITHOUT THE COCOON of electricity, Mallory realized, you were more aware of the natural rhythms of the world. When the sun rose, its warm light touched your face and stirred you out of sleep, the same way it woke the birds and squirrels in the park across the street.

She lay there as long as she could, savoring the misty, glimmering morning and the gentle weight of Tyler's arms around her. They hadn't slept long, spooned together in that sleeping bag, but it had been a deep, sweet sleep. His lovemaking had left her so weak that when the waves of pleasure had finally moved through her, she found she couldn't move her arms or hold her eyes open.

He had pulled her body against his and kissed the nape of her neck. She'd sighed, drained and yet aware that she wanted more. Deep within her, a tiny interior vibration had still tingled, ready to throb to life at the slightest invitation.

Besides, he had done all the giving this time. She had meant to turn to him, to tell him that he should lie back, that she wanted to seduce him now, the way he had seduced her.

But when she tried to move, he made a soft "shh" sound, and held her closer. He stroked her back rhythmically, blurring the line between waking and sleeping, between lovemaking and love. She dreamed a graceful collage of hands and lips and quivering skin wet with moonlight, but she never woke up again.

Until now. And now it was too late.

Though it couldn't be eight o'clock yet, already she heard the deep rumble of trucks approaching—power trucks, tree surgeons, roofers, street sweepers. The army of specialists that were right now being deployed all over Heyday, so that order could be restored.

The businesses were first on the list—their presence kept the little town's economy alive. On a normal day, Mallory would have felt lucky to get help so soon. But today she felt an irrational resentment. Why should she have to rush to return to normal? Her one enchanted evening had been far too short.

Behind her, Tyler's face was still in shadows. The sun couldn't penetrate that far, couldn't touch his dreams and tell him to wake up. She was glad. Perhaps, as she had done, he would dream of making love.

She slipped out of the sleeping bag, found her crumpled gown and pulled it over her head. Then, taking a deep breath for courage, she stepped over the low railing, back onto her own balcony. Back into her own world.

She looked back one last time, to the soft shadows where he lay sleeping. She tried to ignore the pinch in her chest. She had no right to feel sorry for herself now. When she had asked for this, she had known it would be brief and beautiful. She hadn't deluded herself that it would outlive the night.

The first thing she did was check her cell phone messages. She had nine, mostly from friends, like Claire McClintock and Lara, offering sympathy and offering to help. A few others were from her fellow merchants, suggesting a noon meeting to discuss joint cleanup efforts.

Nothing from Mindy.

Mallory decided that, though she didn't want to badger, if she didn't hear from Mindy by the end of the day, she was going to make the call herself. It had been five days. She was really starting to worry.

She showered and dressed quickly, work clothes only, as this would undoubtedly be a sweaty, grungy day. And then she went downstairs to face the damage.

The bookstore hardly even looked like the same place. Her friends had screwed sheets of plywood over the broken bay window, to protect against the elements and intruders. But it shut out almost all the light, and turned the interior the dim yellowish color of dirty water.

To brighten things up a little, she left the front door open. That was better. She might actually be able to see what she was working on. At least five hundred books lay scattered on the floor, their pages fluttering in the breeze from the door. She'd have to inspect each one carefully to see if it could still be sold as new.

She could hear the trucks, their gears grinding more loudly now as they made their way down the street. Across Hippodrome, a chain saw started whining as someone went to work on the trees, and within seconds the sharp scent of sawdust drifted in through the door.

She glanced through the side window at the staircase that led to the apartments. The world was bustling noisily toward recovery. How long would it be before the chaos woke Tyler, too?

She should start reshelving the books. But she couldn't make herself settle down and focus yet. She knew what she was waiting for. She was waiting to see Tyler, to gauge the expression on his face, to see if she could guess what, if anything, last night had meant to him.

So she wandered the store, trying to absorb the extent of the damage. The children's area hadn't been touched, thank goodness. The stuffed animals still smiled from their perches on small plastic chairs and brightly colored pillows. The jeweled tones of the painted calliope, visible even in the minimal light, looked as cheerful as ever.

But on the other side of the cash register, she saw with dismay, her case of antique and collectible books had fallen over. Its contents were spilled all over the floor.

She hurried toward it, frowning. She could swear that case hadn't fallen during the tornado. Or had it? Things had been crazy, and her attention had been focused on Aurora, and then the McClintock men, and then, of course, the cleanup.

But she distinctly remembered the keen relief she'd felt when she saw it standing intact. Those were her most precious books, the ones that meant more than money. Some of them were so rare she'd have no way to replace them even if she could afford to.

And yet now the case was on its side, just as the others had been. The beautiful books lay at all kinds of weird angles, their spines bent backward and straining, their pages torn and bent.

She knelt and picked up the nearest one. *Lorraine and the Little People.* Though it wasn't the most expensive book in her collection, it was one of her favorites, full of color and fantasy. But now several of the illustrations were bent and almost ruined.

She folded them out carefully, closed the book and set it on the counter. She was steeling herself to check the next one when a shadow fell across her. Someone was standing in the doorway.

She looked over her shoulder, feeling an adrenaline flush shoot through her. She knew it had to be Tyler.

And it was.

He must have been up for quite a while. His dark hair was wet and he was neatly dressed. He showed no signs of having camped out in a sleeping bag on the balcony all night. He showed no signs of—

Of what? She was being ridiculous. Why should he look any different today? Having sex didn't leave a brand on a person's forehead. Even after a night of fabulous sex, people got up in the morning and went about their daily chores, unchanged.

He moved into the store, looking at the mess in front of her.

"What happened here?" He frowned. "That bookcase wasn't on the floor yesterday."

"I don't know." She put her hands helplessly in her lap and surveyed the disorder. "That's what I thought, too. But we must be wrong, don't you think? It must have gone down in the tornado. There really isn't any other way—"

He shook his head. "We're not wrong. I checked every inch of this store when I got back from the ER. That bookcase was completely undisturbed."

An uncomfortable tension had begun to gnaw at the pit of her stomach. She watched as Tyler moved around the bookcase, running his hands over every edge, peering into the shadows of the empty shelves.

Then he squatted down and began sifting carefully through the books.

"What are you thinking?" She knew, of course. But she wanted to be wrong. She wanted so much to be wrong.

He looked up at her. "Someone came in here. It must have been while we were gone, working on other houses. It couldn't have happened while we were here, not even while we were sleeping." He glanced over the tumbled books. "Whoever did this made a lot of noise."

It was strange. Five minutes ago she'd been heart-broken about her books, but now that he was here, all she cared about was whether he would say anything more about last night. "While we were sleeping." The phrase rolled so easily off his tongue, as if it had been just another normal night. As if they hadn't spent the night wrapped in each other's arms, naked and on fire.

"But who?" She picked up another book, a first edition of *The Moonstone,* and rubbed her palm against the wrinkled pages. "And why?"

"I don't know." His voice was thoughtful. He flipped over a couple of books to get a look at the titles. "Some of these are pretty valuable, right? Is anything missing?"

"I can't tell yet. It's all such a mess. But a couple of the rarest titles are still here. If you were going to steal books, why would you leave the best behind?"

"You wouldn't." He stared at the books, as if the answer might lie on their pages. "It must be a message, then. Someone just wants you to know he was here."

"The blackmailer," she said.

"It has to be. Anything else would be too much of a coincidence. He's done it before, with the flowers, remember?"

Of course she remembered. "But this is different," she said. "This is so much more—"

"More personal. Absolutely. And that's a bad sign, Mallory. It's a—"

Suddenly, he bent down, as if to get an even closer look. He swiveled and checked the window behind him. "Did that glass break during the storm? Could there have been any water damage over here?"

She shook her head. "No. The only window that broke was the front bay, where the branch hit. I'll have to replace the cushion on the window seat, but other than that—"

She broke off suddenly, a sick feeling oozing through her. "Why do you ask? What do you think you see?"

"I'm not sure." He bent again, even closer, and this time when he straightened, his face was somber. He looked angry.

"What?" She pressed her hands to her stomach. "Tyler, what is it?"

"I think our blackmailer has left a calling card behind. It would take an expert to be absolutely sure, but my best guess would be that, before he left, he urinated on the books."

She felt the blood drain out of her face.

"Oh, my God," she said hoarsely. She touched the edge of the bookcase for balance, because she felt dizzy. "Oh, my God."

"Mallory, listen to me," he said in a firm tone that somehow helped to steady her. "I know it's horrible. I know it's hard to think. But you have to. This is someone you know. There's a lot of anger here, and, whatever he might say on the phone, the anger is not directed at Mindy. It's directed at you. Who do you know who could have done this?"

"No one," she said numbly. She had touched these books. She thought she might be sick. That was what he had wanted, wasn't it? He would foul the books, and then, when she touched them, it would be as if he had fouled her, too. "No one could do such a thing."

"But someone did, Mallory. Think. Who was it?"

No one, her mind insisted. *No one.* This was Heyday. Hadn't he seen yesterday that Heyday was a special place, where people cared about each other? There were no monsters here.

Tyler rose to his feet. He motioned that she should do the same, and somehow she managed it. "You have a bathroom, don't you? Where is it? You'll feel better when you've washed your hands."

Yes, he was right. She needed to wash her hands. She scrubbed them so long, under water so hot, that she thought she might scrape the skin from her fingers. Then she splashed cool water on her face and she sat on the edge of the toilet, trying to pull herself together.

By the time she emerged from the bathroom, Tyler had already packed away about a third of the books in an empty box, which he must have found in the back room.

"These are the only ones affected," he said. "The rest are fine. I'm going to put these away for now. Do you have a storage area, someplace you don't use much?"

"Put them away?" She shook her head. "*Throw* them away. I don't want them anywhere near me."

"We can't do that," he said matter-of-factly. "They can incriminate him, Mallory. These books can prove who did this to you. We'll give them to the police, and—"

"No," she said. "No police. Not yet. I'll keep the books if I have to, but no police."

For a minute she thought he might lose his temper, might shout at her for being a stubborn fool.

But shouting wasn't Tyler's style. He set the box of books down and went into the bathroom to wash his own hands. He left the door open.

When he returned, wiping his hands on a paper towel, she saw that the anger in his face had subsided, replaced by something that looked like pity.

"I'm sorry," she said. "I know you'd like to—"

"She's never going to tell him, Mallory," he broke in. His voice was flat. "Not unless you force her to. In your heart, you know that."

"I—you don't—"

Without warning, her eyes began to sting and she had to look away. What could she say? It was true.

But how could he have known the exact sentence that had been haunting her for days? At first, all her anxieties had focused on how Freddy would react when Mindy told him, and how Mindy would handle that reaction, whatever it might be.

But before the tornado, as she had waited for the telephone to ring, she had suddenly understood that it wasn't going to happen. Mindy wasn't ever going to tell Freddy. Not unless she was forced to.

How could Tyler know that? What kind of magic did he use to see so clearly inside her soul?

She faced him again. "You're right," she said. "I do know that now. But I still have an obligation to see this through in whatever way will cause the least damage."

"The least damage for Mindy, you mean," he said. His voice was bitter.

"Yes, for Mindy. I wouldn't expect you to understand this, Tyler, but I love her, and I have to take care of her. My mother isn't able to do it, and I know she is counting on me to protect her the best I can."

His anger seemed to be building. "What exactly is it you think I can't understand, Mallory? What it means to love people? Or what it means to coddle them until they're so weak they don't know how to take responsibility for their own mistakes?"

She flushed. She hadn't realized how insulting her words had been until he threw them back at her like this. "I'm sorry," she said again. "That wasn't exactly what I meant. It's just that, for you, it's all about the story. All about the book."

"Is that so?" His eyes were hard, the blue blazing through narrowed lids. "What about last night, then? Do you think that was all about the book? Do you think that was just some hands-on research to spice up Chapter Ten?"

She didn't answer. She wasn't sure what to say. Of course she didn't think their night together would show up in the pages of his book. But she also didn't believe anything that had happened between them had changed his mind about writing it.

When she remained silent, he made a low, scoffing sound.

"Oh, that's right," he said. "You've already decided that every time I touch you, it's part of my master plan to control your mind and your body, so that you'll do my evil bidding."

She could hardly meet his eyes. She remembered well saying almost exactly that.

He laughed. "Well, that kind of manipulation can go both ways, Mallory. As I remember it, last night *you* were the one making all the advances. Have you ever considered that maybe, from where I stand, it looks as if you offered your lovely body to me as a bribe? Sex for silence. Carnal favors for cooperation. It's been done before. It's even been done to me."

He might as well have slapped her. Her cheeks burned, but she lifted her chin and met his angry gaze squarely.

"Is that really what you believe?"

He shrugged. "It's as legitimate an interpretation as the one you've adopted. You tell *me*. Is there any reason why I would believe anything else?"

"No," she said softly. "Apparently we're just hopelessly stranded on opposite sides of this situation. And the past—" She bit her lower lip, which was threatening to tremble. "The past has taught both of us not to trust. So I'm afraid you're just going to have to do whatever you think is right."

She glanced at the toppled bookcase. "And I'm going to have to do the same."

AN HOUR LATER, when Tyler was long gone and the glaziers were busy installing new squares of glass in the broken bay, Mallory went into her office, shut the door and picked up the phone.

Mindy's number rang only once before she answered. She must have been sitting by the telephone.

"Hi, Mal," Mindy said, her voice strained. "I'm sorry I haven't called you. I was just about to."

"That's okay." Mallory picked up a pen and began turning it over and over, trying to keep herself steady. It wouldn't help if Mindy sensed Mallory's own distress. "But I do need to know what's going on, honey. Have you told Freddy yet?"

The silence lasted only a second or two, but that was long enough. Mallory dropped her forehead to her hand. "You didn't, did you?"

"No. I couldn't. I tried, but I couldn't." Her voice broke slightly. "You don't understand. You just don't know how much I love him."

"Yes, I do," Mallory said as calmly as she could. Logic, not emotion. That's what they needed here. "And that's why you have to tell him. When you love someone, you can't keep secrets from them. Especially when those secrets could end up hurting them."

"I'd never hurt him." Mindy began to cry softly. "You don't understand. You and Dan—that was different. It wasn't ever really…real."

Mallory let that go. In a way, it was rather perceptive. At nineteen, Mallory had married Dan because she wanted to grow up, get free, stop being such a burden on their mother. She had wanted the security of love, the comfort of love. But she hadn't really *been* in love.

Not until she met Tyler.

"This kind of love…" Mindy sobbed. "I love him so much it hurts."

Oh, yes. Mallory knew all about that now.

But if they both collapsed into tears, that wouldn't help anyone. Mallory toughened her heart, just a little, and forced herself to wait for the storm of sobbing to pass.

"He has a right to know, Mindy," she repeated gently when there was silence on the other end. "No matter how hard it is, you have to tell him."

"You don't understand," Mindy said on a fresh, anguished sob. "I can't. I'm—"

She struggled to control her voice and failed. Her next two words sounded as if they were made of tears.

"I'm pregnant."

CHAPTER FIFTEEN

At THREE-THIRTY that afternoon, Mindy sat on one of the few undamaged picnic benches in Heyday's central park and watched as Freddy chatted with Mayor Dozier by the band shell.

Even now, when things were so complicated, the sight of Freddy still made her feel just a little bit stronger and safer. He was so handsome, so tall and smiling, a stark contrast to the mayor, who was pinch faced and beady eyed. Mindy couldn't remember ever seeing Mayor Dozier smile.

As if he sensed her attention, Freddy glanced over at her and tossed her a sunny smile and a cheerful wink. The casual sweetness nearly brought tears to her eyes. She smiled back and said to herself, *This is how I want to remember him.*

But wait…hold on, for heaven's sake. *Remember* him? That was pretty fatalistic, wasn't it? She might not have to tell him anything. She might still be able to make Mallory understand.

But even so, she found herself watching him with a poignant ache in the pit of her stomach. As silly as it sounded, she felt as if she needed to imprint his image on her mind, just in case she never saw him again.

Oh, she had to stop this morbid stuff. If only Mallory would get here, Mindy could start making her case. Surely, now that there was a baby on the way, Mal wouldn't really want her little sister to risk alienating her fiancé just for the sake of clearing her conscience.

But where *was* Mallory?

Mallory had set up their meeting here at three, and, though she'd forgotten her watch, she was sure it was at least three-thirty. The location was so odd, too. Why here? Why not in the bookstore? Mindy had glimpsed the bookstore on her way in, and, aside from the window, which was only about half repaired, the tornado didn't seem to have messed it up all that much.

Mallory had been strange on the phone yesterday, so adamant that Mindy tell Freddy about the Heyday Eight. Even when Mindy confessed about the baby, Mallory had refused to back down.

"I want you to come to Heyday, Mindy," she'd said. "Come tomorrow. We need to discuss this face-to-face."

Mindy had tried to talk her out of it, but Mallory had been surprisingly stubborn. No, she couldn't come to Richmond and have their talk there. No, she didn't care whether Freddy liked the idea of Mindy spending the whole day away from him.

Even when Mindy grew teary and hinted that she

was troubled by morning sickness, Mallory didn't relent. That shocked Mindy more than anything else. In the past few years, Mallory had been extremely gentle, backing down from any demand whenever she thought Mindy was sick or emotionally fragile.

This time, though, she had been unshakable. Convenient or not, pregnant or not, Mindy must come. Freddy would just have to live without her for one day.

To Mindy's relief, when Freddy heard that she was driving to Heyday, he hadn't been annoyed at all.

"I'll come, too," he'd said eagerly. "That area was hit pretty hard by those tornadoes Friday, and I can probably pull together a small press conference. I'll get dad's press secretary to write something, *Our hearts go out to the people of Heyday, we'll make available every possible resource,* stuff like that."

So here they were, at the heavily damaged park, where the citizens of Heyday had organized a cleanup party, complete with free hot dogs, snow cones, slices of pizza and beer for anyone who carted away a carload of debris.

Freddy had been ecstatic. It was the perfect venue for the speech he carried in his pocket. He didn't seem at all self-conscious to be the only suited, manicured man among a park full of hardworking guys in dirty jeans.

Mindy stuck her feet out in front of her and stared at her strappy sandals. She should have worn sneakers. And blue jeans would definitely have looked a lot more appropriate than this overpriced yellow sundress.

Not that she had any idea how to operate a chain saw. Not that she would have had a chance of lifting one of those huge circular sections of tree trunk.

But she could have raked, as Claire McClintock was doing over by the playground area, baby Stephanie strapped to her back in a cute carrier. Even little Erica Gordon was dragging branches to the piles by the street.

"Hey there, honey, sorry I'm late. I was helping Slip Stanton clean some debris out of the Black and White, which took a lot of damage yesterday." Mallory kissed Mindy on the cheek, then instinctively glanced down at her stomach. "Are you all right? You look a little pale."

Mallory was dressed like all the others, just jeans and a T-shirt. She looked sweaty, and she had bits of leaves and sawdust in her hair. Still, she looked pretty. Mindy liked it that Mallory was finally letting her hair grow out.

"I'm fine," Mindy said. "Just a little tired. Freddy came with me, did you see? He's going to make a speech from the band shell in a few minutes. He's got a message from his father, some emergency assistance information and stuff like that."

Mallory looked as if she might comment on that, but she didn't. She just wiped a small chip of wood from her cheek.

"Yes, I saw him. Actually, I'm glad he's here. That way, if you'd like me to be with you while you talk to him, I can do that."

Mindy felt a streak of panic. Mallory was talking as if this was a done deal. "Mallory," she said, wishing she could think of the perfect words, "I know you think I should tell him, but now that I've discovered I'm going to have a baby, I—"

"Mindy, no." Mallory put her hand on Mindy's arm. That sympathetic gesture, combined with the soft, pitying look on her face, scared Mindy to death. Mallory looked like a person at a funeral. Deeply sad, but already accepting the finality of the loss.

"The baby doesn't change anything, honey."

Mindy had promised herself she wasn't going to cry, but already she felt her eyes stinging. How could Mallory be so insensitive?

"It changes a heck of a lot for me," she said hotly.

"I know." Mallory's tone was gentle. "But you need to listen to me first, and then I think you'll understand better. There are—a lot of things I haven't told you. Things I hoped you'd never have to know."

Mindy's stomach was alive with fluttering nerves. She put her hand over her belt and pressed. "What things?"

"Someone knows, honey." Mallory took Mindy's free hand and enclosed it between her own. "Someone knows about Dorian Swigert. And they're threatening to tell Freddy."

Instinctively, Mindy glanced around the sun-dappled park, to see if anyone had heard. *Dorian Swigert.* That was a name she hadn't been willing to speak aloud in nearly three years.

"*Who* knows? How could anyone know? There was only Greta and me. And Greta promised she wouldn't tell. If she'd broken that promise, my name would have appeared in Tyler Balfour's articles three years ago. No one knows, Mallory. There is no one who possibly could."

But she could hear the racing panic in her voice, in the strung-together denials. And then a terrible thought struck her.

"Oh, God. Is it Dorian himself? Is that what you mean? He knows, of course, but why would he tell? He could be arrested. He doesn't even live around here, and…"

She realized she was making a fool of herself. Mallory had just been sitting there, with that sad face, waiting for her to run out of steam.

"I don't know who it is," Mallory said when she got a chance to talk. "The man calls from an untraceable number. He uses a machine to disguise his voice."

As the words sank in, Mindy felt herself sinking, too, as if they weren't words at all, but a physical weight being yoked to her shoulders.

"Oh, my God," she said softly. "We're being blackmailed."

Mallory nodded. "For quite a while now. I've been paying this man a thousand dollars every two weeks."

Mindy didn't answer. The sum was staggering, too much to fully absorb. She didn't make that much in a month, and she didn't think Mallory cleared much more than that, either. Where was she getting it?

Mindy glanced at Freddy, seeking the happiness fix he always gave her, but he had climbed onto the band shell and was looking at the microphone, tapping at it and frowning. He seemed very far away from her suddenly.

"I'm so sorry, honey," Mallory said. "I have tried to pay this man as long as I could, just to buy you some time. But he's getting—upset. I think he broke into the bookstore yesterday and defaced some of my books. I honestly don't think it's safe to let it go on any longer."

Mindy nodded mutely. Then, confused, as if nodding might not be the appropriate reaction, she shook her head. Then she just stared at Mallory helplessly. She couldn't seem to get anything to stick in her head except the basic information.

Someone knew about Dorian. And that someone was going to tell Freddy.

And, when he did, the fairy-tale life she had miraculously pieced together out of the ashes of her youth was over.

It was like watching time-lapse photography in a movie. She looked down at her hand, which didn't really seem to belong to her. She felt herself growing heavy and tired. Duller. Older.

Mallory chafed her hands gently, as if she wanted to get the circulation going. Mindy wondered if her fingers were cold. She felt too numb all over to be sure.

"I'm so sorry, sweetheart," Mallory said again.

Mindy shook her head. "Why are you sorry? You've

done everything you possibly could to save me. The fault is mine. I'm the one who decided to become a hooker. I'm the one who—"

"Honey, hush. This isn't about assigning blame. This is about being honest with the man you love. It's about coming to terms with your past so that you can have the future you deserve. You're ready to do that. It's even more important, now that you're going to be a mother."

Mindy closed her eyes and touched her stomach again. A *mother*. For the first time she caught a glimpse of how profound this change in her life was going to be. She knew how she'd ended up pregnant. She hadn't exactly wanted it to happen, but she hadn't tried very hard to prevent it. She'd been careless with birth control, encouraged Freddy to be careless.

Sometimes she had daydreamed about having a baby, a warm, living creature, who would love her no matter what. In her imagination, the sweet sleeping body nestled against her heart had felt so comforting.

But now she saw that she had merely been playing with the idea of a baby, just as she had played with the idea of being a prostitute. She had, once again, landed herself in the middle of something she couldn't handle.

But this wasn't a club she could drop out of. She was going to have to *learn* to handle it.

Tears burned at her eyelids, but she refused to give in to them. Crying wouldn't change anything. Only a child thought it would. How could she be a mother if she was going to keep acting like a child herself? An irresponsible child causing trouble to everyone who loved her?

She looked at Mallory. "You're sure there's no other way."

Mallory nodded. "I'm sure. It's time to do the right thing. Even if I had a million dollars, even if I could afford to give this guy whatever he asks, I wouldn't do it anymore. You and I are both better than that. We're both braver than that."

Mindy wondered how much Mallory had already paid to buy the blackmailer's silence. She wondered how she would ever pay her back. If only she hadn't decided to wear this new dress today, she thought. It had cost three hundred dollars. If only she hadn't taken the tags off this morning, she could return it, and that would be one little bit of the debt she could pay off right away.

But then she looked into Mallory's sad, steady face, and she understood how typically immature such thoughts were. This wasn't about one dress. This was about a long-term change. It was about character, about courage and self-denial.

Terrifying words. She had precious little experience with any of them. It frightened her to think she might not, in the end, be up to the challenge.

"You can do it, honey," Mallory said, as if she'd read her thoughts. "You're strong, stronger than you realize. You'll *find* the courage. For your own sake, and for the sake of the baby."

"I have no courage at all," Mindy said quietly. "I've been borrowing it all along from Freddy." She smiled, hoping it didn't look as weak and watery as it felt. "And, of course, from you, though I don't think I realized how much until this very minute."

Mallory squeezed her hand. "Well, you'll always have me, Mindy."

But Mindy noticed that her sister didn't mention Freddy.

Mindy looked over at him one more time. He stood at the microphone, smiling as he began to deliver his speech. The band shell was planted all around with wildflowers, yellow stargrass and blue phlox, which matched exactly his sunshine hair and smiling blue eyes.

Yes, she thought, fighting down the knot in her throat. *This is how I want to remember him.*

TYLER FOLDED UP his newspaper and, laying it on the car seat beside him, stared down the empty tree-lined street irritably. He was getting tired of playing games with Greta Swinburne, now Mrs. Ray Woodley. She'd stood him up Friday, and it looked as if she might be going to do the same today.

Frankly, this wasn't the day to mess around with him. He was in a seriously bad mood. He wanted to be in Heyday, keeping an eye on Mallory and helping clean up the park.

Bryce had asked if Tyler would stand in for him at the cleanup day. Apparently Lara had warned Bryce that, if he tried to do any more work with power tools while his arm was in a cast, she'd take a chain saw to *him*.

Tyler had apologized, explaining that he had an out-of-town meeting, but that he'd try to stop by when he got back if it wasn't too late. Bryce had made some easy quip, assuring him that it didn't matter, but Tyler could tell he was disappointed.

So Greta had damn well better show up, and information had better pour out of her like water from a pitcher. She'd held out on him three years ago. She'd caused him to run a story that missed a lot of basic facts, like the fact that it had actually been the Heyday *Nine*.

But she wasn't going to hold out on him today. Today there was a lot more at stake than a story.

Finally he saw her car pull into the driveway of the upscale, two-story brick colonial house. The garage door, activated by remote, began lifting noiselessly. She pulled in, but Tyler joined her just as she swung two long, shapely legs out of the silver Mercedes.

"I couldn't help it," she said defensively, looking up and obviously recognizing his frustrated expression. "Ray's plane was late taking off. I couldn't just leave him there. He would have been suspicious."

This had been her excuse for missing the Friday meeting, too. Her husband had a trip planned, and only when he was safely out of town would she agree to talk to Tyler. But Ray's flights, she said, kept being delayed.

"Let's go inside, okay?" She grabbed an Ann Taylor bag from the seat next to her. Obviously she'd done a little shopping to help buck up her courage for this interview. "Want some coffee?"

"What I want," he said, "is some answers."

"Well, I want coffee. I need some caffeine." She stuck a key in the door to the house and went in, without showing any interest in whether Tyler followed her.

But he did, and it was a nice view, watching her glossy brown hair swing from side to side, so long it just skimmed her rear end. Her bright green dress fit her so tightly that he could see the muscles in her thighs move as she walked. The only thing that kept that dress from being criminally oversexed was the fact that she'd paid about five hundred dollars to make sure it didn't cross the line.

The interior of the Woodley house was cool and smelled as fresh as a model home, as if no one lived here at all. The plasma television in the living room was at least fifty inches, and the ceiling-high picture window looked out onto a shady brick patio and bright blue swimming pool.

Tyler raised his eyebrows. He'd heard that Ray Woodley, who had been Greta's favorite client during her Heyday Eight days and then had become her husband, was well-off, but this was impressive.

According to Tyler's research, Ray was forty-eight, a day trader who worked from home, and something of a legend in model-train circles. The adjective that most often came up about him was "obsessive." The second favorite was "weird."

But Greta had been having sex with Ray for years, in exchange for the money to buy pretty things. So Tyler suspected this arrangement, which at least came with a legal contract, suited her fine.

She led him into a large kitchen, where everything was ultramodern, done in elegant shades of copper and beige. She tossed her large key ring onto the counter. To Tyler's surprise, her little gold tiger, the highest prize of the Heyday Eight, was attached to the key ring as a decoration, right between a medallion with the Mercedes insignia, and a silver charm that read "#1 Wife."

He lifted the tiger and looked into its diamond eyes. "Cute," he said. "I'm surprised you've still got this. What does Ray think about that?"

She laughed. "Ray *doesn't* think about it. He's never even noticed it." She took it from Tyler and rubbed her fingers across the tiger, as if to polish its golden surface. The gesture was a little wistful.

"Sometimes respectability can be a little bit boring." She glanced up at him, smiling wryly. "So I keep this to remind me that sometimes excitement isn't that great, either."

He smiled. She never had been the type to sugarcoat the truth much. He liked that.

"So have a seat," she said, indicating the comfortable, high-backed bar stools that lined the counter. "Want a hard-boiled egg? That's really all there is right now. I don't cook a lot. Ray likes pizza, thank God, so—"

"Greta," he broke in, though he tried not to sound too impatient. "I've already waited more than an hour, and I don't have a lot of time. I need to ask you some questions."

She kept her back to him as she took out a bottle of instant coffee and stuck a mug of water into the microwave, ignoring the glossy, high-tech coffeemaker right next to her elbow.

"I still don't know why you're so hot to talk to me," she said. "I know about your book, but I told you everything when you were here before. If it wasn't for me, you know, you wouldn't have had a story at all."

"And if it wasn't for your willingness to talk to me and to the D.A., you might have ended up in jail. But there were some things you didn't tell either of us, weren't there?"

While the microwave counted down the seconds, she turned to Tyler, putting her hands on her hips, a move she'd perfected to accentuate her tiny waist. "Things like what?"

"When you gave me the list of your clients, you left somebody out."

The microwave beeped at her, and she turned to tend it, but not before Tyler observed the flash of awareness in her pretty green eyes.

He was relieved to see it. His worst nightmare was that her list *had* been complete, which might mean the blackmailer hadn't ever been one of their clients. Then the best lead, the Heyday Eight connection, would dry up completely.

"Didn't you, Greta?"

She was busy spooning an amazing amount of artificial sweetener into her coffee. "Gosh," she said. "I don't remember. We had a lot of clients. You'd be surprised how many men get turned-on by the idea of doing it with a pretty little college girl."

She glanced over her shoulder with a teasing grin. "Or would you? I always thought maybe, if you hadn't been even *more* turned-on by the idea of writing our story, we might have been able to come up with something that interested you."

Now there was the Greta he remembered. Bright, sassy, really more a salesman than a prostitute. A graduate of the Moresville College School of Business Management. Good at reading people, knowing what they wanted and then offering it to them.

Tyler smiled. "You certainly tried your best."

"Yeah, but you're tricky," she said. She leaned one curvy hip against the counter and eyed him curiously. "Most men, they fall into one of two categories. They like to boss, or they like to *be* bossed. Right off, I pegged you for a boss. You've got testosterone vibes that just bounce off the walls, you know? Of course, later I found out you were a McClintock, which explains that."

"Greta. You're trying to change the subject. Tell me about the list. How many people did you leave off?"

She sipped her coffee. "What makes you think I left

anyone off? I mean, I told you about Ray, but that was off-the-record. You can't write about that unless you find proof somewhere else. I checked about what *off-the-record* means before I told you anything."

Yes, Greta was quite the businesswoman. Ray's Heyday Eight association was so secretive that Greta hadn't even told the other girls, though it meant she had to work harder to earn her little gold tiger pin. But it had worked. Even the cops hadn't been able to pin anything on Ray. And her loyalty had paid off. Now she was Mrs. Ray Woodley, and had about a hundred thousand dollars worth of expensive kitchen equipment she didn't use.

"I'm not talking about Ray," he said. "Who else?"

"Nobody."

But Tyler had done a lot of thinking about this. Greta had left Ray's name out because she had high hopes that their relationship could lead to marriage. And she'd left Dorian Swigert out because she was trying to protect Mindy, their newest initiate, the ninth girl, the only one who had any hope of escaping undetected.

So what other reasons were there for her to hide a name? Tyler could think of only two good ones. The man could be so powerful that he could retaliate in some way. Or he could be physically dangerous, someone who just plain frightened her.

Given what he'd seen in Mallory's bookstore yesterday, Tyler was ready to bet on the scary guy.

"Think harder, Greta. There was somebody…

maybe somebody who actually made you nervous. You said you serviced two kinds of men. The ones who liked to be dominated and the ones who liked to do the dominating. Was there one of them who liked it a little bit too much?"

She gave him a long, appraising look over the rim of her coffee cup. "Something's not right here," she said slowly. "I don't believe you're just pushing to get more names all for no reason, you know? So I'm thinking…has something happened?"

Tyler had to make a quick decision. What kind of person was Greta Swinburne Woodley, really? Did she have enough basic decency to care what happened to other women, now that she was safely out of the whole mess?

In spite of everything, he thought maybe she did.

"Well?" She looked serious. "What is it? Has somebody been hurt?"

"Not yet," he said honestly. "And I'm trying to make sure it stays that way. But I need help. I need names."

She screwed her mouth up sideways and squinted her eyes, a habit she'd always had when she was thinking hard. It had the effect of making her look very young, in spite of the heavy makeup and the tight green dress.

"Can you keep me out of it?"

He nodded. "I think so. I'll do my best."

She grinned a little. "I'll bet your best is pretty good, too." Then, sobering again, she put her coffee cup down and took a deep breath. "Okay, there were two names I didn't give you. I was ready to see the club get put out of business, but I wasn't ready to get any of the girls hurt, you know? And these two guys were really jerks."

He nodded. "Okay. Who were they?"

"One of them was the mayor. Heyday's mayor. He was a hitter, liked to slap you around, and sometimes it got out of hand. Toward the end, Pammy Russe was the only one who would even take an appointment with him."

Tyler wasn't particularly surprised. Joe Dozier was fairly smooth himself, but his wife had that terrified mouse look that often meant abuse. It could be just emotional abuse, of course, but Tyler wasn't shocked to learn there was a physical component, too.

"And the other one?"

"A low-rent guy named Slip Stanton. Another hitter. He owns a couple of bars and a motel just outside Heyday. The Absolutely Nowhere, which is where this guy is going, if you ask me. He used to like to take the girls to his motel, because that way the room didn't cost him anything. Sometimes he was okay. But if he'd been drinking, he could really mess you up."

Slip Stanton. The guy who had bought the Black and White Lounge from Tyler just a couple of months ago. Greta was right about the low-rent comment, though Slip would have been furious to hear it. Slip was a blue-collar guy desperately trying to bleach himself into the white-collar world. Tyler hadn't liked him much, but he'd put his aversion down to Slip's smarmy social climbing.

"Did either one of them show an unusual interest in Mindy Rackham?"

Greta's eyes widened. "Wow, you *have* been doing your homework! Poor kid—I hope you won't put her in your book. She nearly puked her guts up the one time we sent her on a date. Even if your articles hadn't shut us down, we wouldn't have kept her. That kind of flower just wilts too easily, you know what I mean?"

"Yes," he said. "I think I do. But did either of those men seem particularly interested in her? Did they ask for her? You told me once that only you knew all the names of the Eight. But could they somehow have found out that she was joining the club?"

Greta frowned. "I don't remember if I told them. I did tell one guy, and—" She broke off abruptly. "If you're looking for somebody truly creepy, there's someone else you might want to think about. Someone who *was* on our list."

"Another hitter?"

She shook her head. "No, that's what was so weird. He never did anything wrong, exactly. But he insisted on being the first to get any of our new girls. He had a thing for virgins. Pretty damn medieval, don't you think? My theory is that a fetish about deflowering virgins usually means you've got some serious masculinity issues, you know what I mean? Maybe some psychiatric issues, too."

"But he never did anything violent?"

"Not exactly. By the end, though, none of the girls wanted to date him. They said he creeped them out. So when he asked for Mindy, I said no way. I knew she couldn't take it. And besides, I told him, that's just too bloody weird for me, buddy. Aren't you still married to her *sister?*"

CHAPTER SIXTEEN

THE POWER COMPANY HAD HOPED to restore electricity to the downtown area by the end of the day, but so many hundred-year-old trees lying on top of downed lines, and power poles broken like toothpicks, had proved too much for them.

They planned to work through the night, they said, but many businesses, including Mallory's bookstore, were still dark and might well remain that way for at least another twenty-four hours.

Meanwhile, they'd have to struggle on without benefit of electricity. Mallory hadn't ever been without power for more than an hour or two before, and she had a new appreciation for the comforts it provided.

She'd worked in the bookstore, in the dark, for almost two hours, after she left Mindy at the park.

Mindy had insisted that she wanted to talk to Freddy alone. Though Mallory had found it wrenching to abandon her, she understood why Mindy needed to slay this dragon by herself. All Mallory could do was try to infuse their goodbye kiss with all the courage and confidence she could muster.

Though the main phone lines were out, Mindy had Mallory's cell number, and she'd promised to call as soon as she had the privacy, and the emotional equilibrium. She had warned Mallory that, if things didn't go well, she might not feel up to talking about it for a little while.

Reluctantly, Mallory had agreed to wait without calling. She had promised not to hover.

It was a harder promise to keep than it was to make. Mallory had busied herself downstairs as long as she could, reshelving books until the light was so bad she couldn't even read the authors' names. Then she'd gone upstairs, and, for want of the electricity needed to do anything more productive, like laundry or bookkeeping, vacuuming or e-mail or even checking the news, she tried to distract herself by straightening up the stacks of books.

But her mind kept wandering. She kept realizing that she was always listening for the sound of her cell phone.

Or the sound of Tyler's footsteps on the stairs.

She wondered where he was. Several people at the park cleanup had asked her about him. But she had no answers. She hadn't seen even a single glimpse of him since their argument this morning.

Perhaps he'd gone straight to the police station.

But if he had done that, wouldn't someone be here already? Wouldn't they want to investigate the crime scene, the ugly, ruined books, now packed away and out of sight, but still, she knew, covered in incriminating DNA?

For a moment she wondered whether he might have

left Heyday completely. Could he have decided he would rather be back in Washington, where the stories he investigated were significant? Not tawdry and pathetic, like this one.

But, of course, there was still the book. *The Heyday Eight.* That tied him here, at least for a while. The book had the power to hold him, a power that apparently the town, his inheritance, his brothers—and even Mallory herself—did not possess.

She heard a noise on the stairs. Her heart lifting, she hurried back into her apartment and pulled open the door to the back hallway. But the corridor was dark and, apparently, empty. Disappointed, she closed the door quietly. She must have imagined the noise.

From that moment on, though, she felt slightly on edge, the skin on her back prickling, as if something unseen disturbed the air behind her. She heard creaks and whispers that were undoubtedly normal to the old building, noises that ordinarily were smothered by the drone of air conditioners, refrigerators, televisions and computers.

She went outside so that she could take advantage of what light remained. Out here, at least she could hear the distant sounds of people still working at the south end of the park, and that was comforting. She didn't feel quite so alone.

Looking down, she realized there was a figure standing at the edge of the park just opposite her store. The light was too dim. She couldn't tell whether it was a man or a woman.

It could have been someone taking a break from the hard cleanup work. Any one of the shopkeepers along this street might stroll across to the park for a few minutes, just to escape the practical worries of drenched merchandise, soggy carpets and spoiled food.

She knew she had no reason to be filled with dread. And yet her nerve endings shimmered with a primitive, inexplicable alarm.

She rubbed her arms, irritated with herself. This was ridiculous. She needed to take action, not just sit around here twiddling her thumbs, waiting for Mindy to call, waiting for Tyler to appear. She knew what needed to be done, and she was perfectly capable of doing it.

She glanced at the motionless figure one more time. Then she went back into the apartment, scooped up her purse and cell phone, dashed down the outside stairs to where her car was parked and drove to the Heyday Police Station.

MINDY STARED curiously at her hands.

At least she assumed they were her hands. Except for the fact that they were attached to her arms, she would never have recognized them. Every single one of the pretty pink fingernails, which she had shaped and oiled and buffed and painted into perfection, was broken down to the quick. She had three bleeding knuckles, a coating of sawdust, and dirt in every crease.

But the strangest, most foreign thing of all was what she *didn't* have on those hands.

She didn't have a diamond ring.

But right now she was just too darn tired to cry about it. Which was, of course, what she had hoped would happen when she joined the cleanup crew two hours ago.

"Hey, squirt." Roddy Hartland came up behind her and tickled her hair with the leaves of a small branch he had just picked up. "Didn't anyone ever tell you not to play in the dirt with your party clothes on?"

"Sorry. I hadn't heard there was a dress code for this event," she said, turning around and countering his branch with a thrust from her own handful of twigs. "Or maybe I shouldn't mention dress codes. I hear that's a sore subject with you. Where *is* your skirt, by the way?"

"Mal told you about that?" He grinned. "I've got it on under my jeans. Wanna see?"

"God, no!" She grimaced, but she wasn't really annoyed. She was actually relieved that he'd finally come over and broken the ice. The two of them had both been out here for at least an hour, but he hadn't said a word to her. And she had been too emotionally drained after the discussion with Freddy to make the first move.

It was ironic, really. In the past two hours her body had become exhausted, but her heart had grown a little bit stronger. Maybe, she thought, physical labor really was good for the soul.

And so was Roddy. Her own obnoxious, lovable pretend big brother. Just having him around to trade insults with made her feel like herself again.

Soon, though, the cleanup would be finished, and Roddy would go home just like everyone else.

She looked around the park, which was gradually emptying out. Most of the big tree trunks had already been sectioned and carted away. The sun was falling, casting a glaze of honey light over everyone. She wished she could make it freeze in the sky so that she could go on tugging and digging and hauling…and never have to go home alone and think.

"Have you seen Mallory?" Mindy had thought her sister would have come back by now—unable to resist the urge to check up on Mindy. "She left a long time ago."

"No." Roddy glanced around, too. "That's weird. I haven't seen Tyler, either. You think maybe they've run away together? I've been hearing all kinds of rumors about them. Apparently there've been lots of smoldering glances and stuff. When Tyler got cut up in the tornado, the man was damn near bleeding to death, but he wouldn't go to the hospital until he found out whether Mal was okay."

Mindy tried to cover up how surprised she was to hear that. Tyler and Mallory? Tyler *Balfour?* Could it possibly be true? Or was Roddy making one of his usual over-the-top jokes?

Certainly Mindy hadn't picked up any vibes, hadn't seen any signs that Mallory was interested in Tyler.

The last she'd heard, Mallory hated the guy. But then, Mindy hadn't really been paying much attention lately to anyone but herself. Mallory could have tattooed "I love Tyler" across her forehead, and her self-absorbed little sister wouldn't even have noticed it.

Roddy plopped down on the top of a picnic table and wiped his filthy face with an equally filthy hand. "You know, there oughta be a law. Those McClintocks are making off with all of Heyday's best-looking chicks."

She smiled. As if he couldn't have any girl he wanted. He had a zillion dollars, and he had the best body in town. He was shirtless right now, and even sweaty and covered in grime, that inverted pyramid torso and washboard stomach were just about perfect.

"Thanks a lot," she said. "And here I thought I was one of Heyday's best-looking chicks."

Roddy leaned back, as if the picnic table were his own massage pad, and groaned as he stretched out tired muscles. He twisted, trying to crack his back.

"Used to be, you were," he said between cracks. "Now you're just another cookie-cutter ingenue in training to be a trophy wife. Borrrrr-ing."

She knew he was goading her, but, on this subject, at least, she didn't have the spunk to fight back. She tried to think of something to say that could dodge the subject completely, but there was just a pulpy, unformed mass of pain in her mind where all the sharp comebacks used to be.

As the silence dragged on, Roddy gave her a frowning look. He rolled slowly to a sitting position, unwittingly showcasing those iron abs.

"Squirt? Are you okay?"

She opened her mouth, but nothing came out. She shook her head and put up her dirty palm, asking him to let it go.

He frowned. "Hey, I was just kidding, squirt. You know I think you're—"

"No," she said. "It's not that. It's just that—" she held out her bare ring finger "—Freddy and I have called off the engagement."

If she'd thought Roddy would gloat or make fun, she had underestimated him. He took her muddy hand gently, by the fingertips, as if he were a knight ready to bestow a respectful kiss. He rubbed the empty spot on her finger with his callused thumb.

He looked at her. "What happened?"

She suddenly wished she'd spent her afternoon thinking up a good story. One that would help her save face. A story that might make her feel less like a piece of trash that had been crumpled up and thrown away.

But the truth would have to do. Wasn't it trying to hide from the truth that had gotten her into this mess in the first place? Supposedly all this sacrifice was about starting over. If she began with another lie, then what was the point?

And if she couldn't tell the truth to Roddy, then who could she tell it to? Roddy was the least judgmental person she knew.

"I had been lying to Freddy," she said. "I had an

ugly secret in my past, and I'd been keeping it from him. Finally I decided I had to—"

She stopped. "No, that's not exactly true. Mallory *convinced* me that I had to tell him the truth. I was afraid to, but I didn't have any choice. So I told him, even though I knew it would probably mean we'd break up."

Roddy was still frowning. "And did it?"

"Yes." She had to shut her eyes for a minute. She could still see Freddy's face. He had been so shocked, so betrayed. So heartbroken.

Much as she'd like to demonize him, make him the bad guy in this story, she knew that he had loved her, and that losing her was tearing him up inside. It was just that they both knew he couldn't give up his dream, not without coming to hate her in the end.

Roddy growled. "God damn the man. I knew he was a stick, but I didn't know he was a gutless son of a bitch."

"He's not," Mindy said. "I was the gutless one. I let it go too far. I should have told him six months ago."

"Told him what? How bad could it be? Unless your dirty secret is that you're really a guy under all those curves, I can't see how it would make a damn bit of difference."

She hesitated. Even now, it was hard to say it.

"It's pretty bad," she said. She licked her lips and gathered enough breath to force the words out. "I—I was a member of the Heyday Eight."

He stared at her a long minute, not even blinking.

Oh, God, she was going to lose him, too. He'd been her best friend, her protector…and now this.

"Just once," she said. "Just one night. One man. But it's enough. You know how ruthless campaigns can get, and if Freddy were ever running for office, and this got out—"

Without warning, Roddy stood and took her into his arms. "Aw, squirt," he said, his voice strangely husky and warm. "I'm sorry, sweetheart. I'm so damn sorry."

She held herself stiffly erect for as long as she could. All day, she had tried so hard not to cry. And she'd been successful. Even with Freddy, she hadn't broken down.

But then, because Roddy's arms were familiar and completely safe, she finally let go. She cried without noise, but without embarrassment. She cried until the tears had washed her face clean. And then, as soon as she'd cried herself dry, he relaxed his hold on her and let her go.

"Is that all?" He reached out and straightened her hair, which had plastered itself to her cheeks. "That's your only secret?"

She touched her hands to her belly. "No. I'm also going to have a baby."

"No." Roddy squeezed his eyes shut and groaned. "Aw, man. The *stick's* baby?"

She frowned. "Roddy."

"Sorry." He shrugged. "It's just that…well, I don't give a damn about that stupid Heyday Eight stuff. It bothers me a heck of a lot more to hear you're going to have the stick's baby."

"Roddy!"

He grinned. "Sorry. *Mr. Earnshaw's* baby. Yeah, that's definitely more of a problem to me."

That surprised her. He was so unconventional himself, and he came from a long line of rebels. Besides, his mother had always volunteered at a charity for unwed mothers. Once, during Roddy's high-school years, when the "safe home" was overcrowded, the Hartland family had housed a couple of the girls. That had provided lots of great jokes about whether any house with Roddy in it could possibly be considered safe.

"I know you must be disappointed in me," she said. "I know I have been irresponsible. But I intend to be the best mother I can possibly be. I'll—"

"God, squirt, would you please stop talking to me like I'm your obnoxious great-uncle? *Disappointed* in you? What a load of moralistic bunk." He seemed to be working at trying to hold in his frustration. "Look. I don't have the right to be disappointed in you, and even if I *did* have the right, I wouldn't be."

"Well, what is it, then?" She really was confused. "Why does knowing about the baby upset you more than—"

"Because—" He scratched his chest, and a dusting of sawdust sprinkled to the ground. She had his sawdust on her lips, she realized, from crying on his shoulder.

He sighed. "Look, squirt, the timing here couldn't be worse, I know that. But this helpless, abandoned, unwed-mother thing is going to make you even more adorable than ever. If I don't speak up, some other guy is going to ride in on a white horse and rescue you, and I'll lose my chance."

"Your chance for what?"

"To tell you that I'm crazy about you. That I love you, and I always have."

This time she was speechless. She just stared and wondered what the punch line of this joke was going to be.

"Well? I'm pretty sure you're supposed to say something now," he said, laughing. "Like, 'this is so sudden,' or 'I never knew,' or even 'how could you, when you know my heart will always belong to the stick?'"

She ran her hand through her tangled hair, perplexed. "How about, 'you've got to be kidding?'"

He nodded. "Okay. That's a start. Then I say, I'm *not* kidding. I really do love you. And you say—"

"I—" She shook her head helplessly. "This is so sudden. And I really never knew."

"Very good." He arched his brows. "And?"

She smiled. "And it's too soon, Roddy. Too soon for me to be able to think about anything like this." She looked down at her bare left hand, feeling the twinge that she knew would soon become a torment. "I really loved him, you know."

He grinned. "Yeah, I know. But he blew it. And eventually you'll get over him. And then it's going to be my turn."

She had no idea what to say. Nothing on earth could have shocked her more.

But she didn't have time to think of a sensible response, because suddenly she saw Tyler Balfour running across the grass toward them.

"Mindy," he said without preamble. "Where's Mallory?"

"I don't know," she said, startled by the urgency in his voice and the automatic assumption that, if she knew the answer, she would be willing to tell him.

She had met him back during the Heyday Eight investigation, of course. She couldn't have missed him. He'd always been hanging around their café. But since then the two of them hadn't exchanged a single word, and she had hoped they never would. They hardly qualified as intimate friends.

Still, something in his face made her put all that aside and answer frankly.

"She was here a couple of hours ago, but then she left." She glanced over at the stores on Hippodrome, which, she noticed for the first time, were still dark and without power. Oh, she should have called Mallory hours ago, as she'd promised she would. "Have you checked the bookstore, or the apartment?"

"I came here first, but I'm going there now." He handed her a scrap of paper on which he'd scribbled some numbers. "If you hear from her, tell her to call me. Tell her it's important."

And then he turned around and began loping back toward the street.

The blackmailer.

He's getting edgy, Mallory had said. Mindy knew instinctively that something new had happened, something that disturbed even the cynical Tyler Balfour.

Mindy, whose heart was suddenly racing in her chest, looked at Roddy for about half a second. And then, without saying a word, they both began to run after him.

CHAPTER SEVENTEEN

MALLORY RETURNED to the bookstore a mere twenty minutes after she left it. And she felt only slightly better.

Both Heyday deputies were out trying to round up looters who had been seen removing jewelry and electronics from some of the unguarded homes without power in Riverside Park. There was no one in the station right now to come out and look over Mallory's damaged books.

The dispatcher who had taken her statement was very nice, and had considerately asked whether Mallory believed there was any emergency. If not, she promised to have an officer come by Mallory's store the minute one of them was free.

That would have to be good enough. In the meantime, the woman had suggested that Mallory might want to secure the evidence. If she'd left it in a building where security was compromised by broken doors, windows and so forth, Mallory might want to consider putting it somewhere safer.

For now, Tyler's new security system was inoperative on both floors, as it relied on electricity. But at least if Mallory kept the box of books upstairs with her, no one could take it without her knowledge.

She wasn't nervous about going into the store alone, not really. Still, she had to admit she did look first to see if Tyler's car was in the parking lot.

It wasn't.

But she refused to be childish about this. Why should she let a little darkness make her afraid of her own store? She'd left small handheld lanterns at all the entryways, so she'd be fine.

When she let herself in the side door, though, the lantern wasn't there. She knelt and felt around with both hands but encountered nothing.

Rats. In her haste, she must have forgotten this door. There was definitely a lantern at the cash register, she was sure of that. She made her way across the room like a blind person, remembering where every piece of furniture was placed, and feeling with her hands for anything that might have been disarranged by the storm.

Her instincts started prickling, sending a weird shivering across her scalp, just about the time she heard a tiny noise. She didn't have enough time to process what kind of noise it was—small, scurrying animal? rustling paper? something more sinister?—before her hands, groping at chest level, ran into something big, something firm enough to be a piece of furniture, but shockingly warm, as if alive.

She let out a small cry, because her instincts knew

even before her conscious mind understood. It *was* alive. It was a man.

"Who—"

But she never even got the word out. A large hand came out of nowhere and clapped hard across her mouth. A rough arm wrapped her across the chest, smashing her painfully, back first, up against the man's torso.

No. She writhed, trying to get leverage, trying to slip out of his grasp. But he was strong, and he held her so firmly that as she struggled, his arm burned and pinched her breasts, sending red flashes shooting behind her eyes.

She tried to bite his hand, but he covered her from nose to jaw, and she couldn't find an opening anywhere, not even one small enough to let through a little air.

She kicked backward, but there was no force behind it. She fought harder, stretching her arms until the sockets burned, searching for anything big enough, or sharp enough to hurt.

There was nothing. He just stood there, holding her like a disobedient kitten, enduring her scratching and kicking without even breathing hard.

She hated him, whoever he was. She hated that he had violated her store, her books, her life. She hated his big, horrible hand that choked off the air so casually, as if she had a right to breathe only if he decided to let her.

She would have killed him right now if she could.

But how much longer could it go on? What would she do if she couldn't get free?

She felt her lungs pulling desperately, her jaw straining to move, to open, to break the seal…and getting nothing.

Her head began to spin, and the red lights of pain started to flicker with a strobe effect. And then, suddenly he released her. Stumbling away from him, she knew she should scream, but first she had to feed her lungs, which were burning and heaving, as if, in that short horrible starvation, they had forgotten how breathing worked.

And then she felt the gun. Up against the small of her back. The thrust of its nose was grotesquely sexual. He pushed, then pushed harder, until she was bent over the cash register's counter, the gun still nestled in the hollow at the base of her spine.

"You shouldn't have come back, Mallory," he said.

Shock made her whip her head around, which seemed to infuriate him. He put his meaty hand against the crown of her head and forced her face into the countertop.

But why should he be so afraid of her seeing him? She didn't need to see this man to know who he was. She'd know that voice anywhere. She'd heard it every night before she went to bed and every morning when she woke up for six long years.

It was Dan.

"What are you doing here?" She hoped he could understand her words, even though the countertop smashed her lips strangely, and her voice sounded muffled even to her own ears.

"I'm getting something that belongs to me," he said. "You aren't supposed to be here. You shouldn't have come home."

She tried to swallow, but something on the desk, something hard, was cutting into her throat, and she couldn't do it.

"You're the one, aren't you?" She tried to turn her head again, but he wound his fingers into her hair and forced her face back down. "The one who's been blackmailing me."

He laughed at that, as if it were the most ridiculous question on earth. "You made it so easy," he said. "I knew it would be. I knew you couldn't think straight when it comes to that little bitch."

"You mean Mindy," she said. Of course he meant Mindy, but now that her head was clearing and she was getting over the shock of finding out who it was, she felt a little less panicked, a little more focused.

The big bad anonymous bogeyman had somehow been much more terrifying than Dan Platt could ever be. Dan was mean and petty and obviously a very dangerous man. But he was still just Dan, and she knew there had to be a way to outsmart him.

The most important thing was to buy some time. This was her store, her turf. She might be able to make something out of that. If she failed, at least the police were aware that she had asked for help. They'd show up sooner or later. So, perhaps, would Tyler.

Or Mindy…

Fear began to race through her again. Not Mindy. Of all things, she must keep Mindy away from this.

She forced herself not to think about Mindy. Right now she just needed to keep Dan talking.

"Would you really have exposed her, Dan?"

He laughed again. "Hell, yes, I would. She's a stuck-up little brat, and she needs taking down a peg. Both of you do. You always thought you were so much better than I am, didn't you? What a joke. A frigid bitch and a dirty whore."

"We didn't think that we—"

The gun pushed so hard into her that she felt the rim of its nose scrape her spine. She arced her back, trying to escape the pain.

"Yes, you did," he said harshly. "You married me, God only knows why you did that, and then you froze me out. You refused to touch me for six months. And then how shocked and disgusted you were when I found some warmth somewhere else."

You didn't find it, she thought. *You bought it.*

But she didn't say it out loud. She could only imagine how strung out he was already, how tense that finger was upon the trigger. She had to find a way to keep him from pulling it.

"But you've found another girl now, Dan. Jeannie is warm. Jeannie loves you."

"That's right," he said. "And you're going to try to spoil that, too."

"No," she said. "No, why would I do that?"

He twisted his hand in her hair viciously, pulling at the roots so hard it brought stinging tears to her eyes. "I saw you tonight. I saw you go to the police station. You are going to give them the books, aren't you? The books I left you as a little present."

"No," she said. "The books are still here. You can take them."

"Bullshit. You just want me to take this gun out of your back. You'd never give me all of them. You'd always keep one, to put me in jail with. You've seen my new wife. Do you really think she'd still be sitting around waiting for me when I got out?"

She didn't answer. She couldn't focus on him right now. She had finally thought of a plan, and now she just needed the courage to carry it out.

There was a very large, very sharp pair of scissors in the left-hand drawer of this counter. She kept them there to cut open cartons of books as they arrived. Wally sometimes took them out and pretended to clean his nails with them, amused that they were so huge.

She was pretty sure she could reach them, as long as he kept her stretched out like this across the counter. But she also knew he'd hear the sound of the drawer opening, and, if he realized what she was up to, he could reach out and slam it shut on her fingers before she had the chance do anything.

Or else he'd take the easy route and shoot her.

So she had to create a diversion. She had to pretend to panic, make some noise, flail about wildly. Anything to keep him from suspecting that her movements were deliberate, that she was reaching for those scissors.

It was going to hurt dreadfully. Already her breasts, with the edge of the counter cutting into them, were on fire with pain. Her nose throbbed from slamming into the counter. The instinct was to stay as still as possible, to keep from making the torment worse.

But she had to fight that instinct. And she had to do it quickly, before he decided to move her to another spot.

"Dan," she said, "please let me go. I can't breathe. I can't breathe."

She began to wriggle. She twisted, ignoring the red-hot pincers of pain that shot through her chest and shoulders and spine. She felt the warmth of seeping blood where her breasts were scraped raw.

But she couldn't let herself stop. She made choking sounds and began to move her arms in terrified, jerking motions.

He laughed. "Too bad you didn't have this much fire in you when we were married." He stepped closer and ground his pelvis against her a couple of times obscenely, unaware or uncaring that she was nearly torn in two with pain. "I might not have needed to go out looking for love in all the wrong places."

The bastard. She thought of the years she had let him make love to her. She thought of him standing over her books, soiling them. She was afraid she might be sick, which would be disastrous, with her face pressed painfully against the counter.

So she took her horror, her revulsion and her fear, and she used it to push away all awareness of pain. She jerked and twisted.

"Let me go, let me go, let me go." She went slightly mad, and finally he was panting, too, just trying to hold her still.

"You're going to get it now, you hellcat." He released her hair to free a hand so that he could unzip his pants. "It's time somebody taught you a lesson."

But finally her hands had touched the cold metal of the scissors. She couldn't find the holes, so she grabbed them around the shaft.

And then she reached back and drove them into his leg.

He screamed, backing away. She heard the gun fall to the floor.

She didn't wait to see how much damage she'd done. She began to run. But he was running, too. Then there was a gunshot. He had found the gun again, even in the dark. He had found it. And now he was going to kill her.

She almost made it to the front door. But then she tripped on a battery-operated fan someone had left there to help dry out the carpet. She banged her head on the CD display case as she went down. She felt her limbs go limp.

She heard him coming behind her, but she didn't seem to be able to do anything to get away.

And then, miraculously, the front door burst open. She saw a confusion of torchlights, and a lot of bodies, lots of men and noise. Was it the police?

Or had Tyler finally come home? If she was going to die here, there was something she'd like to tell him.

More gunshots rang out. A man yelled in pain. More people called out, more jiggling, crazed torch beams.

One of the beams caught her in its glare. And then Mindy was suddenly there, kneeling beside her.

"Mallory," Mindy cried. "Mallory, are you all right?"

"I'm fine," she said, or at least she hoped she said that. Her throat felt bruised, and her mind was a little fuzzy. She started to mention that her chest was bleeding, and something warm was running down her temple, but that didn't seem to matter right now. It was so good to feel Mindy's arms around her.

"Sit still, you son of a bitch," a voice in the darkness said irritably, "or we'll shoot you again."

Mallory raised up on one elbow. That was Tyler's voice. "Tyler?" Her voice sounded raspy and unfamiliar. "Is that you?"

"Yes," he said. "I'm here. I brought some friends, just in case you needed help."

"You brought the police?"

"Not exactly," another voice said. She knew that voice, too. It was Bryce McClintock. "All he could find was a little band of brothers, but apparently that was enough to do the trick. Dan here—it is that asshole Dan, isn't it? He's not going to be bothering you anymore."

Suddenly, there was a crackle, a flicker, and then a

flood of lights. The power company, working around the clock as they had promised, had finally prevailed.

Mallory blinked, squinting, unable to bear the sudden illumination. She ducked her head into Mindy's lap and, as she did, it occurred to her that this was the first time she had ever turned to her little sister for help. It had always been the other way around.

Mindy stroked her head gently. It was, surprisingly, one of the most comforting feelings in the world.

When her eyes could see again, she looked at the scene before her, trying to figure out what exactly had happened. Dan was kneeling on the floor, holding his right arm and moaning. There seemed to be a large crowd of men standing over him.

Tyler and Bryce, but that wasn't all. Kieran, too. And Roddy. Poor Dan, she thought with a stupid smile. He hadn't had a chance.

Tyler was making sure Dan stayed put, but Kieran seemed to be holding a gun, staring at it bemusedly.

Bryce chuckled and patted Kieran on the shoulder. "You did great, bro."

"I don't shoot people," Kieran said. He scowled at Bryce. "You shoot people. It's your gun, damn it. You should have been the one to do it."

Bryce held up his cast with a smile. "Can't. I'm on injured reserve. Besides, Lara said I'm not allowed to shoot anybody anymore."

Kieran glared at Tyler. "We should have made *him* do it," he said. "Mallory is his girlfriend. How come we didn't make *him* do it?"

Bryce shook his head. "He would have killed the guy. Remember? We decided Tyler couldn't be trusted not to go for the throat."

Kieran still looked grumpy, but Bryce seemed to think it was hilarious. "Oh, get over it. You didn't kill anybody. You're just ticked off because you know this is the end of that Saint thing."

Then the police arrived, and then some EMT guys, and it took two of them to pick Dan up off the floor. Dan squealed. "She stabbed me!"

One of the emergency technicians reached over, checked his leg and then slowly pulled the scissors out of Dan's meaty thigh.

"Two inches, at least," Tyler said admiringly. "Way to go, Mallory. Looks as if maybe you didn't really need us at all."

She had about one full second of basking in the warmth of his tone. It was true, wasn't it? She had done okay, all things considering.

And then she fainted.

CHAPTER EIGHTEEN

AS SHE SAT in the front office of Valley Pride Property Management Inc. the next morning, Mallory gazed at Elton Fletcher with extreme distaste. Not only was the guy much too militaristic and supercilious, he was too darn slow. He was supposed to be giving her the exact location of where Tyler and his insurance adjuster were working right now, but it was taking forever.

"Let's see," he said, hovering over his document protectively, as if Mallory might be planning to steal some of his addresses. "I know he was going to try to hit all the affected properties this morning, but in what order? I had a list, but—"

Mallory tried to be patient. "Why don't you just give me all the addresses, and I'll take responsibility for tracking him down?"

"Oh, that wouldn't be efficient," Elton said with a note of horror. He frowned at his desk, as if it had somehow disappointed him. "I have a list here somewhere."

It was a good thing Mindy had offered to open up

the bookstore for Mallory this morning because, at this pace, Mallory was never going to make it back in time.

It was just one of many humble, helpful gestures Mindy had made in the past twelve hours. Mallory had been afraid that her little sister might blame her for the collapse of her engagement. After all, it had been Mallory who insisted that the truth be told.

But to Mallory's amazement, Mindy had never seemed to consider that possibility. If anything, she took on too much of the blame. Even when Mallory explained that Dan's rage was at Mallory herself, that Mindy was just the weapon he had chosen to hurt her with, Mindy wouldn't let herself off the hook.

After Mallory had been checked out at the hospital last night, and released with only a couple of bandages and a prescription for a painkiller, Mindy had driven her back to the apartment and spent the rest of the night tending to her every possible need.

Tyler had disappeared much earlier, with Dan and the police. Roddy had been assigned to follow the ladies to the hospital and make sure everything was okay.

Mallory had hoped, at first, that Tyler might come back, if not to check on her, at least to his own apartment. But he never did. She had no idea where he spent the night.

Luckily, she didn't have time to brood over it. She and Mindy had so much to talk about.

They had hardly slept at all. They'd talked about Dan, and the blackmailing, and the horror in the bookshop. Talking it out helped, Mallory discovered. It made it seem less monstrous and unmentionable.

Later they'd discussed the inevitability that Mindy's involvement with the Eight would finally be made public. Mindy seemed amazingly calm about having her secret exposed—she said she'd already told everyone who mattered, and she could handle the rest. But she wasn't able to share her emotions about Freddy and the breakup yet. The grief was too raw.

At the very last, they'd talked about the baby. And after the tears and shame had spent themselves, they'd found joy in the prospect. They had giggled and dreamed and invented crazy names, like Peacock Glockenspiel for a girl, and Bowtie Juggernaut for a boy.

"You know, Ms. Rackham, I believe he has his cell phone with him," Elton said, eyeing her a little suspiciously. It apparently had just occurred to him that, if Tyler had wanted to see Mallory, then Tyler would probably have told her where to find him. "Why don't I call him now and tell him you'd like an appointment?"

Mallory shook her head. "I would rather surprise him," she said. She couldn't say the things she needed to say over the telephone. It had to be done in person.

Of course, they could call and simply ask him where he was right now, but, as Elton so shrewdly guessed, she couldn't be certain that Tyler would even want to see her. The last time they were alone together, they had both said hurtful things. He might not have forgiven her, in spite of the way he rode to her rescue last night.

"You're not looking to buy, are you?" Elton was watching her carefully. "Because if you are, you probably should leave a bid with me now. Mr. Balfour is in a hurry to liquidate all his assets in Heyday. That's why he rushed the insurance adjuster out today. He isn't planning to rebuild any of the damaged structures. Just tear them down and sell the land at bargain-basement prices."

Mallory stared at the fussy little man whose clothes looked so stiff they might have been made of plastic. His tight face made him look cruel, but he was probably speaking nothing more than the truth. The master plan he'd just outlined definitely fit with everything she'd ever heard Tyler say.

"Mr. Fletcher," she said. "Please give me the most likely address. Otherwise, I'll have to call Kieran and tell him you were unable—or unwilling—to help me."

Elton sniffed, clearly offended that she had pulled rank. She and Kieran had been friends since childhood.

"Well, I'd assume the most problematic property is the house on King's Mirror Lake. It has a historical designation, so I'm not sure he can just tear it down. He may be stuck with that one."

She knew that house, though she hadn't realized that Tyler had inherited it.

It was, in a way, the house of her dreams if she'd ever allowed herself to dream about owning a house, which she didn't, as it was obviously out of reach.

But this house was a beautiful mansion from the early 1900s that had been built on the edge of town. The owner had believed the city would grow out to meet it, but most development had moved toward Grupton, in the other direction. The marvelous old house still sat in isolated splendor, with at least ten acres of unspoiled land all around.

She made her way there quickly. What had seemed quite remote a hundred years ago was only a ten-minute drive today. And the owner's dream just might be going to come true before too long. Someone had erected a billboard announcing the arrival of Heyday's newest gated community, King's Mirror Lake Estates.

Several cars were parked in the semicircular driveway in front of the house. One of them, she saw with relief, belonged to Tyler. She pulled up next to a large iron statue of a ringmaster, complete with top hat, red tails and, thank goodness, a baton instead of a whip. She patted the iron man on the head for luck and went up the driveway toward the house.

You could tell this place had been built after Moresville changed its name to Heyday. The circus theme was everywhere.

The elegant double front door had stained-glass sidelights, and in each one a zebra stood on its hind legs amid a backdrop of bright green leaves. The black and white and green color scheme was repeated everywhere—on the house, on the mailbox, in the flower boxes and plantings and drapes that blew softly through the many large, opened windows.

The only other color in the picture came from the lake, which you could just glimpse on each side of the house. King's Mirror was one of Heyday's largest natural lakes. And, as its name implied, it was elegantly oval, eternally placid, always mirroring back the condition of the sky overhead.

And today the sky was a clear and royal blue.

She wondered if Tyler really would tear down this house if he could. She didn't want to believe it. If he could look on this much history, this much atmosphere and charm, and be unmoved...

Well, if he could do that, then perhaps her old opinion of Tyler was the correct one. Maybe all the new, more sensitive things she thought she'd glimpsed in him had been merely wishful thinking.

She heard voices out back, so she didn't bother knocking on the door. She walked around the side of the house, past a regal, spreading oak that had probably been planted the year the house was built. At the very back, a group of men were standing beside a huge toppled elm, which had fallen straight onto the kitchen roof.

Two of the men were holding chain saws, and two more were holding clipboards, making notes. The rest of the men were McClintocks. Tyler, Bryce and Kieran were all studying the problem, talking quietly together.

Kieran saw her first.

"Mallory!" He came over and gave her the gentlest of hugs. Obviously he hadn't forgotten all the smears of blood on her clothes last night. "What are you doing out here? I thought we gave you strict orders to take today and stay in bed."

Bryce came up with his usual rakish smile and, bowing, took her hand and kissed it. "This lady doesn't take orders, Kieran, she gives them. Just ask our friend Dan Platt."

More slowly, Tyler made his way over, too. It obviously would have looked odd if he hadn't kissed her, so he gave her a careful, fraternal peck on the cheek. He looked tired, she thought. She loved the McClintock boys, but right now she wished Bryce and Kieran were anywhere on this earth but here.

"Hi," Tyler said, a little stiltedly. "How are you feeling?"

"I'm fine," she said. "Much better, thanks."

Kieran and Bryce exchanged a grimace. Together, as if they were twins with one mind, they patted Tyler on the back.

"Well, we'd better get going," Bryce said. "Urgent business in…um…where was that urgent business of ours, Kieran?"

Kieran grinned. "I forget." He winked at Mallory. "But we'd better get going or we'll be late. See you later, Tyler. I'll get John Gordon to draw up the papers. We can sign everything tomorrow."

Tyler nodded. "Great. Tomorrow will be good."

And then, with another round of careful kisses and backslapping, the other men were gone.

"I'm sorry," Mallory said, watching Bryce and Kieran walk to their cars, still laughing and teasing each other mercilessly. "I didn't mean to break up your meeting."

"We were already finished," he said. "Besides, I'm glad to see you. Are you really fine? Last night was very difficult, I know. I would have come to check on you, but I thought you and your sister might need some time together."

"Yes," she said. "We did. It was good for us. But I—" She hesitated. "I missed you."

He looked out over the lake. "How's Mindy?"

She flushed. The change of subject was so abrupt it was almost painful. He could hardly have been more clear. He didn't want to talk about personal things. He had gone back to his detached-journalist persona.

"Good," she said, attempting to match his neutral tone. "She's doing well. She's going to stay in Heyday for a couple of days, just to be sure I'm okay. After that, she needs to go back to Richmond, at least for a couple of weeks. She says she can't quit her job without giving notice, but then she's coming back to Heyday for good."

Mallory had been surprised to hear that, but Mindy had insisted that it was time she gave Mallory a little help, both with the store and with caring for their mother. Running away from her past meant that Mindy had run away from her obligations, too.

From now on, Mindy had vowed, things were going to be different.

"That's great. She'll need family right now." He turned to her with a somber look. "I'm sorry to hear the engagement is off."

She nodded. "Yes, it's very sad. But it was just too big a hurdle. About Freddy—of course you were right all along."

A pulse worked in his lower jaw. "I would rather have been wrong," he said. "I hope you can believe that."

She wasn't quite sure how to begin, but this seemed like an opening, a chink in the fortress he'd built of deliberate, careful indifference. She knew she had to seize it.

"I do believe it," she said. "That's why I've come. I know you're leaving soon, and I wanted you to know that I appreciate the many ways you've befriended both of us—last night, of course, but many times before that, too. Sometimes I was so caught up in my own emotions that I couldn't see when you were giving me good advice."

Somewhere behind them a worker cursed colorfully, and then they heard the sound of a chain saw spinning into action.

Out front, she heard more cars pulling into the driveway. The insurance adjuster, perhaps? She knew she had very little time left, and she'd better make it count.

"I—" This was so important, but confusion tied up her words in knots. What should she say? In some ways, this man she saw before her now felt like a stranger to her.

It was as if there were two Tyler Balfours.

One was the professional Stranger, not the type

to get involved. An observer, never a participant. He had made it clear he'd come to Heyday to do a job, not to adopt a new family, a new woman or a new town.

And yet his actions contradicted that over and over again. Whether he meant to or not, he *had* become involved. He'd cared for her when she was sick, tended her store, even visited her mother. He had climbed into a flooding car to pull his half brother, a man he supposedly didn't care about, to freedom.

He had made love to her in the moonlight.

And, last night, he had been ready to kill a man for hurting her.

So which one was the real Tyler? The distant, detached stranger who saw everyone as material for his book? Or the warm lover who had protected her at every turn?

Maybe Elton Fletcher was right. Maybe Tyler couldn't wait to get out of Heyday. But maybe, just maybe, the little man was wrong. Maybe, in spite of his best intentions, Tyler had come to care about Heyday and the men here who were tied to him by blood.

And what about her? Had he come to feel anything about her?

If she didn't take a risk right here, right now, she might never know.

"There's something else I wanted to say. The other night, when we—" She swallowed, the movement stinging a little, one of the echoes of last night that would take a little while to die away.

"When we made love," she finished firmly. "I want you to know that I didn't have any ulterior motives that night. And I don't believe that you did, either. I think we both had wanted that for a long time, and it just happened, that's all. I want you to know that I'm not sorry it did."

"You're not?" He lifted his shoulders slightly. "I am."

She felt stung, and yet part of her couldn't believe he was serious. It had been good. It had been *great*. He had more experience than she did, obviously, but some things didn't take experience. You just knew.

"You're sorry we made love? Why?"

He gazed down at her. She noticed that his eyes were as blue as the lake behind him. "Because there will never be another night like that for me."

The words were spoken softly, with an honesty that took her by surprise. Though her heart beat high in her throat, she owed him honesty in return.

"No," she said. "There will never be another night like that. Unless—"

"Unless what?"

Oh, this was too hard. But she had told Mindy to be brave, to speak the truth whatever the consequences. And Mindy had found the courage to do exactly that. How could Mallory do any less?

So she swallowed her fear and let her heart speak for itself.

"Maybe someday—" No, that was wrong. She started over. "I know that while you're in the middle of this book you can't get personally involved with anyone here, anyone you might have to write about. I'm not asking you to set aside your principles. I'm just saying that maybe, when the book is finished, you might consider coming back to Heyday."

She took a deep breath. "You might consider coming back to me."

His handsome face did not change. He still looked somber, giving no clue to his own thoughts.

She stood her ground, refusing to look away in shame. The truth might be difficult, but there was no shame in it.

"You're right," he said finally. "Objectivity is a serious ethical issue. When I'm writing this book, I must have no personal ties to anyone involved."

"I understand," she said.

"And that's why I've decided not to write it."

What? She frowned. What did that mean? Not write it? He had already signed a contract. He'd devoted months to the research. *Deciding not to write it* couldn't possibly be an option.

"I don't understand," she said.

"Neither do I." He put his hand out and touched her cheek. "I don't understand how, in such a short time, you've come to mean more to me than anything else in my life, including my career, but you have."

The world around them seemed suddenly filled with a spring sweetness, as if the wildflowers had all burst into bloom.

And yet, afraid to believe, she held her breath. "Tyler—"

"The book means nothing to me anymore. If I could take back any of the pain I've ever caused you or your family, I would. I certainly can avoid causing any more. I've already told my publisher I won't exploit the tragedy this town has suffered. I've bought my way out of my contract."

She couldn't believe what he was saying. As one of Anderson McClintock's heirs, he wasn't exactly poor, but it must have cost him many, many thousands to free himself from this commitment.

"Why?" She shook her head. "Why would you do such a thing?"

He smiled. "Because I love you, of course. Because I love you more than I thought I was capable of loving anyone."

She caught her breath. She reached up and put her hand over his. "Tyler," she said again.

But he wasn't finished. "And because when I thought Dan Platt might have hurt you, when I thought we might get there too late, I nearly went insane. I don't know how you broke down every barrier I ever built, Mallory. I just know you did. I'm exposed, for the first time in my life. It scares the hell out of me, but there's no way for me to go back behind those barriers now."

"Don't try," she said, her voice suddenly urgent. "I

need you out here with me. I'm as exposed as you are, Tyler. And I'm scared, too."

His hand tightened. "Does that mean you love me? In spite of all the mistakes I've made in the past?"

She felt such a rush of joy she couldn't help laughing. How could he even question this? Wasn't her love written all over her face? It was certainly written in her heart, and in her soul.

"You mean can I love you in spite of how you taught me that the truth really does set us free? In spite of saving me from Dan—not just once, but twice? In spite of helping me see that my sister needed a chance to grow up and learn to respect herself? In spite of showing me how magical it can be when two people come together with real passion? Yes," she said, smiling. "I can love you, in spite of all that."

He took her in his arms then, cautiously. She wanted to tell him it was all right, that Dan had not hurt her so very much, but she loved the tender, careful look on his face.

"Can you love me," he said, "if I sell everything I've inherited to buy the *Heyday Herald?* Can you love me if I'm just a hand-to-mouth, small-town journalist?"

"Yes," she said. "Speaking as a hand-to-mouth, small-town bookseller, I think I can."

"And what about my obnoxious brothers?" He grinned in a way that made him look very like those brothers. "Can you love me in spite of the fact that I seem, after all, to be a McClintock?"

"Yes," she said. "I bring a few sibling issues of my own, you know. So yes, in spite of your terrible brothers, I can."

His arms grew tighter, and his eyes began to take on that smoldering look she was learning to adore.

"And what about the home I'll bring you to? It's the only one I've kept, and the historical society won't let me change a thing. Can you love me in spite of the fact that you'll have the tackiest front door in all of Heyday?"

She looked over at the beautiful white house. In an instant, behind those windblown curtains, she thought she could see their whole future. They would be happy here. They would sing in the kitchen and make love on the porch. He would write by lamplight, late at night in their bedroom.

Their children, and Mindy's children, and Bryce's and Kieran's children would climb these trees and splash in the clear blue lake.

And, tacky or not, she knew that they would love the stained glass leaping zebras. Perhaps they would even name the zebras. Peacock Glockenspiel and Bowtie Juggernaut might work just fine....

"Yes, I can," she said again, lifting her face for his kiss. "In fact, the only thing I can't do, Tyler, is marry anyone but you."

"*Darn right* you can't," he said, pulling her close and growling softly.

And in that moment, she observed with delight, Tyler Balfour had never looked more like his brothers. She rested her head on his chest, knowing that everything was just as it should be.

The last of the heroes of Heyday had finally found his way home.

* * * * *

Watch for Kathleen O'Brien's next book,
Happily Never After, a Signature
Select Spotlight book available in
August 2005.

HARLEQUIN® *Super*ROMANCE®

Come to Shelter Valley, Arizona, with
Tara Taylor Quinn...

...and with Caroline Prater, who's new to town. Caroline, from rural Kentucky, is a widow and a single mother.

She's also pregnant—after a brief affair with John Strickland, who lives in Shelter Valley.

And although she's always known she was adopted, Caroline's just discovered she has a twin sister she didn't know about. A twin who doesn't know about her. A twin who lives in Shelter Valley...and is a friend of John Strickland's.

Shelter Valley. Read the books. Live the life.

"Quinn writes touching stories about real people that transcend plot type or genre."
—Rachel Potter, *All About Romance*

SPECIAL EDITION™

THE ROSE COTTAGE SISTERS

Love and laughter surprise them at their childhood haven.

What's Cooking?

SHERRYL WOODS

**Silhouette Special Edition #1675
On sale April 2005!**

Fleeing a burgeoning romance with a renowned playboy, food editor Maggie D'Angelo escapes to Rose Cottage, vowing to put love on the back burner. But Rick Flannery intends to turn up the heat, and soon Maggie is face-to-face with the sexy fashion photographer who makes her blood sizzle!

**Meet more Rose Cottage
Sisters later this year!**

**THE LAWS OF ATTRACTION—
Available May 2005**

**FOR THE LOVE OF PETE—
Available June 2005**

Only from Silhouette Books!

If you enjoyed what you just read,
then we've got an offer you can't resist!

Take 2 bestselling
love stories FREE!
Plus get a FREE surprise gift!

Clip this page and mail it to Harlequin Reader Service®

IN U.S.A.
3010 Walden Ave.
P.O. Box 1867
Buffalo, N.Y. 14240-1867

IN CANADA
P.O. Box 609
Fort Erie, Ontario
L2A 5X3

YES! Please send me 2 free Harlequin Superromance® novels and my free surprise gift. After receiving them, if I don't wish to receive anymore, I can return the shipping statement marked cancel. If I don't cancel, I will receive 6 brand-new novels every month, before they're available in stores. In the U.S.A., bill me at the bargain price of $4.69 plus 25¢ shipping and handling per book and applicable sales tax, if any*. In Canada, bill me at the bargain price of $5.24 plus 25¢ shipping and handling per book and applicable taxes**. That's the complete price, and a savings of at least 10% off the cover prices—what a great deal! I understand that accepting the 2 free books and gift places me under no obligation ever to buy any books. I can always return a shipment and cancel at any time. Even if I never buy another book from Harlequin, the 2 free books and gift are mine to keep forever.

135 HDN DZ7W
336 HDN DZ7X

Name	(PLEASE PRINT)	
Address	Apt.#	
City	State/Prov.	Zip/Postal Code

Not valid to current Harlequin Superromance® subscribers.

Want to try two free books from another series?
Call 1-800-873-8635 or visit www.morefreebooks.com.

* Terms and prices subject to change without notice. Sales tax applicable in N.Y.
** Canadian residents will be charged applicable provincial taxes and GST.
All orders subject to approval. Offer limited to one per household.
® are registered trademarks owned and used by the trademark owner and or its licensee.

SUP04R   ©2004 Harlequin Enterprises Limited

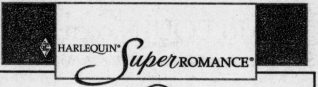

HARLEQUIN *Super*ROMANCE®

On sale May 2005

With Child by Janice Kay Johnson
(SR #1273)

All was right in Mindy Fenton's world when she went to bed one night. But before it was over everything had changed—and not for the better. She was awakened by Brendan Quinn with the news that her husband had been shot and killed. Now Mindy is alone and pregnant…and Quinn is the only one she can turn to.

On sale June 2005

Pregnant Protector by Anne Marie Duquette
(SR #1283)

Lara Nelson is a good cop, which is why she and her partner—a German shepherd named Sadie—are assigned to protect a fellow officer whose life is in danger. But as Lara and Nick Cantello attempt to discover who wants Nick dead, attraction gets the better of judgment, and in nine months there will be someone else to consider.

On sale July 2005

The Pregnancy Test by Susan Gable
(SR #1285)

Sloan Thompson has good reason to worry about his daughter once she enters her "rebellious" phase. And that's before she tells him she's pregnant. Then he discovers his own actions have consequences. This about-to-be grandfather is also going to be a father again.

Available wherever Harlequin books are sold.

www.eHarlequin.com

HSR9ML0405